Praise for *The Book of Knights*

"At once sharp and humane, revealing just what it means to be human, however strange one's world. *The Book of Knights* offers a fantasy with a refreshing difference, and wisdom."
—*Locus*

"One of the brilliant new-generation writers coming out of the recent extraordinary growth period of Canadian speculative fiction, Yves Meynard manages to be both lyrical and tough at once, writing fluent and evocative stories in either English or French. His stories create a gestalt of literary and genre traditions from classical to cyberpunk."
—Candas Jane Dorsey

"Yves Meynard is an exciting new voice, refreshingly different."
—Robert J. Sawyer

"I read Yves Meynard's *The Book of Knights* in one sitting. It's a lovely, lively, truly enchanting book, filled with wonders and nightmares, and not a little wisdom."
—Susan Palwick

"In *The Book of Knights* Yves Meynard has written a novel that is *about* something. From the ancient materials of myth, folklore, legend, he has fashioned a work that is wonderfully new and wonderfully wise. Here is literary alchemy of the highest order, resulting in seamless Art."
—Terence M. Green

"Enriched by both American and European fantasy traditions (a twisted reminiscence of Hoffmann, for instance), here is a deftly spare picaresque novel, a story looking sideways, with love and gentle irony, at the traditional, even archaic, tropes of fantasy. A Don Quixote in his own way, the young but no-nonsense hero believes enough in the marvelous to make the world of his Book of Knights real, even while he returns to his mundane world to transform it. The characters, the places, the tone and mood, all seem to indicate a possible successor to Jack Vance. And better yet, he will still be Yves Meynard."
—Élisabeth Vonarburg

THE
BOOK
OF
KNIGHTS

YVES MEYNARD

TOR®

A TOM DOHERTY ASSOCIATES BOOK
NEW YORK

This is a work of fiction. All the characters and events portrayed in this novel are either fictitious or are used fictitiously.

THE BOOK OF KNIGHTS

Edited by David G. Hartwell

A Tor Book
Published by Tom Doherty Associates, Inc.
175 Fifth Avenue
New York, NY 10010

Tor Books on the World Wide Web:
http://www.tor.com

Tor® is a registered trademark of Tom Doherty Associates, Inc.

Library of Congress Cataloging-in-Publication Data

Meynard, Yves
    The book of Knights / Yves Meynard.
    p.   cm.
    "A Tom Doherty Associates book."
    ISBN 0-312-86482-5 (hc) (acid-free paper)
    ISBN 0-312-86831-6 (pbk) (acid-free paper)
    I Title.
  PR9199.3.M4524B6   1998
  813'.54—dc21
                                                        97-34387
                                                        CIP

First Edition: February 1998
First Trade Paperback Edition: April 1999

Printed in the United States of America

0 9 8 7 6 5 4 3 2 1

For Nathalie, who liked the idea
of Adelrune going to knight school

THE
BOOK
OF
KNIGHTS

1 THE BOOK

ADELRUNE'S EARLIEST MEMORIES WERE OF FINDING THE *Book of Knights*, hidden away in the attic of the four-story house of bricks where his foster parents lived.

In retrospect, it seemed unthinkable that he should find a book, any book, in that dour and austere house, apart from the Rule and its twelve accompanying volumes of Commentaries, which garnished the oaken shelves of the parlor. How often had he heard Stepfather repeat, with smug relish, the words of Didactor Moncure: "All the wisdom of the world is to be found in the Rule and its Commentaries. All other texts are but a waste of parchment."

Yet he had found the book in his foster parents' house: in the attic, wedged between a great empty trunk and the rearmost wall of the house, further camouflaged by clotted spiderwebs and decades of dust. He had pulled the book out, dropped it in his lap; wiped the cover clean, and seen the gilt letters come to life—or rather, half-life, since he did not yet know how to read, and so could not understand the patterns they formed.

He was at that age when miracles cannot be distinguished from ordinary occurrences; the discovery awoke in him no sense of awe, nor dread, nor wonder. He accepted it with the terrible serenity of the young, and so broke the preordained pattern of his life. Had the book been naught but text, all might still have returned to normalcy, for Adelrune, already trained to be methodical at the age of five, would have swiftly grown bored with the meaningless letters and put the book carefully back in its place, thereafter forgetting all about it.

But there were pictures. Adelrune had seen pictures before, large pictures in color, painted on the walls of the smaller Canon House, where young children were brought while their parents went to Temple, to begin their acquaintance with the Rule. On one wall stood the pictures that illustrated the Precepts of the Rule, with the rewards it entailed to follow them; on the other were portraits of famous men whose exemplary lives were deemed to optimally embody the Rule. Adelrune had been allowed, indeed encouraged, to pore over these pictures to his heart's content; yet they had not impressed him much.

The illustrations in the book were in faded black ink, and quite a bit smaller; and yet to Adelrune they were infinitely engrossing. Looking upon them, he felt nothing at first but intense curiosity: the thought formed in his mind that somehow he must understand what the pictures meant. And on the heels of this thought came another, an odd thought for him: that he must keep quiet about his discovery. He must not tell Stepmother, nor Stepfather. He already sensed that they would not approve.

They told him often enough, both in words and not, that he should be *grateful*. Grateful for everything in his life, since nothing had ever been owed him. He wasn't a child like any other: he was a foundling, abandoned at birth by his true parents. Stepmother and Stepfather had taken him in, sheltered him, clothed and fed him. It was a measure of their great devotion to the Rule—almost, it might be inferred, their saintliness—that they had bothered to do so, that they continued to undertake so many sacrifices for his sake.

And Adelrune did feel grateful, conscientiously, taking pains to make it clear in words at least once a day. Often Stepmother found more concrete ways as well for him to express his gratitude: fetching small things, dusting low shelves, cleaning the kitchen floor. All aspects of a good boy's life: obedience to one's parents prefigured obedience to the Rule.

Adelrune knew, from some place at the back of his mind, as dusty and quiet as was the attic, that looking at the book would not be construed as obedience or gratefulness. He had not been forbidden it, but then it was likely neither of his foster parents knew of its existence. Having been carefully brought up, he would not, could not, disobey a direct interdiction. But as long as they didn't know of the book, he could look at it and at least pretend to be blameless.

And so it was in secret that he came back to the *Book of Knights,* again and again, day after day. The pictures were his first doorway into the book, all that year before he learned to read.

There were twenty-two, scattered across far more pages than Adelrune could hope to count. The main subject of every illustration was a man—never the same one, though some resembled each other as brothers might. Usually the man wore armor, though sometimes he wore only clothing, and in one picture he was nearly naked—most definitely a breach of the Rule, though it might be that his clothes had been stolen by the crowd of bird-headed men who surrounded him, leering and jeering.

Adelrune soon grew to know each picture by heart, to recognize in each its own innate character. Some of the pictures were serene and almost gay; they enjoyed being looked at. Like the drawing of the mustachioed man in baroque armor, lying on a bed of moss, being fed grapes by a cohort of small girls with huge eyes and little horns poking through their hair.

Other pictures were reserved and made the boy want to turn the page after a brief while. In one of those a man stood in a courtyard, holding a bloodied sword in his left hand and looking down at the ground. Bodies lay all around him, apparently slain by the man's sword. None wore armor or carried weapons. There were clouds massing, visible over the rim of the surrounding wall. The sun was sinking, and half the courtyard lay in shadow from the walls. At the edge of one patch of shadow a hand was visible—someone hiding from the man?

Five of the twenty-two Adelrune grew to call the Angry Pictures; those forced the boy to stare at them, tried to prevent him from ever tearing his gaze away. What they showed made him unwilling to even touch that area of the page. The worst one was a winter scene. It showed a man, his hair an unkempt mane and his cheeks roughened by a nascent beard, strapped to a contraption of metal and wood full of spikes, saw-toothed blades, and hooked thorns. At first Adelrune had believed this some sort of torture rack, and felt disgusted. But then he'd understood the frame was a kind of armor, that it moved with the man, made him into a ten-foot giant whose every surface was deadly. The huge double-bladed cleaver at the end of one arm wasn't hinged to disembowel the man, it was a weapon meant to destroy others. What the boy had taken for snowdrifts all about the man now appeared to be the coils of some colossal wormlike being. And the too-perfect icicles that stabbed downward in the foreground, were they not the translucent teeth of the beast? Meaning that the vantage point of the illustration was from within its very mouth.

For all the fear—and, always, oddly, sadness—that these images evoked, Adelrune looked at them often at the start, until in time he learned to avoid opening the book to their pages. Still, he would sometimes dream of the Angry Pictures at night. When he thought of the book, always these five images hovered in his mind just beyond the book itself. *Remember us. We are as real as the others, if not more so.*

The mysteries of the pictures did not pale with time, as might have been expected. Rather, they awoke in Adelrune, more and more fiercely, the desire to understand the signs on the pages of the Book of Knights. It seemed to him only logical to assume that the letters on the pages were the same as those used in the Rule and its Commentaries. Therefore—this leap of logic took him a few days—if Adelrune were to learn how to read those books, he would also be able to read from the *Book of Knights.*

Adelrune conceived of a clever plan to that effect. That evening, after dinner, the three of them left the kitchen table and went into the living room. Stepmother sat in her usual chair as Stepfather went to his single shelf of books and pulled out one of the Commentaries on the Rule. Normally, Adelrune would have sat down on his own chair, a tiny wooden one brought down from the attic, and remained there. He never fidgeted; he had only had to be told twice and hit once to remember forever more that it was not proper to squirm while the Rule was being read out.

This time, however, he waited by Stepfather's leg and cleared his throat.

"What is it, boy? You have to go?"

"No, sir. I wanted to sit at your side. I want to learn how to read the Rule."

Stepfather had started to frown, but he now stopped. He looked to his wife for advice. She said in a soft voice, "Why not allow him, Harkle? It's a good thing to learn to read early, isn't it?"

"Hmpf. Very well, Adelrune. Climb up here and look at the pages, but don't touch the book and especially don't fidget."

"No, sir. Thank you, sir."

While Stepfather read aloud, Adelrune stared at the page and tried to figure out the script. He remained very quiet and still, once painfully stifling a sneeze.

" 'As the Eighty-ninth Precept instructs us, we must in all things keep an awareness of the boundaries of the Rule. This must be understood in detail: it is not enough to know that one is within the Rule, but also how far from the limit of proper conduct one stands. Praise to the righteous man, secure as he is in the very heart of the Rule, knowing himself as distant as may be from the least form of misconduct. Beware the potential sinner, who leans deliberately close to the boundary of what is allowed; for in time, if he should not feel the burning need to return to the center, then he shall surely get ever closer to the unallowable until he steps over the boundary and transgresses against the Rule.' Do you understand that, boy? It means you've always got to do your absolute best at all times. If you shirk your duty, even though you don't do anything wrong, you're bad. You understand?"

"Yes, sir. I'll always do my best."

Day after day this went on, Adelrune sitting carefully by Stepfather's side, trying to follow the man's words on the page, not daring to ask whether it was this word or that which was being read out. At times, overwhelmed by the task, he would lose his focus completely and let the words wash over him without bothering even to figure them out; then Stepfather would turn a page and Adelrune jumped at the chance, knowing that the first word spoken must be at the top left.

Once Stepfather was done reading, Adelrune was sent to his room, though he was allowed an idle hour before bed. One evening, perhaps two weeks since he'd started his reading program, he came down to the kitchen to get water from the pump. He carefully set his assigned tumbler at the bottom of the sink and worked the handle until water gushed into it. He was about to leave when he heard his name spoken. Thinking he'd been called, he went toward the door to the parlor, but stopped short when he realized he was in fact being talked about.

"I don't know," Stepmother was saying. "That's a lot of money, and for what? You said yourself the masons' guild won't take him, for all that he should be entitled, being your son. What good will an education do him? Juhal offered to take him as an apprentice if he grew strong enough, and there's Rodle who said . . ."

"Yes, yes, all your friends' unguilded husbands looking for cheap work. And that's well and good, 'earning a modest wage is a clear path to righteousness,' not to mention our cut on his salary. I agree: that's the safe way. But, Eddrin, he could be more than that. He wants to learn. He respects the Rule better than many children his age. Why not try to get him into the ranks of the hierarchy?"

"It's a hard regimen. If he fails, we'll look like we were trying to get above our station."

"Bah, what does a woman know about hardship? He won't fail. Think what it'll be like to have a son who's an adjunct to the Didactors."

"They won't let him rise high. An abandoned child, born of unknown parents? They'll never allow a bastard to—"

Stepfather cut her off: *"Don't* use words like that in my house. Adelrune is a foundling, and we've given him a decent, righteous family. It's true that the Didactors won't let him rise too high, but he could still go all the way up to deacon. Wouldn't that be something? It would repay us for all we've done for him, all the sacrifices we had to make to raise him. Our son, a deacon."

"Well, yes, that *would* be nice. . . . A deacon." She tried on the word for size and feel. " 'The other day, my son Adelrune, the deacon . . .' " Her voice trailed off into a mumble.

"I'll enroll him at the Canon House starting next week, then."

"As you will, my dear," said Stepmother obediently.

There came the noise of Stepfather's footsteps. Adelrune went hurriedly up to his room, lest he be caught eavesdropping and immediately ruin his chances. Schooling! He would never have dared to dream of *that.*

Adelrune found the school regimen unpleasant but, ultimately, bearable. The various indignities he was forced to endure, the meaningless rote and drills, those he could stand, so long as he was eventually given the key to the book that awaited him each day as he returned home.

And he learned. Slowly, but steadily, he learned. What each letter signified and how they went along with each other, how these arrangements made words. Until one day, as he labored to shape proper *f*s on his slate, along with a dozen other pupils, something turned over within him and he knew that he was ready. All this time he had held back from actually looking at the book, since it would be worse to be able to read only a few words here and there than not to understand them at all. Now he need no longer put it off.

The revelation shook him. His *f*s began to grow more and more crooked, all trembling stems and oblique crossbars. The young Didactor in charge of the class took one disgusted look at Adelrune's handiwork, cuffed him on the side of the head, and ordered him to erase his slate and do it all over again.

The pain was almost welcome, since it distracted his mind from the revelation. Adelrune sponged his slate clean and redid his letters with care, eliciting a nod of approval from the Didactor. The rest of the day, the boy managed to keep his mind on his duties, thrusting away any thoughts of the book. At long last, four o'clock was rung from the bell tower in the center of town. The pupils rose and intoned that day's hymn, led by the Didactor's off-key baritone. Once that was over, the Canon House's dismissal bell was rattled; children poured out from the various classrooms.

Adelrune made his way home, walking as fast as decency allowed. He went up to his room, put his vest away and brushed his shoes clean—remembering always the Eighty-ninth Precept, which was even more popular at the Canon House than at his home. Once all his obligations had been discharged, he went to the attic on trembling legs, pulled the book out of its hiding place, and set it in his lap.

He read the cover first; the gilt letters, after a space of nearly a year, finally able to deliver their import to him: "A History of the Famous Lives and Deeds of Valor of Many Brave Knights."

At the Canon House there was no talk of knights, no hint that anything existed in the world outside the boundaries of the Rule. But sometimes, going to the House, he would walk behind a group of other children, close enough to overhear. In their conversations, knights might be mentioned, in the same breath as kings, castles, and magicians. But even the children seemed to think that all these were equally fanciful, the product of wild imaginations. If he had tried to write down all that he had heard of knights, Adelrune would have produced only a very short list. But it was as if the word itself, when spoken, carried most of its meaning; for if he had tried to write down all that he *knew* of knights, his list would have been significantly longer. And this book, now, this huge book that had so many pages they needed three digits to be numbered, this book was so many, many times longer than the imaginary list he had in his mind. When he had read it, how many times more would he know?

Adelrune opened the book and shattered the chains of his destiny.

Didactor Moncure still said, when he visited Adelrune's foster parents: "All the world's wisdom resides in the Rule and its Commentaries. Any other books are a waste of parchment." Adelrune would stare at the floor and bite his lower lip, almost breaking the skin. He was nine, and the book had been his only companion for four years. He had read it seven times, cover to cover, omitting not one sentence, not a single word. At school he had now graduated to Third Index and was well on his way to Fourth; the phases of the Rule were being drilled into him diligently, and he appeared to learn with equal diligence. Yet all his learning was rote, and though he could recite Precepts with an accuracy exceptional for a child of his age, he believed none of them. His mind had been set on a different course, and he was lost to the Rule forever, though as yet not even he knew it.

"Look at me straight, boy," the Didactor would chide indulgently, and Adelrune would have to meet the man's gaze. "Now recite the Eleventh Precept for me." And Adelrune would recite the Eleventh Precept, flawlessly. His foster parents would beam, and Didactor Moncure would smile.

Stepfather would invite the Didactor to sit in the black armchair, which was a signal for Adelrune and Stepmother to leave the room. From behind the closed door of the parlor came the murmur of male voices, then the pungency of tobacco. Step-mother would retire to the kitchen to knit, and Adelrune was allowed an hour's idleness before sleep.

He did not go out of the house to waste that hour playing in the narrow street. His foster parents preferred to know where he was at all times—and besides, he had no one to play with. It had been a constant of his life as far back as his memory ran. It had not occurred to him to question it until quite late, and then he deduced it had to do with the circumstances of his birth. Lacking parents of his own, he was set apart from the other children. The Eighteenth Precept of the Rule, third verse, stated, "Let no one scorn he whose parentage is not known, or of low repute." Adelrune never tried to quote it to the children who ignored him when making teams for dive-ball in the court of the Canon House, or to those who fell silent as he approached. He had grown to understand that the Commentaries upon the Rule were often more important than the Rule itself, and that they usually said the exact opposite of the Precepts they were intended to illuminate.

Rather than going out to play, he would climb the stairs, ostensibly to his room on the fourth floor. But instead of the door to his room, he would open the small door that gave on the attic stairs, and climb those noiselessly, skipping the squeaky second and ninth steps. He would sneak to the back of the attic, pull open the old curtain that masked a tiny window. In the last rays of light from the setting sun, he would read a page of the *Book of Knights*.

In that way, in small daily doses, he made his way through the *Book of Knights* and its stories. He learned to name all the knights in the pictures. He learned the stories behind the pictures, and the reason for the particular character of each.

He had expected that perhaps, once he'd learned the stories, he would find the impact of their illustrations lessened. He already understood that imagination could fill the world with fancies more beautiful and terrible than any reality. But in fact, when he read the stories behind the pictures, he found they were stranger than what he had imagined. The near-naked man surrounded by bird-headed monsters was named Sir Tachaloch, and they had not stolen his clothing: he had shed it himself, that he might be able to anoint his skin with grease and pass through a mile-deep fissure in a black glass mountain to reach the chamber where a sorceress had lain in an enchanted sleep for centuries, warded by demons summoned by the King of Eagles. . . .

The *Book of Knights* told its stories to Adelrune, one by one. As promised, they recounted deeds of valor and life histories. There was some joy but also much sadness in the tales, for knights often died on their quests. Sir Athebre, he who had fought an offspring of the World-Girdling Serpent on a snow-bound island, wearing an over-armor he had cobbled together from what he had salvaged of his shipwreck, had perished in his fight. Years after his defeat, his fate had become known when the tide had cast ashore the mangled bones of his hand, fused together by the pressure of the wyrm's jaws, his family ring still borne by one clenched skeletal finger.

More than stories were to be found in the *Book of Knights*. There were considerations of the adventures, sometimes even snatches of dialogue between unnamed characters, discussing the comparative valor of this or that knight, wondering whether Sir Ancelin had truly done best by refusing to free the Shade of Gedrue when he'd had the chance. . . . Adelrune, used to Commentaries on the Rule, found these interjections normal and absorbed them with equal interest.

One in particular came to have greater and greater importance to him. It began the third chapter of the book, in this way:

> *To become a knight, training is a necessity. A prospective knight must find a mentor, one who will guide him in the proper path that leads to knighthood. Such men are not easy to find. One whose name lives still is Riander, who dwells beyond the forest, in a sheltered valley*

within the hills, three days' journey from town. Those who come to him must present a record of their deeds, to show they possess the seeds of knightly mettle. Many are those he turns away, few are those whom he accepts as his students. But those few all swear that of all teachers, he is the best a knight could aspire to. . . .

On the day he turned ten years old—in celebration of the occasion, he had been granted a respite from his chores—Adelrune read this passage in the Book, for perhaps the twelfth time. And when he reached the bottom of the page, he made a resolution. Though the Rule forbade a child to disobey his parents, though it asserted no virtue could be found outside the dwellings of the righteous, Adelrune resolved to leave home; to seek Riander, and become, in his turn, a knight.

The attic was growing dark. Adelrune found he was shivering, as if it were the feeble light which seeped through the window that had kept him warm. "I do not believe in the Rule," he whispered to himself, stating a fact so obvious he had never as yet realized it.

He went down to his room in silence and crawled under the bedclothes. He felt as if his foster parents would be able to sense his apostasy, as if the house itself, which Stepfather had built, might start to creak and groan and disclose his secret.

Nothing happened. Nothing gave him away. At the Canon House, his performance remained the same. He memorized Precepts and Commentaries with diligence, earning his teachers' commendation for the excellence of his recall. He understood finally what he had known in an inchoate fashion before: that the Didactors who instructed him did not and would never concern themselves with whether he truly possessed faith, that his mastery of the rote and apparent respect of the Rule was their sole measure of him.

And so he began to practice dishonesty. On his way home, he tried dawdling, found that as long as he kept his delays small they were never noticed. He managed to wring as much as ten minutes of free time from his schedule. It seemed to him an eternity.

He began to cast about for ways to employ this new freedom to best effect. Staring at the weeds that grew in cracks, or trying to entice ants onto his fingers, soon grew uninteresting.

Eventually he thought of the toy shop. He had never been given any toys. When he found the need for them, he would bring his hands together to make strange many-legged characters, with thumbnails for eyes; or he would set down all his fingers save the middle ones, and create a pair of long-necked dogs. Yet he had been growing somewhat jealous—in spite of the Thirty-seventh Precept—of the other boys, who sometimes brought playthings their families had bought them to the Canon House and displayed them at recess.

A single person in Faudace was the source of all these objects: Keokle the toymaker. On the infrequent occasions when Harkle and Eddrin took Adelrune on a Sunday walk, they would pass by his shop and allow the boy to look for a minute or two, but only from the outside. No matter how much he yearned for one of the items displayed in the shop, it had always been understood on both parts that he would get nothing.

Adelrune began to use his newfound freedom to visit the shop most afternoons, as he came home from the Canon House. Detouring by the shop cost him a significant amount of time, so he had less than five minutes at his disposal to enjoy the shop's displays. He never went inside: that would have been presumptuous. He might have been expected to buy something. Even limiting himself to window-shopping, Adelrune still feared that Keokle would denounce him to Stepfather. He would therefore walk by and glance to the side as if not truly interested, only to return and station himself in an inconspicuous spot, stealing looks through the windows, finally leaving when his anxiety became too strong.

Keokle's shop-front was wider than it was deep. Next to the right wall, an immense stuffed heron stood. It had been given a crown and a pectoral of malachite; the tarnished brass of the crown glimmered dimly. Facing it, across the width of the shop, was a large puppet meant to depict an evil emperor. All in black,

even to the crown of iron upon his head, the emperor leered at
the stuffed bird, who ignored him stonily. So their relations had
stood as long as Adelrune had known them, as no one either
wanted to purchase one of the pair or was able to meet Keokle's
prices.

Closer to the storefront were racks of string puppets, wooden
boats and chariots, simulated weapons, and miniature dresses in
the fashion of ancient royalty. These varied with the months and
the particulars of Keokle's whims, yet in essence never truly
changed. Adelrune could easily have lost himself in the contem-
plation of the puppets. Their features, whether hewn from wood
or shaped from porcelain, were strikingly lifelike. Their dresses
were finely detailed, their articulations apparently perfect. The
strings were tied to the crossbars in such a way that the puppets
would keep a dynamic pose. A king in a robe of red and white
held out his right hand in a gesture of benevolence; a dancer held
her hands above her head and kept her legs crossed at knee and
ankle, ready to twirl on herself. The puppet Adelrune preferred
above all showed a knight in armor, holding a shield and wield-
ing a shiny sword. His sword arm was thrust forward, the blade
raised as if to parry a blow or deliver a masterful counterstroke.
It seemed to Adelrune the emblem of a future destiny.

2 THE DOLL

TIME PASSED. THOUGH ADELRUNE'S RESOLVE TO BECOME a knight did not waver, he found himself unable to implement it. How to leave his house he had already planned out; it was a fairly simple matter. But *when* to leave was a real problem. A boy might become a squire, a knight-in-training, as early as twelve; so said the *Book of Knights.* Yet he might not do so rashly, for no particular purpose. Sir Elwydrell, for instance, had been refused thrice as a knight-apprentice by the mentor Hertullian, until the day he'd come bearing news of reavers and vowing to rid the land of their presence. Then, his purpose clear, he had been accepted.

What would be Adelrune's purpose? What quest could there be that only a knight might fulfill? Should he undertake to defend Faudace against marauders? But there never were any. Who was there around him who needed succor? No one. Devoid of any knightly purpose, Adelrune felt he could never legitimately petition Riander for instruction.

One afternoon, shortly after his twelfth birthday, Adelrune left the Canon House and went by Keokle's shop. In recent months, its attractions had started to pale; Adelrune had spaced his visits more widely, as he might sip ever more sparingly from a glass of juice, to make the pleasure last. He had been thinking perhaps he should dare to enter. He still had no money of his own, but he had heard some of his schoolmates relate their visits to the toy shop, and it seemed that Keokle did not demand purchases of his customers, as long as they were well-behaved.

The boy approached the shop with a trepidation almost as great as it had been the first time he'd risked this. He stationed himself a bit to the side, swept his gaze across the closest shelves. There was nothing new to be seen. Nor was the owner himself visible. When he was absent, Keokle would hang a small placard by the door. On those occasions, Adelrune had been able to stare brazenly at the inside of the shop. This time, there was no placard. Conceivably the door was still unlocked.

Might he go in? There were mysteries in the depths of the shop Adelrune would have liked to pierce. . . . If Keokle was absent, he need never know anyone had been there. . . .

Peering between the objects hung closer to the window, the boy could discern three shelves along the far wall, to the right of the door that led to Keokle's private apartments. Various toys rested on the shelves, a jumble of shapes that were hard to make out. The lowest shelf was unoccupied but for a single toy: it looked like a particularly large doll, though it was little more than a vague shape in the dimness.

At that moment someone opened a window, in a third floor room on the other side of the street. The angled pane of glass caught the sun's light and cast it slanting down into Keokle's shop. An elongated rectangle of orange light appeared on the far wall.

It was indeed a doll that rested on the lowest shelf. She was tall, maybe two feet high, perfectly proportioned. She wore a fine dress of deep blue with white lace at cuffs and collar. Her hair was blondish brown; her eyes were dark. Her face appeared distorted; not from lack of skill in the crafting, not through exaggeration of her features, but because she bore an expression of tragic despair that twisted her whole visage. On her cheeks, blood mingled with tears.

She seemed to be looking at him. Adelrune met the doll's

look, dizzied and oblivious. Her face tore at him, awoke something within him he could not place. He was as stirred, if not more, as when he had first seen the pictures in the *Book of Knights*. For ten or twenty heartbeats he stared at the doll, and then the window was moved again, opened farther or closed. The rectangle of light slid away, and Keokle's shop was dark again.

Adelrune was too wrought up to hesitate any further. He went to the door, worked the handle. The door was locked. Adelrune rattled it with increasing force. He heard movement from within; Keokle was speaking, though not to him. A brief silence, then hurried footsteps and noises. Adelrune abandoned the door, peered through the window again. He saw Keokle emerge from the rear of the store, shutting the inner door behind him, then moving to the front door.

The toymaker opened the door, stood on the sill, looking about. He appeared somewhat flustered. "Yes? What is it?" he demanded.

He was a man of middle years, his dark hair shot through with white, a neatly trimmed beard framing a strong mouth. He wore a dark gray shirt and dark brown trousers, garments somewhat austere in their lack of color and ornament. Adelrune faced him, momentarily at a loss for words.

"I . . . There was something that I wanted to talk to you about," he said. He had memorized the cadences of the Rule and its Commentaries so well that his own speech was always somewhat formal. Perhaps it was this refinement of manners that made Keokle invite him inside instead of keeping him on the threshold.

Adelrune stepped within, intimidated by the toymaker but driven by his memory of the doll. Keokle stood regarding him for long seconds with a disquieting attention. Then the man's expression changed, as if he'd dropped a mask—or put one on. "You've never yet come inside my shop, young Adelrune," he said in a tone of strained jollity. "What can I do for you?"

The boy didn't pause to wonder how it was that Keokle

would know his name. He cleared his throat, forced out the words.

"I have just seen a doll in here. . . ." He pointed to the lowest shelf on the far wall; it was empty.

"What kind of doll? Do you mean one of the puppets? They're all very nice, and not so expensive as people think. You must tell your parents I would give them a good deal if they came to purchase one."

"No. A doll . . . a large doll, of a girl. Wearing a blue dress . . ." Adelrune looked at Keokle, and it was clear to him that the man knew very well what he meant. The toymaker darted a glance to the door that led to the rear of the store. Adelrune hadn't dreamed the doll's existence; Keokle had whisked it in back while he rattled the door impotently.

"I have no doll like that in here," said Keokle, the lie plain on his face.

It did not occur to Adelrune to wonder why Keokle would lie, and that he might be ill-advised to press on. He insisted, doggedly.

"I saw her. You know she was there; on the shelf. There was blood on her face. She—"

"Be silent. You disgusting little animal! How could you dare pretend I'd shape such perverted toys?" Keokle's face had grown scarlet and his whole body trembled. "Filthy little bastard of a liar! Get out! Get out!"

Keokle raised a hand to strike; Adelrune was used enough to blows from adults that he barely flinched and managed to stand his ground. But then the toymaker shouted, his hand still poised for a blow, "Wait until I tell your parents! How you disobey the Rule and spread untruths!"

At this, Adelrune's nerve broke; he swung the door open and fled the toy shop, running all the way home. He kept expecting to see Keokle striding after him, but there was no visible pursuit. He forced himself to slow down as he approached his house; he must maintain the pretense of innocence.

All the rest of the afternoon he spent in dread of being denounced, starting at the least noise, presently exasperating Step-father and earning himself a good whack of the switch. Despite all his fears, no one came to the door of his house to reveal his dereliction. Evening came, with the routine of the house still in-tact. Adelrune was given the dishes to wash, dry, and store, and then left on his own. He climbed up to his room and shut him-self in.

He spent a restless night, sleeping in brief snatches only. Shortly before dawn he sat up in his bed with a start, having re-alized that at long last he had found the purpose he needed. Though she might be only a doll, still there was someone im-prisoned in Keokle's shop who must be succored.

He was ready to leave now. There was nothing that held him back and ample reason to leave: should Keokle come to the house and make good on his threat, Adelrune's life might well take on an unpleasant turn.

He put his long-rehearsed plan into action. He slipped from his room, barefoot and in his nightshirt. He went first to a cup-board across the hallway, in which were stored various pieces of linen that were not in current use. From this he plucked an old pink tablecloth. He carried this downstairs, to the larder. He filched food from the shelves, took a chipped green-glass bottle from a nook and half-filled it with the water left in a carafe on the table—he dared not work the noisy pump and risk waking up the household.

After securing the food and drink inside the cloth, he crept back up to his room. He gathered up the totality of his personal possessions: thirteen sheets of paper, a quill and inkpot, and four court playing cards lost from a deck ages ago, which Stepfather had bestowed upon him in a rare fit of generosity.

The Fifth Precept echoed in his mind, with its injunction against stealing. Adelrune shook his head. He was already flout-ing the Ninth Precept, which stipulated obedience; what was one more transgression?

He dressed carefully, tied and retied the tablecloth until it felt secure, and sat down on his bed. The sun would be rising shortly; it was time to go. He felt an impulse to fetch the *Book of Knights,* to bring its marvels along with him on his journey. Yet the very thought of removing it from its place behind the great empty trunk seemed blasphemous. The *Book of Knights* belonged in this house, where he had found it. He might suffer niggling guilt at appropriating his foster parents' belongings: that merely came from the Rule. To take the Book was not a matter of the Rule, but of right and wrong—and it would be wrong. Besides, it had been nearly seven years since Adelrune had found it, seven years in which he'd read it constantly; he knew it by heart now, from the first word to the last.

He stood up, went carefully down the stairs to the ground floor and the front door. The latter he unlocked with a minimum of noise and swung open. He drew it shut behind him; the latch clicked and he knew himself to be free. A dissolute son, a reprobate, a flouter of the Rule; a free man.

He set off along the narrow lanes of the town. Only a few souls strayed about, this early in the day. Some had come in from the surrounding farms, to set up their stalls in the market square; Adelrune avoided that area and walked deserted streets. It was early spring, and the mornings could still be brisk. The boy shivered and walked faster to warm himself with the exercise.

It was obvious that he couldn't take the main road out of town; he would surely have been noticed and reported. Instead, he slinked hurriedly across the bridge over the river Jayre and struck out through the fields, toward the chain of hills known as the Beriods.

Faudace spread mostly to one side of the Jayre; on the other bank of the river, there were only a few streets, less well paved and whose houses ranged from mildly shabby to decrepit. Adelrune was not bothered as he made his escape.

Soon all the houses of Faudace had fallen behind him. For a space he followed a dirt path that had been mud the previous day, when it had rained, and still harbored patches of wetness here and there. Reflecting that carts from the farms would run along this path, and not desiring any one to see him, Adelrune presently walked off the path and into the surrounding vegetation. Bushes and wild grasses grew here, along with patches of burdock and the odd clump of tiny flowers. Adelrune made his way through the tangle of greenery as if through a maze, detouring around the thickest parts, trying to keep his orientation more or less constant toward the hills.

Around mid-morning, he reached cultivated fields. Farms were visible in the distance. He intended to keep well away from them, fearful more of blackdogs than of the farmers themselves. He thus detoured around the fields, keeping at their margins, where his progress was much faster than it had been.

At last the farms were behind him. He left the margins of the last field. Between him and the hills lay a forest. He made for the line of trees that marked its outskirts.

The day drew to a close as Adelrune entered the outskirts of the forest. Among the trees, the going was much easier since the undergrowth was sparse; however, it was quite difficult to tell where exactly he was headed, since his sight was blocked in all directions. Adelrune's legs ached; his feet had blistered, and the blisters had burst, and the flesh beneath had bled, and the blood had dried to a blackish red crust. If only to put an end to these metamorphoses, he thought to pause for the night.

Adelrune ate some of his food, and drank a careful measure of the water in the bottle. By the time he was done, it was becoming very dark under the trees; more so than Adelrune had expected. He had never been among anything denser than a copse of birch, and had assumed a forest to be no more than a very large copse.

The boy squatted on the ground, and drew quill and inkpot from his pack, along with two of the thirteen sheets. In the rapidly-fading light, he wrote at the top of the first sheet: *Gained Knowledge of Forest Density*, then, on the second sheet, sketched in a map of his travels so far. A large round dot was Faudace, three or four tiny crosses marked the farms he had avoided; he decided against drawing blackdogs there, as they would take up too much space. A dotted line figured his course; near its terminus Adelrune indicated a fringe of trees, the limit of the forest. He drew a hollow circle at the end of the line and labeled it *The First Camp*. All along the line he wrote *One Day's Travel*. He finished the last stroke of the *l* just as the last of the day ebbed away.

The boy put away his things and took stock of his surroundings. The moon was a day or two old, enough for him to see his way, albeit dimly. Not far away stood a trio of oaks, their wrinkled trunks so close together that they created a pocket of enclosed space between them, like an endlessly tall hut. Adelrune squeezed himself through a gap and landed on a soft mulch of dried leaves. The air was rich with strange smells: a sweet, ancient vegetable rot and some undercurrent of musk. Adelrune hung the pink tablecloth from a twig and settled down to sleep.

In the morning green-stained light filtered between the massive trunks and awoke him. The night had been cold, but the oaks had offered adequate shelter. Adelrune uncurled painfully—he had slept all hunched up, his back in the shape of a question mark—and reached for his pack.

He stopped his gesture in amazement and with some degree of dread. What he had thought, in the darkness, to be a short, thick twig growing—however incongruously—from the main trunk, was in fact a slim dagger, blistered with rust and spotted with moss. The blade was sunk two-thirds into the tree, and around it the wood had puckered like a mouth in a sour frown. In the pommel of the dagger was a tiny gem that sparkled bluely.

Very carefully, Adelrune unhooked his pack from the dagger. Then he pondered his next action. A knight needed a weapon. At home, he had not been able to find anything that might be used as such, save for dishonorable or simply ludicrous implements like frying pans or knitting needles. But here was a true weapon, designed specifically for combat, something a knight might wield without incurring dishonor.

Yet the weapon was not his. True, its state argued that it had long been abandoned, and therefore that it might be claimed by anyone. Still, how could he be sure?

After a space, Adelrune thought of a way out of his predicament. Taking the third of the thirteen sheets of paper, he wrote on it, in his best hand:

> *To Whom it May Concern:*
> *The Dagger that you Left Here is now in the Possession of the Knight Adelrune of Faudace, who Thought to Borrow it in your Absence. Should you now have Need of it, please Seek out the Knight Adelrune, and he shall be Honor-Bound to Render it back to you upon the Instant.*
> *(Signed) Adelrune, of Faudace, Knight*

Adelrune signed, paused thoughtfully, then took up the quill again and added under his signature:

> *(A Brief Delay may be Unavoidable should a Battle be in Progress at the Time)*

The boy wedged the sheet of paper into a crack in the bark, made sure it was firmly affixed. Then he grasped the handle of the dagger and pulled. There was some resistance, which abruptly vanished, and the blade slid free. The portion of the blade that had been sunk into the tree had not rusted, but it had developed a yellowish green, mottled luster. Adelrune stowed it in his pack, vowing to clean it as soon as he found the means. Then he stepped out of his refuge.

At first the going was painful, for not only did his back pain him, but his blistered feet protested. It was like walking on small coals; but after a time the coals grew less hot, and his pace increased somewhat.

The forest was now suffused by the sun, yet it seemed far less hospitable by daylight. The heat of day stoked some rank odor out of the ground, and the distant noises disturbed Adelrune: he could fancy that he heard snatches of speech, the tinkle of bells, a gasping, choked cry repeated again and again. He told himself that these were only birds, the breeze through tree branches, perhaps the murmur of water—but he could not truly believe it.

That there were dangers in forests he had always known in a dim, detached fashion. Cuprous owls and liar-snakes, bloodrock, the Three Dreads, all those he had heard about from the other boys in the courtyard of the Canon House, but they had not borne upon his existence in Faudace and so he had put them out of mind. The *Book of Knights* did recount several tales of knights overcoming monsters, but these always took place in the middle of a desolation, on a distant island, or deep in the dungeons of a sorcerer's castle. He had not felt that these applied to travel immediately outside the town of his birth; but he realized that he had been wrong. Now the dangers were no longer blackdogs, being caught by his foster parents, or forgetting a Precept of the Rule. Now all the once far-away threats were nearby, now they had to be faced.

For a long moment Adelrune looked back in the direction of the fields, the farms that he could almost see, Faudace itself, which in his mind's eye was a tiny toy city, its narrow tall houses all set together like dominoes in a box, and he wished more than anything else to go back. Then he turned around, faced into the depths of the forest, and wiped his moist eyes. Knights might meet dangers every day, wherever they went. This was the life he had wished for himself; this was the life he would get.

Before setting out, he took out his first sheet and wrote *Overcame Fear & Homesickness.* Then he began marching straight ahead.

The deeper in he traveled, the louder and the stranger became the sounds of the forest. Yet their sources remained invisible. Adelrune heard words muttered so rapidly they blurred into a random string of consonants. There were distant peals of bells and metallic scrapes. Once he heard a gobbling laugh coming from behind a large pine; he rushed around the tree, to find nothing there but a lingering sense of presence.

As the day wore on, Adelrune began to get glimpses of forest life. Birds flittering from bough to bough, squirrels darting across his path, once a pair of hedgehogs dodging under a bush. These looked like the animals he had seen all his life in Faudace, yet he intuited they were not entirely what they seemed. Coming finally across a stream, he drank his fill, topped up his bottle, and cleaned the dagger as best he could, first washing then scrubbing it with a handful of moss. He got most of the rust away, but the sheen over the last two-thirds of the blade remained impervious. For a time he carried the weapon in his hand, but he soon developed a terrible cramp of the palm. Eventually he carefully slid it under his belt.

Adelrune proceeded along his journey. He walked along the stream for a time: logically, going upstream must lead him toward the hills. But after a while he reached the stream's beginning, a mossy hole in the ground; so he went on without a guide once more. He climbed over fallen trees that barred the way ahead, detoured around thickets of brambles. Deeper and deeper in he went. The ground began to slope noticeably; he must be nearing the hills proper.

Late that afternoon he heard a crashing sound; he had barely drawn his dagger when something burst out of the trees, stopped its headlong rush, half-turned to look back at him. It walked on two hooved legs; it had a man's arms; it bore antlers on its head. Glittering eyes were set in a face so inhuman Adelrune almost screamed.

The apparition whirled about and bounded off; the noise of its passage died presently. Adelrune leaned against a tree, shut his eyes, remembered a tale told in the Book. Sir Avary had faced the ghosts of his entire ancestry ten generations back, and survived where others had been found dead; not simply because he had known the spirits would do nothing to him, for many others had known that; but because he had succeeded in convincing himself, without a shadow of a doubt, that it was so. In much the same way, or so he hoped, the boy convinced himself that the being had gone, and would not return. After some long minutes he found he could walk once more, and made himself push onward.

The ground now sloped markedly up, became broken. By necessity his path must take him perpendicularly across the ridges and plateaux, and so the going became strenuous. He had not covered much ground horizontally when he reckoned he must prepare a second camp. Already the afternoon neared its end and the temperature was dropping. Shelves of rock thrust up here and there, and at the base of one of them he found a shallow cave. It was not as warm as the refuge between the oaks had been, and so the boy gathered dried sticks of wood to make a fire. When he figured he had gotten enough, he piled them in front of the cave's opening. While there was still enough light, he drew the second day's journey. The dotted line went on from the hollow circle of the first camp and wound its way into the forest. Adelrune inked in the broken ground and the slope of the foothills. He made another hollow dot, labeled it *The Second Camp (Cave)*. Then he wrote *Another Day's Travel* along the second segment of the line.

He had finished before the light quite went out. He put his pack deeper into the cave, then busied himself making a fire.

In this he was sorely disappointed. It was supposed to be that one could make fire by rubbing two dry sticks together; Sir Oldelin had done this, and so had Sir Khlaum when he was caught in the middle of the Great Steppe. Yet for all his efforts—and he strove till his arms were trembling—Adelrune could not manage it. He lay back against the side wall of the cave. For the moment, he was quite warm from his exertions; but soon the night might grow bitterly cold.

He heard a sound, the rustle of fur or cloth against stone. He drew his dagger, for all that his arm shook with the strain. "Who goes there?" he called, the first time in almost two days that he had spoken.

A great mass shifted and rose, blotting out the stars. It

seemed the thin crescent of the moon could not illuminate the scene for Adelrune to see clearly. There was a reddish glint within the dark mass, as of tiny rubies stitched upon a vast cloak, or a dozen eyes scattered over great filmy wings. Adelrune pointed his dagger. "Come no closer!" he croaked. "I am a knight and may not be trifled with!"

"Your weapon will not harm me," said a voice like dead leaves rubbed together. "I am inured to metals."

A pause. Then the voice added: "Put the blade down. I do not wish you ill."

Adelrune lowered the dagger but kept it in hand. "Who are you?" he asked in a whisper.

The being did not answer his question. Instead, it observed, "You have failed to make a fire. I foresee that in the night you will freeze to death."

"I know a dozen ways to remain warm," said Adelrune, but his tone betrayed the lie.

"I can give you a means to make fire, but you must pay me in return."

"I have little of value," said Adelrune.

"Not true," countered the being. "You are rich in flesh, in life, in youth. Nothing could have greater worth."

Adelrune blindly reached inside his pack and brought out the four playing cards. He attempted a desperate bluff.

"I have other wealth. I own four rare portraits. I will give you one in exchange for fire." And saying this he held out one of the cards at random: the Queen of Cups.

He felt it, not gripped and yanked, but smoothly and nearly imperceptibly eased away from his clutch, as though the being had not really touched it. He heard a drawn-out hiss. Then the voice of dead leaves spoke again.

"The queen. It *is* her. There is still hope then."

Adelrune felt rather than saw movement within the dark shape. Some of the rubies or eyes winked out, reappeared. He became aware that a long strip of parchment and a white stick rested at his feet.

"A fair deal," the being whispered. "On the scytale is written a potent cantrip. Wrap the parchment around the stick and read the words that are revealed to make flame."

Then all the eyes or rubies were extinguished at once; there was a liquid rustle, and Adelrune was alone.

He took the strip of parchment and wound it around the white stick. Letters aligned themselves; they had been written in silvery ink and reflected the dim light of the crescent moon well enough to be read; Adelrune painstakingly made out five words.

Though he had not spoken the words aloud, a tall, quivering flame instantly sprang into being among the dry branches and twigs he had piled up. By its light, Adelrune unwrapped the parchment from the long, straight bone and put both possessions away into his pack. Then he took out the first sheet and wrote on it *Gained Fire-Making Magic from Redeyes,* and now that he had named the object of his fear he found he could no longer deny it. He buried his head in his arms and wailed in terror.

3 THE HOUSE OF RIANDER

ALL NIGHT ADELRUNE STAYED AWAKE, AND HIS FIRE burned hot and bright. His fear had calmed down somewhat, faded into an all-encompassing dull dread. With dawn the magical fire collapsed to ashes; the boy rose to his feet and set off without delay. He was so drunk with fatigue that his eyes could not track. His steps were weaving and twice he fell heavily to the ground. Still he went on. In his head fragments of the *Book of Knights* swarmed and collided with his senses. For brief spans of time, though he walked still, he would dream, and in the dream he would see Sir Julver in his shining armor of orichalc striding by his side, or he would skirt the edges of the funeral feast at which Sir Lominarch had at last recognized the Imp of Nothwerl in the guise of fair Blancean.

After a time, constant exertion overcame his torpor and, though he was still exhausted, his mind grew clearer. Throughout the morning, he gained slowly but surely in elevation. The trees were now sparser by far; there were frequent glades and stretches of tall grass along the edge of rock shelves. Among the grass grew lilies of a black-tinged purple. Bees flew around the flowers. Adelrune saw one enter the calyx, and instantly the whole flower closed up around the insect, trapping it. Elsewhere another lily relaxed its petals; a few chitinous fragments fell out.

The apivorous lilies were the last manifestation of the forest's strangeness. By early afternoon, he had gained the crest of the hill and the forest lay behind him. To his left and right the Beriods extended, their summits clothed in grass and dotted with flowers. Ahead, the land fell and rose, sloping down into an indistinct country.

Adelrune's entire body cried out for rest, for sleep. But he did not dare give in, so close yet to the forest and its denizens. He squatted on his haunches and drew out paper and pen. From the second camp, he extended the dotted line up to the summit of the hill, and wrote along it *Two Thirds of a Day's Journey.*

When he got to his feet, a dazzle of orange and green blotted out his sight for several seconds, and he broke out in a sweat. He forced himself to take one step forward, then another. Slowly he made his way down from the crest of the hill, toward an unknown land.

But now he began to know doubt. The *Book of Knights* had held no specific directions to Riander's house. He brought the relevant passage to mind, almost automatically: *Riander, who dwells beyond the forest, in a sheltered valley within the hills, three days' journey from town.* The boy had never considered which forest was meant; he had assumed that the Book spoke a universal truth, that the fact of undertaking a journey to a mentor's house was more important than the destination one set oneself. If he'd asked Stepfather for his advice, the man would undoubtedly have opined that Adelrune had been an utter fool. Who else would set off with only a destination in mind, and no directions?

Yet, there *were* hills beyond this forest, and the third day of his journey was not yet ended. He still had reason to hope. Sir Berralgis had been foretold he would have to quest a year and a day to find an alicorn; and so he did, from the confines of his sickbed, searching for it in books and ancient scrolls, until three hundred and sixty-six days into his search, the beast had wandered by itself into his room—summoned either by Berralgis's persistence or by a spell he'd found buried deep in some old tome—to lay her horn onto the dying knight's breast and sweeten his leave-taking of the world. . . .

And by the end of his third day of travel, as the *Book of Knights* had promised, Adelrune reached the house of Riander.

He had come halfway down a hill, and now perceived a combe opening on his left. At the far end rose a long low structure of pinkish bricks. It was built entirely of straight lines, but its corners had been beveled so that it did not seem truly angular.

Adelrune made his way down to the floor of the valley and diffidently approached the house. It was already in shadow, save for the topmost floor, whose bricks turned to peach in the sunlight. There was a wide sandy path leading to the front door, which was of heavy, dark wood. Set in the middle of it, a metal plate bore the graven image of a leering gargoyle. From the gargoyle's nose depended an iron knocker.

Adelrune grasped the ring and knocked three times. When the door opened, he lowered his eyes and fumbled out the two marked sheets from his pack. "I am Adelrune," he croaked, swaying and shaking with fatigue and dread, "and I wish to be a knight. I have here my list of accomplishments and a map of my travels. If you should refuse me, I will make no complaint."

The sheets were gently taken from his hands. There was a long silence, interspersed with the rustling of parchment. Finally Adelrune raised his eyes, to find himself looking straight into those of a tall, spare man.

The man was still young, dressed simply but richly. He had a mane of brown hair reaching halfway to his shoulders, but was as beardless as Adelrune himself. There were crinkles around his eyes, and his teeth shone white when he parted his lips.

"Do you have some task to accomplish, some quest to fulfill?" the man asked him.

Adelrune lowered his gaze once more. Suddenly, his purpose seemed to him so silly as to be shameful. Yet he blurted it out, to the extent that he dared.

"Yes. I . . . There is someone in the town of Faudace, held

prisoner by a man. I must rescue her. I am the only one who knows of her existence; if I do not succor her, no one will."

"A noble quest," the man said gravely. "However, if you aim to be a knight, you must learn to look people squarely in the eye when you speak to them." He took the boy's hand and drew him inside. Then Adelrune's legs gave way and he fell in a heap before Riander had finished shutting the door of his house.

For a time he burned with fever. His body spasmed in ague and his mind roamed the shores of delirium. He dreamed he was held in a cage that had molded its shape exactly to that of his body. Then he perceived that the cage was in truth a sarcophagus of porcelain, and that though he wasn't dead, he wouldn't live as long as he lay within this shell. In front of him, against a curtain of painful light, hung a red-and-white flower twined around a lance of ivory. There was the smell of heated metal, then the spicy reek of cloves. He stood on a melting glacier and icy water, stronger than wine, filled his mouth.

Adelrune awoke covered in sweat. By the bed sat Riander, his kind face full of serene concern.

"You have slept a night and a day," said Riander. "I have put you in my room for the nonce, but we will move you to yours as soon as you're well enough." He helped Adelrune sit up in the bed.

At first the boy thought he was still dreaming. He had seen that the bed lay with its headboard against one wall; and that wall made a corner on the right. Now he saw a wall to his left, as was proper; but there was no wall in front of him. The room just went on and on. There were dressers against the right-hand wall, and small tables; mirrors on the left-hand wall, and low chairs, and shelves and writing-desks. Rugs on the floor, one after the other like a tawny rainbow, narrowing down into the distance. There was no far wall, no end to the procession of furniture. Far away, the room grew dim and blurred, not because it was dark but through the accumulated thickness of the air and the eye's limited powers.

Adelrune turned to Riander, who shrugged smilingly. "I will not attempt an explanation. Just keep in mind that you should not move too far from the doors which connect the rooms; they exist only in the front of the house. For now, what would you like to eat?"

Adelrune stammered, "I can—can I stay?"

Riander spread his hands. "Haven't I said so?"

In the space of three more days Adelrune regained his health. Riander made light talk to him all this while: sun and clouds, the music of the wind, the taste of simple food. He hung a curtain across Adelrune's room, so that the endlessness of it was hidden. In much the same way, Adelrune hung a veil across certain of his memories; though they were still there for his inspection, he no longer dwelled on them unceasingly.

One morning—his fifth at the house of Riander, though only the fourth he was aware of—he rose from his bed, dressed himself, and went out of the room and down the stairs to the parlor. Riander was sitting in a tall-backed chair, leafing through a tattered book. Aware of Adelrune's presence, he rose with a smile.

"How are you feeling? Though your dress is answer enough."

"I wanted to thank you again, sir, for your care—"

"Hold. My name is Riander. Call me by it."

"Yes, Riander. I wanted to thank you—and to ask what you will do now that I am hale."

"You came to me to receive a knight's training, did you not?" Riander took the two sheets of parchment from a pile on a desk. "Your list of achievements is rather brief, and your travels weren't extensive—but I am concerned with quality, and not with quantity. You are more than qualified, Adelrune. And as I have said, the quest you have set yourself is a noble one. I hereby formally acknowledge that I will take you in training for knighthood."

Adelrune inclined his head mutely, somewhat at a loss. "No, no," chuckled Riander, "I have told you before, look people in the face! Let's see you keep that chin straight."

Adelrune leveled his face, essayed a smile.

"Perhaps the foremost virtue of a knight is humility," said Riander. "And one of its corollaries is acceptance of drudgery. Go to the kitchen—through the door facing this one—and peel six potatoes for the soup."

Adelrune sketched an awkward bow and exited. In the kitchen, which was tiled in white porcelain and went on forever, he found a bin full of potatoes and a small knife. He set to work. Stepmother had given him this precise chore often enough, as soon as he'd been old enough to be trusted with the peeling knife. His hands moved in a familiar rhythm, and long thin strips of peel spiraled away from the tubers. After a few minutes Riander joined him to help, but found that Adelrune was already finishing the last potato. "Well," he remarked with a grin, "you are handier with this blade than I shall ever be. I guess there is nothing to be done for it but to put you to weapon practice immediately after lunch."

True to his word, as soon as they had finished eating the midday meal, Riander took Adelrune into another room of the house. Its walls were dressed stone; metal brackets of many kinds were screwed into the blocks, for what use was not immediately apparent.

There were wooden stands against the walls, in which rested an astonishing diversity of weapons. Swords straight and curved, wavy, hooked, and tripartite; maces with heads flanged, knobbed, and spiked; bows of all sizes, pole arms, daggers, assemblies of chains, wooden shafts and blades which Adelrune couldn't begin to comprehend.

"Now then," said Riander, "we can start by teaching you to

recognize and name all these, or we can see how you do with a blade in your hands."

"If you please, sir—I mean, Riander—I have spent years in the Canon House learning things by rote. I would like to try a blade."

"Fair enough. Let's see, you are too small for any of these swords. . . . Perhaps this will do."

He gave Adelrune a long, thin blade with a large guard that covered his hand up to the wrist. The boy hefted it, moved his arm about. It was a strange feeling. Riander chose a similar blade for himself.

"Let us work on basic stance. Pretend we're about to fight."

Adelrune dutifully tried to assume a proper fighting stance. Riander quirked a smile.

"Adelrune, what do you hold in your hand?"

"I do not know what kind of sword it is, si—Riander."

"Actually, it's a dueling foil shaped after the Old Szeis fashion. But that isn't relevant at present. I meant to point out that what you are holding is not a candle."

"I beg your pardon?"

"Since it isn't a candle, you should not hold it up like one," Riander patiently explained. "What use do you think it will be this way? Point it forward, slightly raised. That way, if I try to rush at you, I'll get a stomachful of your blade. Yes, like that. Much better. Try to cut at me, now."

Riander parried Adelrune's hesitant swing and sent the boy's sword jumping out of his grasp, to clatter on the flagstones.

"You should have kept your grip on the foil," he declared.

"I tried, but I could not," said Adelrune.

"You may be still weak from your illness; nevertheless, I think your arms are not well-muscled enough. Pull up your sleeve, make your arm bulge. . . . As I thought. I believe a course of weight-lifting is indicated."

Adelrune was embarrassed by his lack; he nodded agreement to Riander's suggestion, barely suppressing an automatic "Yes, sir."

"You are well-accustomed to obey, aren't you?" asked Riander in a softer voice. "While you were ill, you raved. At one point, you kept repeating 'Yes, Didactor' as if someone were giving you order after order. Just now, you lowered your gaze again, and you agreed immediately, with the least possible noise."

Adelrune sighed, explained: "The Ninth Precept of the Rule says the laity must obey Didactors 'without refusal, complaint, or shirkery.' Didactor Elfindle's Commentary adds that 'The laity are as children to the Didactors, and so should children follow the Ninth Precept and obey their parents as their parents obey the Didactors.' In my house, obedience was the foremost of the virtues, after righteousness."

Riander frowned. "Why did you leave then? Surely you weren't sent here by your parents?"

Adelrune felt himself blush. "They could never have; I am a foundling," he said softly. "Harkle and Eddrin are not my true parents."

"You say that as though you're ashamed of it."

"Eighteenth Precept, third verse: 'Let no one scorn he whose parentage is not known, or of low repute.' From Didactor Hoddlestane's Commentaries, chapter two: 'Moral turpitude is passed through the blood. The offspring of those who sin by breeding outside of marriage are therefore inherently flawed from birth and should be treated as the potential degenerates that they are.' Does this answer your question?"

"Your words do not, but your stance does," said Riander. "You look like a pardel about to kill and rend its prey. Look at your hands: you've made them into claws."

Adelrune grew aware of his posture and put his arms straight down at his sides. His heart was beating fast and loud.

"My own mother, when she was still a young girl, entertained a succession of lovers in her bed," said Riander, startling Adelrune by the matter-of-factness of his voice, "and when she finally grew big with me, she was hard put to persuade her latest suitor to marry her. He was no fool; he knew the child might well not be his. For a fact, I never looked much like he did; both he and I knew we were almost certainly unrelated. Still, he did agree to wed her before I was born, making me—barely—legitimate in the end."

"How did he treat you?"

"The same as he did the rest of my siblings who followed. I wasn't a fussy baby, and grew up a well-behaved child, so he never had any real reason to resent me. I never felt that he loved me quite as much as he did the later children that were clearly his. But all in all, it didn't make for a great difference. He was at heart a kind and equable man."

"Did he buy you any toys?"

"Yes. I had a wooden duck on wheels and a warrior puppet with a real metal sword. . . ."

Adelrune let out a painful chuckle. "You were a lucky boy."

"And is it because you weren't that you came here?"

"Not really. It is because I never believed in the Rule. When I was ten, I understood I had always been lost to it. I know all of its Precepts by heart, but I do not put the least faith in them."

"Then did you come here looking for something else to put your faith in?"

The question took Adelrune by surprise. He pondered a moment, and answered: "No. I came here to become a knight. That is all I ask."

"Good. For though I can and will teach you to become what is in you to become, I am not a man who can tell you in what you should invest your faith. Now we shall go to that rack yonder, and I will show you how to use the weights to strengthen your arms."

4 THE PRICE OF TRAINING

DAYS AND WEEKS PASSED. RIANDER COACHED ADELRUNE tirelessly in the various disciplines of chivalry: proper forms of address, the science of heraldry, prowess at arms, and the care of weapons. Their days began with the dawn and ended late. Adelrune at first suffered a hundred aches and pains, mostly in his arms, from stressing muscles unused to such treatment. With time, his discomfort abated as his strength grew. Riander endeavored to train him to be both supple and strong, make him aware of his stance at all times, so that he might move more gracefully and efficiently.

Weapons practice was what tired Adelrune out, but it occupied a comparatively small part of his day. Riander and his books were a deep fount of knowledge, much of which he was expected to absorb. Since his memory was naturally sharp and had been further trained by all his years spent memorizing the Rule and its Commentaries, this aspect of his training was fairly easy.

There were lessons on rhetorics, diplomacy, and even evasion—for though knights did not lie, this did not mean they were always compelled to blurt out the whole damaging truth. Thus, to save Lady Klianther's honor, Sir Gliovold had managed to conceal entirely her brother's involvement in the plot against Baron Blindell's life, while apparently revealing all he knew.

More lessons followed these, dwelling on subtler points of etiquette, elementary symbology, the fundamentals of astronomy and the governing principles of magic. Adelrune was somewhat disquieted as he began his course of magical studies, but he soon realized there was no question of trying to shape him into a wizard. Talent was essentially an inborn trait, not a learned one. And at any rate, Riander—despite the strangeness of the house in which he dwelt—disavowed any direct knowledge of the sorcerous arts. He understood the principles by which they worked, which were useful for even a layman to apprehend, but no spells as such.

It was after a discussion of the ways in which weapons might be enchanted, and of famous magical blades, that Adelrune was reminded of the weapon he had gained in the forest. He fetched it from his pack, the tied-together pink tablecloth which he still kept in his room under his bed, then brought it to Riander.

"Do you think this might have some power?" he asked, recounting how he had come by it.

"Unlikely," answered Riander. "I will admit it is seldom possible to tell outright whether an object holds magic, but as I've just told you, there are many more rumors of enchanted swords and daggers than there are actual magical blades. The sheen is odd, but that actually makes me doubt it all the more."

Riander applied powders and metal brushes to the blade, but despite his best efforts, it proved impossible to remove the weird sheen from Adelrune's dagger. "At any rate, it is a sound weapon," he said once he had capitulated in his efforts to clean it. "Small, but keen-edged, and with a good point. The gem might even be a sapphire, though I can't be sure. By all means, keep it. What comes to us unbidden should not be set aside lightly."

Spring moved into summer. The air grew mild, and then hot. There was a pond at the back of Riander's house—which, from the outside, was about a hundred feet in length—and in this pond Riander taught Adelrune to swim and dive. The water was unexpectedly deep and cool; even in the middle of the day, only the very surface of it was warmed by the sun. Once Adelrune had gained in confidence, he took to diving deep down close to the middle, opening his eyes underwater and enjoying the strange perspective this afforded him. Though he had feared at first that the pool, from within, would be as infinite in extent as was the house, in fact he could touch bottom with his outstretched hand, a layer of muddy earth a fathom and a half down at the center.

Evenings grew long and mild, and Riander slackened off Adelrune's training somewhat, whether because he judged the boy needed a rest or because he himself felt lazy, Adelrune couldn't tell. When the sun slipped below the crest of the surrounding hills, so that the combe was sunk in shadows under a sky still bright, the two would sit outside on a bench Riander had taken out and set beside the door. The mentor would tell long, rambling stories about everything under the sun and nothing in particular, while his student listened with half an ear, knowing that in this case it mattered not a whit whether he retained any of the tale later.

On these occasions Adelrune felt suffused by a joy he had never known in his whole life. He forgot the Rule, its Precepts and Commentaries, the numbing routine of his life in Faudace. His long and dull childhood had at last fallen behind him.

Once Riander had finished his tale, the air would have grown almost chill in comparison to the rest of the day. Adelrune, already lulled almost to sleep, would rise and stretch, then bid Riander good night and make his way to bed. As he let himself fall onto the mattress, he would shed a tear or two. Not from homesickness, certainly, nor from knowing his childhood had ended. It was when he reflected upon how long the years had stretched from his early days with the *Book of Knights* till this moment that he felt a measure of sadness. And also, though he kept the thought at bay, and entertained it only the way one gazes at an object through a veil, he remembered the doll in Keokle's shop. The quest he had vowed to fulfill pricked at his conscience like a needle. He felt a prescience of his return to Faudace, though it seemed oddly distant in time and in space, as far removed in the future as his discovery of the *Book of Knights* was in the past.

As summer cooled toward autumn, Riander increased the pace of Adelrune's training. He showed more and more zeal as an instructor, until the boy could have legitimately complained he was being run ragged. Yet though the pace of his education was relentless, Adelrune did not wither but instead bloomed. His mastery of knightly skills had now become sufficient for him to take some pride in it; perhaps that was why Riander had become so insistent, to make sure that his student did not lose his perspective and forget how much he had yet to learn.

One evening in early fall, nearly six months since Adelrune's arrival, Riander took him far along the endless parlor, both of them carrying a lantern for illumination. There was a long stretch of the room where both walls were hung with portraits. These showed, on one wall, all the knights whom Riander had trained, and on the opposite wall, other knights of repute.

"Here is Sir Hawkins, the first knight I trained. His device is a black falcon on a red field. He favors the mace and wears armor of leather stained in his colors. And there is Sir Pellaunce, all in green save for the blue scarf given to him by a lady who shall remain nameless. And there . . ."

They went on along the gallery of portraits. Adelrune was much taken with the portrait of black-bearded Sir Gliovold, who wielded a strange weapon like a triple-bladed sword. On the opposite wall the paintings were duller and older, in a style less bold. Still the personages of note they depicted cut a fine figure. There stood doomed Sir Ancelin, who gave his own life that a dragon might at long last be slain; there tragic Sir Krag, white and gold armor stained black by the blood of friends killed by his own hand; there the mysterious Sir Cobalt, who hid his identity behind a featureless blue vizor and strove against corrupt King Wyrt of Cuvelair for a full score of years.

It was only as they were returning that something struck Adelrune. "Tell me," he asked Riander, "how long does it take you to train a knight?"

"It varies. A year or two, at most. My students are of the highest quality."

"Yet—there were nearly two dozen knights on that wall that you showed me. You are surely not old enough to have taught them all!"

Riander's voice became somber. "That is involved with the question of payment," he said.

"The Book said none had to pay if they could or would not. . . ."

"Nor will you have to, if you refuse. It is not a large thing, and yet it is. We will talk of it later." Riander paused. "Adelrune, I'm an honest man, and I assure you the Book spoke the truth. No price is exacted from one who will not pay. But know that all my students, without exception, paid the price I asked of them. All, save two, swore to do so before they even knew what it was. Becoming a knight isn't like a stroll through a wood. You will be changed more than you can understand now."

"You frighten me!"

"Did you ever wonder why it is said of so many knights, like Sir Actavaron and Sir Julver, that they knew no fear? It is because in their training, in fact, they did learn to know fear. They experienced the extremes of it so many times that afterwards things that terrify normal men were to them no more frightening than angry insects, when compared to the horrors they had faced."

Adelrune said nothing and went to his room. He cried for a time that night, and dreamed of cages bathed in ruddy light, of tears and blood, and of a great hodgepodge of broken toys like dismembered soldiers. In the morning he returned to his practice and studies seemingly with the same energy as before; nevertheless a pall hung over him and did not dissipate.

* * *

One evening a week or two later, Riander sat down on the rug, next to the hearth, and gestured for Adelrune to do likewise. A fire was burning, though the day had been fairly warm. The boy sat down, gazing down blindly at the patterns of the rug. His mood had not improved; what Riander taught him he still retained, but now almost in the same way he had retained the Precepts of the Rule. He knew the words by heart, but their core was hollow.

For a time Riander gazed at the patterns the flames made. Adelrune saw his face from the corners of his eyes. Then, still not facing his student, Riander said: "Have you ever heard tell of the end of the world, Adelrune?"

"Yes." The boy's voice was bleak. "The Didactors at school talked about it often enough. 'When the Rule triumphs over disorder, from all the fields of law shall men reap happiness in obedience. . . .' "

Riander cut him off. "No, not that; I don't mean the end of time, but of space. The end of the world: the utmost part of it, the land beyond which there is only limitless ocean."

Adelrune raised his eyes. Riander was now looking at him. "At the Canon House," said the boy, "I was taught that the world is round like a ball; it cannot have an end in space."

"You said to me more than once that you never believed in the Rule. Did you trust any of the other teachings at the Canon House, beyond letters and arithmetic? Then why this one? The Didactors were wrong: the world's shape is not something so simple that it can be expressed in a single metaphor."

Riander now had Adelrune's undivided attention. He went on. "Not far from the end of the world there lies a small kingdom, named Ossué. Beyond Ossué, at the very end of the world, is another, very tiny, kingdom by the name of Yeldred. Now, the people of Ossué shun the sea, and keep to land at all times; whereas Yeldred's are fond of water and used to spend most of their lives building tall ships that they sailed on the limitless ocean.

"There came a time when all the forests of Yeldred were exhausted; in all of the land not one tree was left standing, save for the twelve sacred oaks of the royal orchard, and these of course would never feel the axe. So for a time Yeldred built no more ships, its people content with the large fleet they had. But the passage of time was not kind to Yeldred's ships. Some were lost in storms, some foundered upon hidden reefs and were rent beyond possibility of repair, and some sailed away into the boundless reaches of the ocean and never returned to Argalve Harbor. In time, only three ships were left to them, and those badly in need of overhaul, if not retirement.

"At that time the King of Yeldred conceived of a grandiose plan: his people would build ships again, or rather *a* ship. One single ship so vast his entire nation could live aboard it, a ship so heavy storms would shy away from it in terror, a ship so rich it would almost suffice to itself, sailing the shores of humanity and trading for whatever trifles it could not produce itself.

"The three surviving vessels would never furnish anything near what this project required. So the timber to build the nation-ship Yeldred must buy from Ossué. This they have been doing now for decades upon decades. And the people of Ossué sell their wood very, very dear. Every year, seven times seven young men and women among the most beautiful in the land must leave Yeldred forever to go live in Ossué, to breed strong children for that kingdom.

"In this manner, Ossué becomes stronger every year, while Yeldred weakens. The people of Yeldred know this very well. 'But,' they will tell you, 'the Ship gets built.' And to them, this is more important than all the rest."

Adelrune sighed. "You tell me I must be prepared to make sacrifices for my goals, like the people of Yeldred."

"No. I think the people of Yeldred are the utterest fools. I think giving up the flower of their youth in order to build their great Ship is evil. One day their kingdom will be sundered by Ossué's armies, and they will find themselves bound to crosses made of their Ship's own timber."

Adelrune laughed briefly at the foolishness of the people of Yeldred. He started to draw in a breath, but grew aware that his laughter had not stopped, that it had in fact increased. His eyes were burning. Then he was letting himself cry in front of Riander, though he had thought it would make him die of shame to do so.

After a time he wiped his eyes and regained his breath. His apprehension had been purged from him; he looked his mentor in the eye and asked, "What is the price of your training, Riander?"

"Six years of your youth. It is by this exchange that I endure. But I say it again: you are not bound to pay it."

Adelrune recalled Redeyes' claim about his wealth. "What will happen to me if I do pay?"

"You will age six years. In a sense, you will profit, as this will give you a man's body. But in the end, it will be six years of your life that I have stolen away. I won't hide that fact."

"I feared it more when it remained unspoken," said Adelrune.

"That is most often the way of it."

". . . and I will pay the price." Adelrune knew that a true knight could not do otherwise.

The magic was held in a cup of blackest glass, opaque and glistening as wet stone. "See the metal rings that have been set inside," Riander instructed Adelrune. "Once the cup starts to fill, keep your attention on those rings. You must let the level reach the sixth ring, and no higher. At all costs, keep your attention on the rings! If you slip into a trance, you will pour out your whole life into the cup and there will be nothing to be done for you."

Adelrune nodded. He fixed his attention on the inside of the cup, counted six rings and counted them again, marked the position of the sixth one firmly in his mind. From the corner of his eye, he saw Riander take a step back and cross his arms. Adelrune breathed deeply and brought the cup to his lips.

There was no pain as such, just a feeling of lassitude like the onset of sleep. Adelrune felt fluid running from his mouth; it was almost tasteless, but he could detect a faint undertone of wine, if he concentrated. . . . He blinked. Had he been asleep an instant before? His eyes were unfocused, the image of the cup was doubled, the glitter of the doubled rings formed a strange design.

The rings! How high had the fluid gotten? Panic struck Adelrune, brought his mind out of the trance. He retrieved the position of the sixth ring from his memory. The fluid was just now drowning it.

Adelrune wrenched the cup away from his lips and stood panting, covered in a sheen of sweat. Riander stood two paces in front of him, his arms still crossed, a worried expression on his face changing to relief.

Adelrune shouted in anger: "Why did you not stand next to me, to remove the cup if I started to drift away? My attention wandered barely an instant and it was almost too late!"

Riander sighed and looked at the floor. He said, in a soft voice, "I could give you two reasons. First, that it does indeed take but an instant, and thus that only you can seize the proper moment to remove the cup. Second, that this in itself constitutes one of the tests of knighthood, that those who fail it were not worthy.

"Or I could give you the third reason: that with my student Perradis I did stand next to him, that I did pull away the cup when I sensed he had lost himself—that I cannot forget how all the blood of his body gushed out of him then like wine from a slit skin. It is the way of the cup that only he who uses it may withdraw it."

Riander's hands closed on the cup but did not take it from Adelrune's grasp. He said, "You can still turn back; drink back your life from the cup, and all will be as before." But his face betrayed the thirst he felt. Adelrune had made his choice and did not now relent; he let go of the cup. Riander raised it to his lips and drank.

THE BOOK OF KNIGHTS

When he was done, he said, "You have faced down one of the horrors of your training, Adelrune. Now go lie down on your bed. You are exhausted and more in need of sleep than you can realize."

Adelrune nodded and left the room. He knew that what Riander needed most now was to be alone with his own shame and guilt.

Pain woke him, and ravening hunger. A deep ache burned from the marrow of his bones, flowered along his spine, drove nails of pain into his extremities. The coverlet of the bed was tight as a shroud on him; Adelrune jerked his arms and flung it away. Then he sat up, and vertigo spun in him. He called for Riander; his voice broke and grated.

A terrible itch sprang up on his jaw; he reached up a hand to scratch, felt the pricks of stubble on his skin. Then he saw his hand, huge fingers knobby with bone, veins stark beneath the skin, a blackish down mantling the flesh up to the knuckles.

Adelrune had known he would change, but fear still gripped him at the reality of it. He swung his legs out of the bed—how absurdly short his gown was, it revealed his privates, and how ludicrous this nest of wires at his crotch, and his sex swelling monstrously of its own volition, a further note in the concert of pain that racked him, and he tried to take a step, but his legs were so long they would not obey him as they had done before, and he fell onto the tiles of the floor.

Then Riander was there, and helped Adelrune change into clothes of his own, for now they were almost exactly of a size; Riander brought him to the kitchen and Adelrune's mouth was suddenly filled with saliva; frantically, he gorged himself, unable to assuage the hunger that twisted ever more fiercely inside his gut with each mouthful he took. There was a burst of agony and he *saw* his hand grow before his eyes, and he felt his legs lengthen, and with a rattle on the porcelain dish his last baby tooth fell out of his mouth and was replaced by its permanent sister.

After an interminable time it was over and Adelrune found himself lying down on his bed; but it had dreadfully shrunk and he felt as if he was about to roll off it at any instant.

"You've grown almost a foot," said Riander, who was sitting at his bedside, "and are in fact now a whole inch taller than myself, and distinctly broader. I will have to tailor you some clothes."

Adelrune turned his head to look at Riander. The crinkles at the corners of his eyes had faded slightly, and perhaps his face was plumper, but that was all the indication that Riander had recouped six years of life. That and the guilt that simmered at the back of his gaze.

"Tomorrow we will have to return to the very beginning of your training; you have a man's body, now, and must relearn every reflex. On the other hand, you will find all your weapons have mysteriously lightened."

"I regret nothing, Riander," Adelrune said in the deeper voice that was now his. Riander said nothing and smiled sadly.

5 A DEAD FRIEND

AUTUMN WAS HARSH THAT YEAR, COLD AND WET. FROM AN orchard at the back of the combe Riander harvested baskets of fruit, most of which were made into jam. A few days thereafter, Adelrune was awakened before dawn by a great noise, like immense sheets snapping in a high wind. He looked out through the window of his room, saw a blur of confused movement before the house.

Worrying that some enemy might have come to their door, he dressed hurriedly, putting on a leather tunic and buckling a sword to his side. Riander was already at the door, and smiled to see him so accoutered.

"A very fast response," he said. "I am pleased; you have learned well the importance of promptness. However, this is neither an emergency nor a threat. I should have told you I was expecting a delivery around this time."

"Delivery?"

Riander opened the door wide, and Adelrune saw a variety of sacks and cases on the ground.

"Food," said Riander. "An old friend sends his regards and a shipment of goods every fall, via a rather special courier. Come, we should get this inside, it might start to rain again and I don't want the flour sacks to get wet."

They moved the sacks and wooden crates into the house and to the kitchen. Adelrune, still not fully used to the transformation of his body, was surprised by the lightness of his load, though he was clumsy in maneuvering it.

"What friend is it that favors you with such largesse?" he asked Riander as they were storing the last of the food into a pantry.

"Actually, he's dead," said Riander in a wistful voice. "I met him at the beginning of my life, and he was already old then. He passed away long ago, but an imprint of his will remains on this world. Every year his servants, who obey him still, bring me food, to complement what I am able to obtain by myself. As long as the echoes of his volition perdure, this place that he caused to be built shall stand, and I shall dwell in it."

Riander seemed saddened as he spoke these last words. Adelrune, though he was eager to learn more, forbore to ask more questions on the subject for the nonce.

Autumn shaded into winter. Snow fell heavily in the hills. When the winds blew, they gathered up the snow in huge, snaky drifts, which reminded Adelrune of the Angry Picture of Sir Athebre facing the wyrm.

The house of Riander was kept warm by many fires, though the air grew colder the farther one went from the front of a room, where the hearths were. Once Riander raced against Adelrune along the length of the training room, until they should reach a pair of fencing-dummies. The student beat his master by three yards' lead or more. As he caught his breath, he grew aware of the chill in the air. The light was very dim, this far from the front of the room, where anyway only weak, indirect sunlight entered at this hour. Adelrune gazed about, made out shapes in the gloom. Besides the two fencing-dummies, there were a rack of double-bladed weapons, a frame holding a large family tree drawn on parchment, and a little chariot, child-sized, resting on three wheels.

"I will race you even farther," challenged Adelrune, on impulse. "Another hundred yards?"

"That might not be wise," panted Riander. "There'll be hoarfrost farther on, and then perhaps ice on the floor. And it will be too dark to run safely. Let us go back to the front, if you want to race."

"Have you . . . ever been to the end of these rooms?" asked Adelrune.

"How could I? I thought you understood; they truly go on without limit."

"Then what is the deepest in that you went?"

"Once I walked down my room for an entire day, carrying light and provisions, making notes of what I saw. Then I grew scared; going too deep into any magic is dangerous, no matter how benign the spell may be. I returned to the front of the house, and when I saw my bed, lit by a thin shaft of moonlight falling through the window, it was like returning home after a month's absence. . . ."

"Why did your old friend make this house in such a way?"

Riander told the tale, leading Adelrune back toward the front of the room as he spoke.

"You will forgive me if I don't speak his name. What is left of him in this world might hear it, and grow slightly more aware of its decayed state. We may act from beyond the grave only as long as we forget that we are dead. . . .

"He was a strange man, and I don't claim to have understood him. As for myself, when I met him, I had learned next to nothing in my life. I worked at a trade, half-heartedly, producing mediocre work and earning a mediocre living.

"He came one day to the small shop where I worked, asking for a stool to be shaped according to certain specifications. I received his order politely enough, already telling myself I would work the stool as was convenient and demand payment nevertheless. Then he grabbed my wrist and insisted it had to be shaped precisely as he required, as it was a very special stool.

"I was taken aback; it seemed like he had read my mind. And

then he said 'I *have* read your mind, Riander, that is why I've warned you.'

"I grew scared then, but belligerent as well—I didn't know how else to deal with fear back then. I asked him just why it was so important to have legs of this precise shape, and set at such an angle, when a stool's sole purpose was to rest one's arse upon.

"He promised to show me to what use he'd put it, as long as I crafted it the way he required; he added he'd pay me double what I would have taken otherwise. I accepted the offer, pretending to be convinced by his promised explanation, though both he and I knew it was mostly for the money.

"Yet when I was done with the stool, I felt real pride in it. It was the first time that I knew I had done really well. When he came to fetch it, I was nearly more eager to hear his words of praise than to receive his coin.

"He invited me to his house the next evening, to show me what he used the stool for. And so he did: he'd cast magic upon it and given it the ability to move by itself. He'd sit on it, hooking his feet in the loops of the two forward rungs, and the stool's legs bent and straightened, carrying him forward without exertion on his part. He was old already, as I've told you, and he was starting to husband his resources.

"No one in the town knew he was a magician; he'd kept it a secret all his life. We toured his house, he sitting on the stool I had shaped, with an embroidered pillow under his buttocks, and I walking and constantly turning in circles to see all there was to see. I saw wonders, a hundred things I won't attempt to describe—it would take me forever. By the time we'd concluded the tour I had been changed; I burned with desire. It wasn't that I yearned to be a wizard—which was a good thing, since I didn't have the gift. Rather, the mysteries in his house showed me that there was more I could aspire to in life than my present condition. And though I didn't know what I could or would be, I knew I wanted to become someone other than I was. I wanted to exist as intensely as my friend—the man who would become my friend—existed."

"And so he taught you to teach knight-aspirants?" asked Adelrune.

"Oh, no. He knew nothing about knighthood. Prowess at arms, heraldry . . . Dead subjects for him. But he could teach me how to *learn*. I returned to his house often after this first meeting. He taught me strange syllabaries and gave me lessons in history, but the really important thing I learned from him was how to pursue the truth.

"I found other mentors for myself, in time, though I returned to him always, to renew his gift of the fire of learning. Through him I found myself, learned to know who I was. He couldn't so much read others' minds as see to the core of them. He hadn't heard my thoughts in the carpentry shop, when he'd come to order a stool. Rather, he'd seen what kind of a man I was and he'd known what that kind of man would do with such an order.

"He'd also seen the kind of man I could become. This talent of his he passed on to me, and only in this way might I claim to hold any magical power. It was because he'd seen what I could be that he'd taken a chance on me, that he'd risked taking me to his house.

"I fulfilled my promise. And, once having been transformed through my friend, I sought to repay his gift in the only way possible: by training others. I couldn't pass on the thirst for learning, as he could; but I'd found out that I was gifted with weapons, and disciplines of the mind as well as the body. I had grown up hearing tales of knights, especially brave Sir Vulkavar, who had been born in my own town in my father's time. I believed it was within my abilities to train others to attain that estate.

"When I had resolved to become a knightly mentor, I sought out my friend. His life was drawing to a close; the ravages of time, which he had long put off through his art, were being wreaked on him with a vengeance. He was growing feeble and now moved about, not sitting on the magic stool, but lying full length in a bed equipped with six arms and a dozen legs.

"I told him of my project. I only asked for his benediction, but in fact he gave me far more. He raised and furnished this house for me, in the last and greatest expenditure of his arts. It was, so he said, something he'd wanted to do all his life; he was delighted that I'd given him a good excuse to try it.

"We parted then, for he'd raised the house in a distant land—it had to be set there, for a whole passel of reasons. I set out the next morning, on foot, and weeping, for I knew my friend hadn't long to live and I would never see him again. . . . And that is the story."

Adelrune was silent a moment, respecting Riander's melancholy. They had reached the front of the house, descended the stairs from the training room into the entry hall. Once they'd reached the ground floor, Adelrune couldn't contain himself anymore and asked:

"You said Sir Vulkavar was a contemporary of your father's?"

"Yes. They were the same age, in fact."

"But . . . from what I read in the Book . . . that was a *long* time ago."

"Oh yes. I am very much older than I appear. All those whom I grew up with are dead; the country I dwelled in has been parceled out into five duchies and patched back up several times. I haven't kept track of my brothers' and sisters' descendants, it would have been too much trouble—and to tell you the truth, I was afraid I would grow to care either too much or too little for the bunch. I chose to center my life on my work, and let the world run its course around me. I have lived nearly all my life in this house, with all its books and wonders, and I have been content with standing at the edge of the mystery, knowing only some small fraction of it. After all, even the wisest person in the world can make no other claim."

Riander remained somewhat wistful throughout the winter, his usually cheerful mood perhaps affected by the shortness of the days and the cold. Still, he trained Adelrune as intently as ever, putting the emphasis now on physical mastery. He spent comparatively little time on matters theoretical, though he told many tales of knights he had trained and some he had not, always with an eye to the general principles to be derived therefrom.

Dwelling in this mix of the physical and the philosophical, Adelrune at last reached the level of balance he had attained before the trading of his youth, and started to progress beyond it. After a long period of confusion, his image of himself had changed to fit his new size; now it sharpened even more, as his adult proportions became fixed in his mind and his reflexes improved. His preferences in weapons shifted from light to heavy: the dagger he had gained in the forest now seemed a trifling weapon, far less fit for him than a claymore or a mace. For a time he even essayed his skill with various exotic weapons, all of which required great strength to be wielded properly, until he grew aware of his limits: had he been a giant of a man, like the near-seven-foot Sir Tachaloch, he would have profited from these colossal blades and crushingly heavy chains and balls. As it was, he did better with somewhat lighter arms.

Then, one morning in early spring, Adelrune came into the parlor to find Riander staring gloomily into the ashy hearth. Sensing something was amiss, he sat down in silence and waited for his mentor to speak. Finally, Riander said, "It is a year to the day that you came to me, Adelrune. And at this time I can only conclude that your training is over."

Taken aback, Adelrune protested. "But there are so many things you have not yet taught me! We never went past the first chapter of the desert kingdoms' etiquette, I have hardly trained with the doubleknife, and there is also—"

Riander shook his head. "You asked to become a knight, not an expert on knighthood. To train you further would make you into a scholar, not a fighting man. What remains for you to learn you must learn by living and doing."

Adelrune objected: "I have not chosen my personal weapon; and where is my armor? We never took care of these matters, I was sure there were months yet before . . ."

"What you are saying is that you do not want to leave." And to this Adelrune had no reply. Riander continued, his tone gentle, "I myself do not want you to leave. Of all my students, you are the one it pains me most to let go. But leave you must, or I will have failed.

"There remains the final aspect of your training, the part that must take place beyond this house, beyond my reach. From that test you will gain your armor, and you will know which weapon shall be your emblem. Once you have completed the test, come back to this house and I shall brand you a tried and true knight, worthy of your title and ready to write your own history."

"You had not spoken of this before. What is that test?"

"I never speak of the final test until it is time. The student must not know it is coming. As to what it is, its specifics vary depending upon the aspirant. You can rest assured it will bear upon the essential virtues I have inculcated in you. You must travel away from this house for seven days and nights, in any direction you choose. At dusk of the seventh day, you will reach a testing place. There, do what you shall perceive is required of you, then come back. I shall be waiting for you."

"But what if I do not come back?"

"You shall. In the end, you can only return."

6 GREEN AND GRAY

ADELRUNE SET OUT THE NEXT MORNING. HE CARRIED with him, in a big leather backpack, all that he had brought with him and all he had gained on his first trip, including the pink tablecloth and the playing cards, no matter that they had no practical use. He took nothing from Riander save for food and water, a sword, and a flint. He had felt odd about taking the weapon with him. When he asked Riander whether it was better to leave it behind, Riander said with a wry smile: "If you depend upon the sword, you will probably find you had no need of it; if you leave it behind, you will have reason to curse your lack of forethought."

Adelrune climbed out of the combe, and as it opened into the hills he turned for a last look at the house. The sun had not yet cleared the hills, and so the valley lay in shadows. Still, he could make out Riander in the doorway, waving to him. Adelrune turned away, but the image had soaked into his mind and become like a painting hung at the back of his thoughts.

Adelrune chose a direction among the hills. Rather than cross them perpendicularly as he had done coming from Faudace, he chose to travel along the length of the chain until its end.

The first few days he spent alternately in baking sunshine and chill shadows, as the sun emerged from behind the slopes to beat upon him, then slipped below the heights to reveal the underlying cold of the early-spring air. He strode along the crests of hills whenever he could; for most of a morning he followed a ribbon of wind-worn stones at the summit of a long hill like a dragon's back, which led down into a meadow spangled with trumpet-shaped flowers.

At the end of the fourth day the hills started to submerge under the land. Adelrune camped in a hollow of rock, lighting a fire with the flint Riander had given to him. He still carried Redeyes' scytale in his pack, but he would not touch the thing unless his life depended upon it.

In the morning he left the hills behind and entered a land whose thin soil supported scanty grass and the occasional dry bush. There were some traces of habitation, but never did he glimpse a human shape in the distance. A tinge of abandonment lay over the land. He spent his fifth night within the ruins of a small tower. The place was the ideal home for a ghost, but if there had been ghosts here before, it had grown too lonely even for them, and Adelrune's sleep was left undisturbed.

Throughout the sixth day he traveled westward, and now he discerned a smell upon the wind—the sea. He came to it at day's end, and he stood at the edge of a cliff and watched the sun drown itself, until the brisk wind drove him to find shelter.

On the seventh morning he needed to make a decision: turn northward or southward? Since Faudace had lain to the north of Riander's house, he chose to go toward the south still. The sun rose to his left, to his right the sea sounded on the shore.

The land lowered slightly and by mid-afternoon the cliff was no more than a score of yards high. The land remained deserted and Adelrune started to worry about his test. While traveling, he had been able to put it out of his mind, but now the time drew near. He began scanning the horizon, but saw nothing special, nothing to indicate that *there* a test lay in wait for a knight-aspirant.

The day ended, the sun sank beneath the ocean. Adelrune dropped the few sticks he had manage to gather throughout the

day—combustibles were scarce in this land—and, striking sparks
from his flint, soon made a fire in a little hollow. He wrapped
himself in his blankets and shivered. He thought of the scytale,
and pushed the image away from his mind. He was not at that
point of desperation yet.

Of a sudden a strong wind rose, and blew so hard on his
meager fire that it extinguished the flames. Adelrune cursed and
crouched in front of the branches to shield them from the wind,
fumbling to retrieve the flint from his pack. Then he grew aware
that the flesh of his hands shone dimly in the darkness, as from
reflected light; he turned around and saw a greenish corona
spilling over the lip of the cliff. His chill forgotten, he approached the edge carefully, sword in hand.

The source of the light was clearly visible: at the base of the
cliff, a hole opened into the rock, and from this opening a radi-
ance flowed forth, staining the rock and the waves with viridian.

Adelrune examined the face of the cliff; soon he identified
what appeared a practicable route down to the rocky beach. He
went to the ruins of his fire for his pack, which he buckled securely on his back; then he returned to the cliff's edge and began
to climb down. As he progressed, the light intensified and soon
he could distinguish his own shadow stretching over the cliff
face; the upper part of his body faded into the night, so that he
could fancy his shadow continued, rising vertically past the edge,
invisible in the darkness.

The way down was easier than it had appeared at first and
swiftly he reached the base of the cliff. He stood on a rocky strip
of beach perhaps ten yards wide, wetted at regular intervals by
tiny waves. The opening lay fifteen yards away. From his present
position he could not see into the cave; even standing at the
edge of the sea, he could not see anything except the cave walls,
which appeared smooth, perhaps worked, although the viridian
glow tended to wash out details. Adelrune listened intently for
a few minutes, but heard no sound of any kind. Finally he went
to the opening.

The glow had no obvious source within the cave mouth; it

appeared to issue from the air itself. The mouth was a roughly circular opening into the cliff, a dozen feet in diameter. Adelrune could clearly see the passage, which curved gently to the right after twenty or thirty feet. It was empty.

Adelrune stepped into the cave and walked slowly forward, using a skill Riander had taught him to minimize the sound of his footsteps. Past the bend, the passage continued straight for two hundred paces. The green glow was even stronger here, brighter than any torch. The walls had definitely been worked; a regular pattern of narrowing and widening, like huge faint ribs, yielded to close inspection.

The passage now widened and turned left. Past the second bend, it opened up into a vast cave the floor of which was in a foot or two of water. Adelrune advanced into the cave, keeping close to the left-hand wall, away from the water. He suddenly noticed that a large white spiral shell lay in his path. Now that his senses had registered the object, he began to notice others scattered here and there, some close to the water but many up on the walls, some as high as his shoulders. He bent to study the one near his foot: like a snail's shell, but big as two fists, and entirely white. A thick yellowish operculum sealed the opening of the shell.

Adelrune picked up the shell in both hands, finding it surprisingly heavy. While he looked at its underside, he suddenly heard a thin voice fluting in alarm.

"Oh, woe! He has taken Kidir, and will smash him upon the hard rocks!"

Adelrune snapped up his head and put his back to the wall. He hefted the shell in one hand, preparing to draw his sword in the other. The voice had come from not far ahead, yet he saw no one. Were invisible beings, hidden by the green glow, waiting in ambush for him?

"See, see," continued the voice, "he holds poor Kidir high in his hand, and will now beat him upon the rocks until he cracks and he spills his life upon the stone!"

With a shock Adelrune realized that the voice came from

one of the white shells nearest him, affixed to the wall at chest height. He almost let go of the shell he held, but forced himself to lower it gently to the rock, and then to take two slow steps backward.

"A miracle!" continued the voice in a trembling tone. "His attention diverted, he forgets his murderous fury and lets his prey down unthinkingly! Kidir, your life is redeemed!"

Adelrune saw the operculum quiver, then withdraw inside the shell. A moment later a whitish, glistening mass emerged; it swiftly bloomed into the shape of a man's upper body, complete in all details save for hair. Two very black eyes glittered in a finely crafted face. The manikin saw him and whistled briefly, whether in fear, anger, or consternation Adelrune could not say. In his right hand the manikin now threateningly brandished a spear of whorled chalk not much larger than a toothpick. The scene was so ludicrous Adelrune could not restrain a bark of laughter.

"Ah, the herald-cry of the kill! Kidir, your foolish display has angered the beast. Now he shall pound you with a stone, slay you, and feast upon your corpse!"

"Will you stop that absurd prattle!" shouted Adelrune. "I am no beast, and I have no intention of killing you, much less eating you!"

The manikin called Kidir looked at him, his tiny features compressed into a frown no human flesh could have achieved.

"I do not mean you any harm," said Adelrune. "You can put down your weapon." Seeing that Kidir still held tight to his spear, Adelrune called out, "You! The talkative one! Show yourself!" The operculum of that shell trembled and another manikin peeked out. Adelrune stepped carefully around Kidir and went to stand next to the shell. It was larger than Kidir's shell, and its manikin looked much like a larger version of Kidir, although his build and features were subtly different.

"I do not mean you any harm," Adelrune repeated. "What is your name?"

"The others call me Kodo, but properly I should be known

as First Brood, Senior-but-three, Acting Senior Offspring Kodo."

Adelrune elected not to puzzle over the weird honorifics. "And my name is Adelrune of Faudace, a pupil of Riander. I came here merely because I saw the glow of your cavern and wished to know its source. I am not your enemy."

"Ah, but are you our friend?" objected Kodo.

Adelrune remembered the story of Sir Hydalt's ill-considered friendships and chose to equivocate: "I see at present no obstacle to our becoming friends in the future, Senior Offspring Kodo."

"Well then," pronounced Kodo, obviously flattered by the use of the title, "I can see there is no need for alarm. Kidir! Put down your weapon, like a dutiful offspring, and return to your previous occupations."

"Pardon my ignorance," said Adelrune, "but I have never before encountered beings of your kind. Who are you, collectively?"

"We are the Offspring of Kuzar," replied Kodo. "All one hundred and seventeen of us, divided into First, Second and Third Broods."

"And who is Kuzar?"

"Our progenitor, naturally, since we are his offspring. The logical relationship should have been obvious. You may be of large size, but I suspect your intelligence is of a lower order."

Adelrune let the insulting remark pass. "I meant," he continued evenly, "to ask about Kuzar's reputation and achievements."

"Kuzar's fame we know little of, having led sheltered lives, but it may be significant that ships never came within three miles of this spot. As for his achievements, every day he stretched forth into the sea and ate a gross of fish, most of those larger than yourself; and of course he gave birth to us."

"And how did he catch those fish?" asked Adelrune, growing irritated by Kodo's boasting.

"Sometimes he used his hands, but mostly he opened his mouth and lured them inside with a bright green glow."

Kodo's tone was perfectly innocent, yet Adelrune felt cold sweat run down his back. He inched his hand closer to his sword's pommel and tensed his legs. He scanned the cavern and noticed that quite a few more shells had opened, their occupants apparently peering at him—with friendly interest, or evil intent? The manikin went on. "It was a glow much like the one that permeates this place, I fancy. That glow is one of the most thoughtful gifts our progenitor gave us before his departure: life would be much less pleasant without it, as we see but dimly in darkness."

"You said Kuzar is gone; where exactly is he now?" Adelrune asked carefully.

Kodo raised a tiny bald eyebrow. "I was using a euphemism, which I suppose must have confused you. It is not considered polite to speak of this in blunt terms, but I will make an exception for your sake. Kuzar is 'gone' in the sense of 'dead.' His long life came to an end, and his body has returned to the primordial waters. Yet, of course, he lives on through us."

"Of course." Adelrune now relaxed. What danger could these people be to him? Kodo must be reckoned ingenuous, and so this was the end of it. Adelrune had learned the source of the green glow that filled the cavern of the mollusc-people, and it was of no concern to a knight-aspirant.

"Well, this has been an enlightening visit, Senior Offspring Kodo. I will bid you farewell and go on my way."

"A moment, Adelrune of Faudace. There is a service which you could do me."

"Yes?"

"For a while now it has been my turn to leave the brood-chamber for the outer sea; I have been procrastinating, but the maturation of all three Broods proceeds apace and I can delay no longer. Could you detach me from the wall and carry me outside? I can do it by myself, naturally, but it is taxing labor."

Adelrune shrugged acceptance and reached for the shell. "Wait," said Kodo, "I must formally transfer the reins of authority. Karel! Are you awake?"

A voice answered in a sour tone, from the outer side of the cavern. "I am awake, Kodo. Just say the words and leave us."

"Karel has long coveted my post," Kodo muttered in an aside to Adelrune. "I have hung on in large part to teach him patience, but it has done no good. Ah well." Then he said in a loud voice: "As Acting Senior Offspring, I, Kodo of the First Brood, transfer my authority to Senior-but-four Karel. Let it be so!"

There was no reply from Karel save an ambiguous snort. Kodo withdrew inside his shell and his voice issued from it: "You may detach the shell now." Adelrune worked at the shell's attachment to the wall and soon broke the adherence. Resting Kodo on his shoulder, he left the cavern behind.

When he had reached the sea, he gently lowered the shell into the water. The operculum opened and Kodo poked himself out. "I thank you, Adelrune of Faudace. I will now travel on the currents until I find a suitable place to anchor myself for the sessile remainder of my life."

"Travel safely, Offspring Kodo," said Adelrune politely. He watched as Kodo's shell closed tightly and, impelled by some means of propulsion he had not hitherto noticed, moved jerkily toward deeper waters.

Adelrune now turned toward the cliff. It seemed he would have to climb back up and return to his dead fire; he could not imagine what else to do.

There was a tremendous splash behind him. Adelrune whirled around and saw a nightmarish winged shape emerging from the water with a white shell clutched in one enormous misshapen paw. From the shell came a thin whine of terror.

Adelrune stood immobile, stunned into inaction. Then his hand reached for his sword. *No, no,* screamed a voice—his own—in his mind, *dive to the side, you fool!* Then the winged creature was on him. Two of its remaining three paws seized him below the shoulders. With a shock that nearly snapped his spine Adelrune was lifted up into the night.

He woke with the knowledge of defeat filling his brain. *Stupid boy,* his voice admonished him, *this was your test and you failed it.* With an effort of will Adelrune managed to silence the inner voice. Nothing was lost as long as he still lived. He recalled the adventure of Sir Aldyve and the Wives of Dust and regained some of his courage.

He now became aware of his situation. A gale blew against his back and darkness surrounded him. He was still clutched in the flying nightmare's paws. Their grip had completely numbed his upper body. He could hardly move his arms, and certainly was not able to draw his sword. There was a salty warmth on his upper lip: he had suffered a nosebleed.

Adelrune drew in a painful breath and called to Kodo, but the rushing air tore away his voice, and he got no reply. He tried to think of a clever plan, but the fact of his present physical incapacity appeared insurmountable.

Time might be on his side. Surely the beast must eventually tire, and decide to land? Adelrune could then attack it—unless it decided to release its grasp on him while still two hundred feet in the air, in which case he would die very unpleasantly.

No, this was a fruitless line of inquiry, Adelrune suddenly realized. Instead of its future actions, the creature's motives must be examined. Did such horrors commonly fish the seas at night for such meager prey as Kodo? Why had Adelrune seen no sign of them before? Had Riander's books or teachings mentioned such creatures, and if not, why not?

Adelrune could not recall mention of similar beings in any bestiary. Indeed, the creature's shape was unnatural, its features grossly mismatched. In all probability, it was a demon. And if it was a demon, it had most likely been summoned by a magician and sent to do its master's bidding. What a magician could want with an offspring of Kuzar could not be imagined; and what a magician could want with Adelrune himself included such a vast range of possibilities that again it was impossible to know.

The rush of air suddenly abated, changed direction. Looking down past his feet, Adelrune glimpsed a flickering gray light, which he assumed must come from the window of a dwelling. The winged demon spiraled in, decreasing its altitude and speed at a rapid pace. The window, Adelrune now saw, was a wide opening in the wall of a squat tower of gray stones, which rose above a domelike structure. The demon made one last loop, then flew straight inside. Adelrune suppressed a terrified yelp as it appeared for an instant he would be smashed upon the wall. The demon's wingtips barely grazed the sides of the window, then it released its grip on Adelrune, who dropped to the floor with no more force than if he had missed a staircase's last step. The demon landed a few feet away, still clutching Kodo in one of its four paws.

A man stood next to Adelrune; he was dressed in gray woolen robes, with a felt skullcap the color of ash on his gray-haired pate and mouse-fur slippers on his feet. In a voice that scarcely raised itself above a whisper he inquired "And what is this bedraggled thing you bring me, Melcoreon?"

The demon answered with an articulated brassy shriek. "It stood on the beach and saw me, master, then it reached for its sword, it did, so I took it prisoner like you said, master, like you said."

"What were you doing on the beach, young man, and why did you threaten my servant?"

Adelrune tried to shake his head negatively, but his shoulders were badly cramped and he could not manage more than a quiver. "I thought it was attacking me, sir. I acted on reflex, not to threaten it. As for what I was doing on the beach . . ." Adelrune paused an instant to swallow, and spent the instant pondering what he would say next. A knight never lied, but might equivocate. "I had been travelling for many days. When I noticed the glow that came from the cavern, I was intrigued and came down to investigate."

The gray magician pursed his lips. "Quite. Well, since no harm has been done to my servant, there is no need for retribution. As a matter of fact, I might be slightly in your debt, since you have been brought here through a misunderstanding. Hmm. A moment, if you please." Then, turning to the demon: "Give me the shell-man, Melcoreon. Ah, he is intact. . . . Well done."

The magician put Kodo under a large glass bell. Adelrune opened his mouth, but thought better of it and held his tongue. The demon spoke in a tone both aggrieved and triumphant.

"Master, he is the third one I bring you, and with the man it makes four, it does, and there are only three left!"

"The young man does not count, Melcoreon, as you know very well. Do not even dream of swindling me, or I will penalize you."

"No, no, master, I do not swindle you, I don't. You keep better count than I. But now morning comes, it does, and I am tired."

"You are always tired. But very well, I dismiss you until next night. Begone!"

Melcoreon spread its wings and made as if to take to the air; but instead of rising it seemed to travel in a direction that fit along none of the three dimensions of space. In a moment it was gone, leaving behind an acrid whiff as the only memento of its presence.

"His kind are efficient workers, but very reluctant to serve," the magician remarked. "They never stop with their whines and complaints. Still, that is nothing to you. I notice the trip has left you somewhat the worse for wear. Allow me to help you up. . . . In the next room I have some salves which should help you, and cotton wads for your nose."

Adelrune let the magician lead him through a curtained doorway—whose curtain parted of itself at their approach—

into a small room crammed full with jars, pots, and vials of glass, ceramic, bone, and metal. The magician selected a small pot of cloudy glass and rubbed some of the greasy ointment therein on Adelrune's shoulders and sides. Warmth filled Adelrune's bruised muscles and within seconds he found he could move his arms as if he suffered from no more than a lingering soreness after weapon practice. The magician now dipped two wads of cotton in the liquid contained in a glazed ceramic jar, then stuffed them into Adelrune's nostrils. An acrid chill spread to the back of his mouth. "Remove them in a minute or so. Your blood vessels will be cauterized."

The magician led the way back to the first room. Adelrune followed him diffidently. This was his test, he felt sure; thus, the confrontation could be delayed no longer.

"Well now," said the gray magician, "you will want to be returned to where Melcoreon seized you, which will fulfill my last obligation to you. It is almost dawn now, and Melcoreon would have refused to fly in daylight. I must ask you to wait until night-fall, when—"

"Bide a moment, sir magician. There is a matter that we must settle." Adelrune pointed to the glass bell under which Kodo lay. He had everted himself and now scrabbled ineffectually at the transparent wall of his prison, his tiny face undone by distress. "This . . . shell-man is . . . well, a friend of mine, and I must ask why you keep him prisoner and what you intend to do with him."

"A friend of yours?" The magician's voice was still barely above a whisper but it now hinted at annoyance, and more than annoyance. "Young man, this so-called friend is now my property and what I intend for him is none of your business."

"One cannot own someone else, sir. That is slavery."

"You are amazingly full of righteousness, for an uninvited guest in the home of a magician. And besides, this is an Off-spring of Kuzar, not a man."

"He is intelligent and free-willed; why will you not grant him the same right to freedom as a man?" Adelrune was badly frightened, yet he would not let himself back down. This was to him now a matter of honor, the foremost virtue of a knight.

The magician's eyebrows came together in a dangerous scowl. "Because if left alone, these vermin will attach themselves to crevices in sea-cliffs and grow to enormous size, until they become a serious danger to navigation. Kuzar was tenscore feet in length if he was an inch, and he could sink a ship through mere petulance. And incidentally, I do not grant anyone any 'right to freedom.' This discussion is ended."

The magician reached for the glass bell. Adelrune tried to weigh his decision. Should he accept defeat temporarily, to return at a later time and redress the wrong? It was indubitably the wisest course; he decided to follow it. Then he heard himself speak.

"The discussion is not ended, magician. I must insist that you release the Offspring upon the instant."

The magician stared at Adelrune angrily. His mouth opened to speak, but he held his tongue.

"I know the question you want to ask me," said Adelrune, boldly. "The one no magician will ask because the principles of balance would force him to answer it in turn. You do not need to ask; I will tell you my name. I am Adelrune of Faudace, pupil of Riander, and I demand that you free my companion at once." Adelrune had heard his voice grow firmer as he spoke. It now carried more authority than he had ever dreamed he could wield. He should by all rights be terrified, yet he felt nothing but a wild exhilaration.

"Indeed." The magician now seemed amused and crossed his arms while leaning back against the table. "It seems, Adelrune of Faudace, that your bravado far outweighs your intellect. An attitude that has much to commend it at times, but not in the present situation, I fear."

He uncrossed his arms, brought his palms together on his belly and knotted his fingers. Staring at his hands, he continued: "I can see that you are quite young, Adelrune, and you must still see the world in shades of black and white, as it were. Yet reality is far more complex and ambiguous than you realize or are willing to admit."

Adelrune started to protest, but the gray magician held up his right hand for silence. "Please, Adelrune, I am not finished. Now, were I in your shoes, I would no doubt feel distress that my companion was being detained, but I would not risk opposing a magician of unknown power." He brought up his other hand. "And, *most* especially," he said, clapping his hands together for emphasis, "I would neither give him my name nor allow him time enough to conjure with it!"

So saying, the gray magician drew his hands apart. Between them now grew a rope thick as two fingers, which he threw at Adelrune negligently. Before the knight-apprentice had had a chance to move, the rope had coiled itself, like a serpent of gray velvet, around his body, and bound him tightly, the upper end stuffing itself into his mouth to act as a gag.

The gray magician looked at him with a sour expression. "I can ill afford the karmic consequences of slaying you outright. Thus, I will not feed you to Melcoreon, though he would dearly love to sup on your liver, and would become a more enthusiastic servant for it. I must be content with holding you prisoner until nightfall, when I will have you transported back to the place you were snatched from. You should consider yourself very lucky indeed, Adelrune of Faudace. Tell Riander that if stupidity and naïveté are what he teaches, he has succeeded to perfection in yourself."

The magician made a slight gesture and Adelrune found that his legs were now free from the knees down. "You will follow me," said the magician. "If you stray from the path the rope will tighten around your ankles, so do not waste your time." He led the way to a staircase and down the steps. Adelrune followed. His eyes darted this way and that as he committed the layout of rooms and corridors to memory.

At the bottom of the stairs a long corridor stretched toward the middle of the dome, and soon gave upon another staircase that corkscrewed down to an underground hall, lit by a sourceless, colorless light. The magician motioned for Adelrune to enter a large bare room. As he did so, Adelrune suddenly unleashed all his strength and tried to snap the bonds. He felt the velvet rope start to give, then there was an annoyed hiss from the gray magician, and the rope grew tight again. Adelrune looked at the magician, and saw a few beads of sweat glittering on his brow.

"Since you will not end this foolishness, I will have to guard you more actively," said the magician. "Move to the back of the room." Adelrune did as he was told, and just as he was about to try another burst of resistance the rope tightened still more, one coil of it squeezing his neck almost to strangulation.

Through a dark haze Adelrune saw the magician leave the room. He tried to regulate his breathing, concentrated on getting enough air through his windpipe. The blood beat hard at his throat, and he wondered how long he could withstand this.

Then the magician returned, carrying a large oval mirror which he set in the middle of the room, in front of Adelrune. "Would you like the rope loosened? You would? Very well, then."

The gray rope released its hold on Adelrune, who gasped in relief, hands to his bruised throat.

"Do not look at the mirror," advised the gray magician. Adelrune's gaze flicked to the mirror, then turned away. He had seen nothing in the glimpse except a reflection of himself and the room. "You are really too cooperative," said the magician dryly, as he took the mirror away. Adelrune's reflection stayed behind. The gray magician motioned to the rope, which obediently slid across the floor to coil up his arm, and without further speech he left the room and shut the door behind him.

Adelrune stared at his reflection. He took a step forward; so did the reflection. He raised his hand; his gesture was copied. Six more steps, and he was close enough to touch. His hand met another hand, cold and hard. He tried to touch the reflection's clothes, but its hand mimicked the movement of his own and all he could touch were the cold fingers. He stepped to one side, but the reflection followed suit and blocked any movement past the center of the room. Adelrune drew his sword and threw it toward the far end of the room: the mirror-sword was thrown symmetrically, and the weapons impacted one upon the other, rebounded back in precisely matched positions. When Adelrune picked up his sword, his mirror-twin remained in perfect synchronism.

He took a step backward and sat down in a heap. Laughter bubbled up his throat and escaped his lips. He did not even flinch when the sound of his reflection's laughter impinged upon his and robbed it of all human overtones. There could be no doubt he was a most excellent fool. Yet, somehow, he still was a happy fool.

Riander had made clear the paradox that there could be no clear code of conduct for a knight. The primary demands were clear: honor and justice; but these concepts were immensely tangled, and must be forever tested against limitations of reality, balancing ideal and possibilities. The Rule, in contrast, had been nothing but an interminable list of commands and constraints, and underneath all had run something suspicious that no one in Faudace would ever dare to name.

The Rule would have compelled him to abandon Kodo and make amends to the gray magician, so much was clear to him. The demands of knighthood were more complex; in the end he had to weigh them himself and decide. And though in retrospect it had been most unwise to defy the magician, still his heart insisted that he had done what was right. And if he could not make rightness and wisdom coincide, so be it.

Now to find a way out of this predicament.

For half an hour Adelrune tried various ways of overcoming his reflection: he had an intuition any break in their synchronism would shatter the spell, but there was no way he could achieve that. He experimented to determine how close the contact really was: taking out his sword, he moved it as close as he could to the mirror-sword and traced a perfect straight line from one wall of the room to the other. The line was double not single, but the division between the two was thin as a baby's hair.

Adelrune leaned against the wall, almost touching his reflection. Was his only choice to wait for sundown, when the magician claimed he would be returned to the beach? That would leave Kodo in the clutches of the magician. Was there nothing in Riander's teachings that would help in situations such as this?

Riander had instructed him in the general principles of magic, which Adelrune understood to the extent a layman could. Spells might have great power, but they could always be unraveled—if one found their weak points. Yet apart from breaking the synchronism, Adelrune could think of no angle of attack on the spell.

His gaze had been returning to the end of the line he had scratched in the stone floor with the point of his sword. Somehow, something was wrong; what? It was not the line itself, but its point of contact with the wall . . .

Then he noticed. The walls of the chamber were large blocks of stone separated by thin lines of mortar. The side walls were exactly twenty blocks wide. The middle of the room was therefore indicated by the line of mortar between the tenth and eleventh blocks.

The line he had drawn was fully half a pace beyond that point. The gray magician had set his mirror a little closer to the door than to the far wall—which meant that the space available to Adelrune was slightly larger than the one available to his reflection.

He turned his back to the reflection and strode toward the far wall. He found himself stopped half a pace from it. Turning his head around, he found that the reflection had reached the wall and could not advance any further. Adelrune pushed furiously against the impediment, but could not advance an inch. He snarled in frustration.

There must be a way. With grim determination Adelrune retreated from the wall until his back bumped against the cold hard back of the reflection. Then he gathered his energy and ran full tilt toward the wall. A step before reaching it, he jumped into the air.

He felt a wrenching sensation just before he smashed into the stone. When the stars had cleared from his eyes, he turned around, holding a hand to his once more bloody nose. Against the far wall lay a glittering pile of glass shards.

Adelrune went to the door and opened it cautiously. Should he retrace his steps to the magician's tower? Not yet. Impelled by curiosity he advanced stealthily along the hall and examined the other doors. None had a lock, but all of them opened onto bare rooms. At the far end of the hall, just beyond the stairway leading up, stood a pair of doors. There was a faint smell of brine coming from the space beyond. Adelrune put his eye to the crack between the doors and perceived a thread of vivid green light. He slowly pushed open the right-hand door.

The chamber beyond was wide and high-ceilinged. There were no other visible openings. The chamber was dominated by a large pool from which came the green glow.

As Adelrune came nearer, a large pale shape suddenly emerged from the water. Adelrune had to stop himself from drawing his sword; instead, he spread his arms wide, indicating a lack of hostile intent.

"I do not wish you any harm," he said softly. "You are an Offspring of Kuzar, are you not? I am a friend of your brother Kodo."

The Offspring inclined his head in assent and spoke in a strong rumbling voice barely held in check. "I am Kadul, First Brood, Senior-but-one, though now effectively Senior Off-spring." He greatly resembled Kodo, save in two respects: he had no shell, and he was a few inches taller than Adelrune. "And who are you? No friend of the magician, I feel."

"I am Adelrune of Faudace. I met with Kodo in Kuzar's cave, and helped him start his journey. But he was captured by a demon just outside the cave, as was I. We were both brought here. The magician detained me in one of the rooms by a spell, but I escaped. I do not know what has happened to Kodo."

"As to that, I can guess. For now he is living in a glass tank in the next-to-last floor of the tower and the magician is force-feeding him to accelerate his growth. When he has attained a foot in length, he will be transported to a pool such as this one."

"What does the magician intend for you?"

Kadul pursed his mobile lips. "I expect he plans to use us to further his ambitions. Not far from here lies a lake whose inhabitants he has tried to bring under his rule, but his spells do not work well on large numbers of people. By binding us to his will, he intends through us to cow the people into submission. Or perhaps he will root us close to shipping lanes and demand tribute for safe passage. It may be he merely wishes to study us. One of his experiments cost my younger brother Koryon his life."

"You must be freed. I will help you escape."

"A brave thought, but impractical. Already I have reached the stage when I may not survive very long out of water. Furthermore, I am too heavy to drag myself around. I should have been anchored weeks ago. I fear that there is little you can do to help me directly."

"I cannot let all this go on unchallenged. How many of yours has the magician seized already, and how many more will he take?"

"He has seized the first four of us. Kyad the Senior he killed in the taking, but then he thought of using his demon to snatch us as we emerged one by one." Kadul was silent for a moment. Then he asked, "If I could make one request of you, I would ask for your sword, whose edge seems fine indeed. I am willing to offer a weapon in exchange."

Kadul flexed a muscle and a whorled lance, nearly four feet in length, emerged from a sheath close to his waist. Adelrune recalled the tiny weapon Kidir wielded. He nodded in acceptance of Kadul's offer, though his heart was heavy.

"Chop at the base, to sever it from my body," Kadul instructed, and Adelrune's sword sheared through the Offspring's flesh cleanly. Then he handed it to Kadul.

"Listen well," said Kadul. "This is what I know: we are one hundred leagues from Kuzar's cave, but whether south, north, or east I know not. Half a day's march west is a large lake, and beyond the lake a forest. The magician sleeps during the day and lives by night, when his demons are active. He is confident of his magic, and so you will be able to escape now. The main entrance is up the stairs, and to your left."

"My belongings are still in his tower. I must get them."

"If you must, but that is running a grave risk. Take nothing that is not yours! The law of balance would enable him to extract retribution."

"And Kodo? The magician does not own him."

"If you would save Kodo, Kuzar's favor be upon you."

Adelrune thanked Kadul gravely and left the room, shutting the door behind him. Then he crept up the stairs, retraced his route. He encountered no sorcerous guards, no warding-spells, perhaps because he kept uppermost in his mind his intention to reclaim his belongings and begone.

Finally he attained the topmost room of the tower. In a corner lay his backpack, which he carefully inspected to verify nothing that was not his lay inside. He even brushed it so that no dust from the magician's house adhered to it.

He went back down the first flight of steps and peered around another door. In the room beyond stood a row of glass tanks, and in one of them Kodo lay forlornly. Adelrune had no trouble getting him out of the tank and into his pack. More arduous was forcing him to stop babbling his gratitude.

Down the stairs again, through the exit Kadul had indicated, and out into brilliant sunshine. Adelrune started to run as fast as he could, and it was not until the magician's dome had vanished from his sight that he allowed himself to slow down.

By nightfall he had reached the shores of the lake. Kodo had become torpid, taken away from the water, and so Adelrune took him out of his pack, woke him up, and prepared to lower him into the lake. As he did this, he felt a sudden wave of sadness, and Kodo shuddered at the same instant.

"Kodo," said Adelrune, "you are now the Senior Offspring of Kuzar. I cannot carry you with me any longer. I will wish you a long and healthy life, though I would advise you to anchor yourself on the other side of the lake, if you can get that far."

"Farewell, Adelrune of Faudace. You have been a good friend, and I shall remember you even as I grow into maturity."

Adelrune let the shell slip from his grasp, and watched it vanish beneath the waters of the lake. Then he shouldered his pack and set out for the forest that brooded over the western shore.

7 THE RIDDLE OF THE WITCH

AROUND MIDNIGHT, ADELRUNE FOUND A SHELTERED SPOT on the outskirts of the forest, where he might rest. He recalled with unease his first journey through the forest mantling the hills between Faudace and the house of Riander; but there came no strange noises to his ears, and no odd manifestations greeted him when he awoke.

The sun was already well up; he emptied his pack of the few scraps of food left in it, and considered his options. He had seen no sign of the lake people last night. They might live anywhere on its perimeter, and would not necessarily take kindly to strangers. Also, the gray magician's attention was often on the lake, as Kadul had indicated. Adelrune felt he should distance himself from the mage as much as possible.

It seemed the thing to do was to continue on his journey until he learned his geographical situation. Adelrune sighed glumly. At the very least, he had a hundred leagues' journey ahead of him. To cheer himself up, he brought to mind the story of Sir Baldazel and the five years of toil he had endured before he regained the house which was rightfully his; but he found the results of the exercise dubious.

Keeping particular watch for edibles, Adelrune moved through the forest. So different was it from the one he had first traveled through that after a time it came to seem almost a friendly place, and while the possibility of threats to his life remained, it felt remote. Under the canopy of leaves the air took on a dark green tinge and a rich smell of decay and moisture. There were no animals to be seen or heard, though there were bird-calls. Adelrune after a time found a large growth of edible mushrooms and picked them all, storing the uneaten half in his pack.

Toward the end of the second day, having exhausted the mushrooms and found nothing else that could fill his stomach besides some scrawny tubers, he came across a trail through the forest. It consisted of a pair of shallow parallel ruts, with the faint hint of a third track between them. The trail was clearly not often used, yet it was undeniably present. Adelrune followed it toward his left, away still from the lake and the gray magician.

The ground now sloped gently down. The trees were too dense for Adelrune to obtain any better impression of the situation. As he traveled, the deciduous trees became conifers, and a burnt-orange carpet of fallen needles spread over the ground. Shrubs and undergrowth thinned away, and visibility improved. What was revealed, however, was no more than row upon row of pines and firs.

The tree trunks had a scaly appearance and were punctuated by globs of deep-yellow sap that had oozed out from wounds in the bark. Black ants ran constantly up and down the trunks, clustered on the globes of sap, feelers waving. Did they eat the sap? Adelrune experimentally pared off a small chunk with his dagger and gave it a lick. For all his spitting, the foul taste stayed in his mouth for several minutes.

Adelrune still followed the trail, which grew no fainter and no more distinct. When night came, he chose a spot for his camp; while gathering twigs and branches for his fire, he accidentally brushed some needles away from a reddish feather as long as his forearm. Adelrune glanced upward uneasily. The feather was more than half-decayed, and its position under the carpet of needles further indicated its age; yet it was a sign of cuprous owl all the same. He spent an uneasy night and his dreams were of the sort no one likes to remember.

The morning was cool and foggy; a white vapor reached above head-height and wrapped every thing in its embrace. Without the trail to guide him, Adelrune felt he might have walked around in circles; the fog was thick enough to restrict his vision to a bare dozen paces ahead, and showed no sign of dissipating, nor did the air get noticeably warmer. Adelrune's stomach growled painfully. His food was all gone and he had found nothing else to sustain him; he would have hunted, but no animals walked the forest; he had climbed trees to find bird's eggs, but without success; and his water-bottle was almost empty.

The ground's downward slope sharpened; the trail now entered a proper valley, perpendicularly from its main axis. Adelrune reasoned that there would be a stream at the bottom of the valley and not only a chance to drink fresh water but many edible plants as well.

The sky was overcast and the sunlight wan and gray. Adelrune trudged onward on the trail. Voices came faintly through the air. He paused and listened. He expected the sounds would fail to resolve, but words became distinct, though they were in an unknown language. Several female voices in concert, chanting or singing.

Adelrune continued on the trail, and the voices grew steadily louder. He kept his senses alert, wary of all possibilities. The fog was still all about him, although it seemed to be finally thinning.

He heard a catch of indrawn breath from up ahead and jumped for cover behind a tree. In a flash of vision, he had thought to glimpse a figure holding what might be a bow.

He heard a faint noise of movement, then nothing. Straining his perceptions, he detected nothing. He risked a peek around the bole of the pine, but this brought no response and he could no longer see the figure. He waited for long minutes, but the forest remained still. From a distance came a bird trill much like those he had heard so far—but was it exactly the same? Could it be instead a clever signal?

Adelrune knew he was at a disadvantage. He could not afford to wait indefinitely, while the other presumably could. It was unlikely the other was alone, so that the odds against him were even worse.

He decided to call out, essaying a friendly greeting. In lieu of answer, an arrow whistled out of the fog and buried itself in the tree. Adelrune muttered an expletive under his breath, desperately wishing he had a shield. Some time passed while he crouched behind the tree. The fog decreased slightly, something which was no longer to his advantage. The chanting female voices had fallen silent, but now Adelrune began to hear murmurs from closer up. The archer had evidently been joined by allies.

"I did not wish to intrude upon your territory," shouted Adelrune. "I apologize for my behavior. Can we not deal with this in peace?"

A chorus of angry yells greeted this overture and three more arrows were shot in his direction. A lone female voice rose after that, taunting him in words he could not interpret.

"This is not fair," raged Adelrune. "I cannot even speak your tongue; you leave me no chance to explain myself!"

"We know man-tongue well enough," came the reply. "Explain all you want, you will still end up skewered."

"What is my crime, then? What have I done for you to try to kill me?"

After a moment of silence the woman spoke up, her tone vibrating with rage.

"You are a male, and you have come into this forest which is ours, defying us! You knew of the penalty; do not think to beg for mercy!"

Several more arrows sped toward him, two of them coming somewhat from the sides, evidence that several archers were now moving to positions which would obliterate his cover.

"I did not know of the penalty!" shouted Adelrune. "Why would males be forbidden to enter these woods?"

"Because of the women you have sullied and abused! None

who have forced themselves upon women may enter the forest and live! Come out now and we will kill you quickly. This is all the mercy you will get!"

"I am chaste!" Adelrune shouted back after a pause. "I have known no women!"

There came the sound of a muttered argument; then the woman spoke again, in a less hostile tone: "The bell has not rung. If you are pure, you will be permitted to live. Come out, and you will not be harmed. You have my guarantee."

Somewhat hesitant, Adelrune rose to his feet and came out from behind the tree. Emerging from the fog up ahead came half a dozen women dressed in russet tunics and mud-colored breeches. Each cropped her hair short on one side of the head and let it grow long on the other, braiding it in a complicated pattern. Their leader strode in front. The woman who walked at her side wore a strange hat made from woven feathers and bones and carried a cleft branch on which swung a black bell.

"I am Challed," said the leader.

"My name is Adelrune."

"What do you do here?"

"As I have said, I did not wish to intrude. I seek my way home, but I am lost and do not know where to travel. I hoped by following the trail to reach a settlement."

Challed spared a glance at the bell, then returned her attention to Adelrune.

"This is the Vlae Dhras. It is well known in these parts that no man is allowed within, save if he is yet pure of body. Did no one tell you?"

"I have spoken with no one of this region."

The bell tinkled softly. Challed frowned and two of her archers pointed their bows at Adelrune's chest.

"You are advised not to lie," warned Challed.

"I did not intend to lie," said Adelrune worriedly, belatedly understanding Challed's previous reference to the bell. "The last person I spoke to lives rather far away, so I did not consider him to be properly of this region—perhaps your bell thinks other-wise."

"Who was he?"

"He did not give me his name. He is a mage who dresses all in gray."

Challed's frown deepened. "We know of him. Did he send you here then?"

"I assure you he did not."

"In any case, the Oula must hear your tale in full. We will take you to her."

So saying she led Adelrune down the trail. When it had reached the bottom of the valley, it turned to the right, and soon gave upon a large clearing through the center of which flowed a small, brisk stream. The fog had finally cleared, though the sun remained mostly obscured by roiling gray clouds.

An encampment occupied the clearing, over fifty tents of black felt scattered over the grounds. At the end of the clearing, on a small eminence, stood a large yurt ringed by a series of crossed poles. Adelrune was bidden to wait for the Oula's plea-sure. He asked for permission to go drink from the stream; an archer lent him a tin cup, and another one offered him some boiled tubers which he ate gratefully.

While he awaited his summons, Adelrune studied the camp. There might be as many as threescore and ten women here, all of whom carried bows and spears. Adelrune saw several of them engage in target practice: their skill was remarkable. There were, in addition to the warriors, two or three women such as Challed's assistant. Those carried neither bow nor spear, but they had short-handled, wicked-looking knives strapped to their belts. They alone of the women wore headgear, fragile con-structions of feathers and bones, no two alike.

Seeing that his guardians now treated him with faint cor-diality, Adelrune felt compelled to make conversation.

"Thank you again for the food." One of the women replied with a foreign word. "Pray tell, what is the language you speak?"

"Woman-tongue, naturally. In this place we try to carry no taint of maleness. So we use our own language, which the brains of men are unable to encompass."

Adelrune nodded understanding and cut short his attempts at conversation. Presently Challed returned from the yurt and beckoned for him.

"The Oula will see you now. You must address her at all times as 'Wise One' and answer all her questions in full."

"Should I not leave my weapons at the door?"

Challed shrugged eloquently. "Nothing you do may harm the Oula; it is all one."

Adelrune elected to keep his lance and dagger and diffidently entered the yurt. Inside, the air was hazy with resinous wood smoke. After a short entrance hall delimited by canvas walls, he entered the central space of the yurt, a circular chamber built around a fire pit in which smoldered several large pine logs.

Across from the fire a human form sat hunched, wrapped in a cloak. At Adelrune's entrance it rose. The firelight glimmered on the huge coppery feathers that made up the cloak. The figure's head rose, and Adelrune stifled a gasp. Under an elaborate hat woven of the same feathers, the Oula's visage had been painted to simulate a pair of enormous staring golden eyes.

"Sit down, Adelrune," said the Oula in a dry voice and Adelrune folded his legs under him, and laid his lance across his thighs.

"I greet you with humility and respect, Wise One," he said, summoning up his etiquette lessons, using a formula recommended for high-ranking tribal chieftains.

"Tell me how you come to be here."

"It is a long story, Wise One."

The Oula sat down in silence; after a moment Adelrune set to recounting his adventures upon leaving the house of Riander.

When he was finished, the Oula cleared her throat and spat into the fire. The flames briefly flared a vivid orange.

"I hear no lie in you. As a knight-apprentice, even though your principles are infected by many absurd male ideals, still they come closer to our truth than those of most men. You have frustrated the designs of the gray magician, who is no friend of ours. And your tale was an entertaining one. In counterpart to those three qualities, I will offer you three boons, and a riddle."

"I am most grateful, Wise One."

"Ask for the boons first, then extend your gratitude."

After a moment's thought Adelrune spoke. "Firstly, I am exhausted and hungry—"

"You will be allowed to rest here, and given ample supplies for the rest of your journey. That is your first boon."

"Secondly, I have no idea where to turn my path—"

"I have never heard of the town Faudace, or any of the locales you have described. But I will tell you what I see." The Oula closed her eyes, whose lids had been stained a glossy black to simulate huge pupils.

"I see you walking westward, coming to a stretch of sand and the water beyond. I tell you now that this is the way you must follow to return home. That is your second boon."

"And thirdly," said Adelrune, daring to trust his intuition, "I have traveled so far without armor, knowing I was to gain my true suit during the course of my travels—"

"Rise and go fetch down what hangs upon the peg to your left."

Adelrune rose to his feet and unhooked a strange garment from a peg set in the fabric wall.

"That is you third and final boon."

"I thank you from the bottom of my heart, Wise One," said Adelrune, bowing.

The Oula gave an ambiguous smile. Her teeth were white and whole in her mouth, and suddenly Adelrune perceived her, not as the crone he had thought at first to discern beneath the cloak and the greasepaint, but as a woman from whom the blush of youth had not yet faded.

"And now I will lay the riddle upon you," announced the Oula.

A house in the woods, doors and windows closed.
The first comes, is denied entry.
Then the second comes, brother to the first.
Being small, he finds a way in
Then opens wide the door to the first.
And now the house lies in ruins.

Adelrune pondered the words for a space, then diffidently asked "How long do I have to think, Wise One?"

"You misunderstand. I don't expect you to answer it at this moment. Only in the fullness of time will you find the key to it. You may leave me now."

Adelrune bowed and thanked the Oula again, and exited the yurt. Challed was waiting for him outside. She took him to an unoccupied tent and bade him rest. "Tomorrow morning, you will be escorted to the edge of the Vlae Dhras."

In the tent Adelrune examined the garment he had won as his third boon. It was made from wide crisscrossing strips of boiled leather, further stiffened by fine metal wires running perpendicular to the strips. Odd armor indeed. It had long sleeves, covering his arms to the wrist, and reached halfway to his knees. Adelrune was not truly surprised to discover it fit as if it had been made especially for him. While not as sturdy as a mail shirt, it was light and did not hinder his movements.

Adelrune pondered the riddle of the witch for a while, but could not hazard any guess. The house was certainly meant as a metaphor, but of what? He made a mental list of all the riddles recounted in the *Book of Knights,* and of those Riander had taught him. None seemed akin to this one.

In late afternoon the women of the camp assembled and began again the chant he had heard earlier in the day, but this time the whole of them joined in, and sang for hours. The song seemed to him both lovely and subtly menacing.

Adelrune thought then, as he had not thought for months, of his foster mother Eddrin, and wondered how life might have seemed from her point of view. The Precepts of the Rule concerning women he knew by heart, as he did all Precepts, but as a matter of fact he had never bothered to understand them in the least, since they did not concern him. He had rejected them implicitly, as part of the Rule, but never actually opposed them.

Now he recited them mentally, trying to perceive their implications rather than simply calling up the words from rote memory. He recalled various snatches of the Commentaries, Didactor Maltrevane's "Exhortations Against the Laggard Wife," Didactor Moncure's pronouncements during his visits, trying to see them as if through Stepmother's eyes.

If these women's native lands treated them as the Rule advised women be treated, concluded Adelrune after a while, there was in fact good reason for them to flee to the forest, band together and speak a language reserved for their ears alone. . . .

And then his thoughts turned to the doll in Keokle's shop. He felt a sudden pang of guilt twisting his innards. He shivered, hugged himself and said out loud "I had not forgotten." But it was a lie, for he had forgotten. He had been absorbed in his training, and then in his adventures. It was, in fact, a very long time since he had thought of the doll he had vowed to rescue.

He found his eyes were moist, and angrily wiped them. Surely he could not be faulted for delay! He was trying at this very instant to return to Riander's house, and thence he would go immediately to Faudace, to fulfill his quest. Even if he had forgotten it for a time, it had brought no harm. Still, he vowed silently not to let the doll stray so far from his thoughts in the future, and sealed the bargain with himself by a childish sign, drawing a cross in the dirt and spitting into the center.

He grew calmer after a time, though guilt still simmered in him. He lay staring out of the tent at the clearing, now washed in russet dusk, which echoed to the women's wailing chant. Presently exhaustion claimed him and he slept.

In the morning Challed came to wake him. She had brought food and water enough for many days' journeying. With her

were an archer and one of the lesser witches. The group set out
through the forest, climbing out of the valley. Shortly before
sundown, they reached the edge of the Vlae Dhras. Challed bade
him a formal farewell and the young witch offered an incom-
prehensible yet presumably benevolent invocation. Adelrune
waved farewell to all and set forth.

8 THE INN OF THE FIVE WINDS

AFTER THREE DAYS' JOURNEY HE WON FREE OF THE FOREST and came upon windy steppeland, under scudding clouds. He thought for an instant to detect a tang of salt upon the wind, but the smell proved imaginary.

Adelrune went his way westward, as the Oula had advised him. The steppe bore no tracks that he could detect. The ground was not flat, as he had first thought, but rolled in long shallow waves. Along the trough of each wave a freshet flowed and spindly reeds grew.

On the evening of his second day on the steppe Adelrune spied a large structure on the horizon. In silhouette against the setting sun, it appeared somewhat foreboding, yet he approached it, lonely for human presence.

From closer up, the structure resolved itself into a three-story house, its walls pierced with many windows. A clearly marked trail ran south to north, a dozen yards from the house. A large courtyard in front of the main entrance, facing west, was paved in pink bricks. Four very tall trees grew to the south and north of the house. A long low building, perhaps a stable, was partly visible, north and east of the house. Adelrune examined the scene from a distance, and presently noted a young girl coming out of the house to sweep the flagstones.

Finally Adelrune sauntered up to the house. The girl noted his approach with obvious curiosity but no apparent alarm. As he came to the edge of the courtyard she called out, "Are you come for a room, sir?"

Then it became clear; what else, indeed, could it have been? In how many tales of knights did a lonely inn figure prominently?

"Well, if you have a room available at rates I can afford, I will take it," said Adelrune.

The girl went back inside, motioning him to follow. Adelrune entered in turn, noting a sign hung over the front door, almost weathered into unintelligibility. With frowning concentration he made out the words "Inn of the Five Winds."

The entrance gave onto a large low-ceilinged common room. The girl's call summoned the proprietor: a stocky middle-aged man with a bald pate and a prodigious ginger mustache. He offered Adelrune a room for the night at a reasonable fee. Adelrune agreed and paid in advance, parting with one of the few coins Riander had given him.

The proprietor, who had given his name as Berthold Weer, eyed Adelrune appraisingly.

"And where might you be from, sir? You wear a hauberk in the style of Intidus, but you don't have the look of an Intidan."

"I am from rather far away," said Adelrune, unwilling to be more precise.

"And which way do you travel?"

"Westward."

At this the innkeeper frowned. "You have arrived from the east, then?"

A knight does not lie. "Yes."

The innkeeper said: "East of here is the steppe and, beyond that, the witches' forest." Before Adelrune could offer a reply the proprietor's hand shot forward and he stroked his thumb along Adelrune's jaw.

Adelrune hopped back, ready to defend himself, but

Berthold Weer had spread his hands palms forward in a gesture of peace.

"Apologies, friend, but one has to be sure."

"I do not understand what you mean."

"I had to test your beard stubble. Once, years ago, a witch from the Vlae Dhras came here disguised as a young man and wreaked her spells on an entire caravan. Five men lay dead when we finally managed to catch her. We burned her according to the rites and scattered her ashes in a circle round the inn to deter her sisters from ever returning. Still, a traveler from the east is cause for caution, if you catch my meaning, sir."

"There are lands further east than the forest of the witches, Master Weer. You might have asked."

The proprietor shrugged grandly. "Bah, no harm done, is there? Come, let me show you to your room."

That night Adelrune came down for supper in the common room, deserted save for himself. The serving girl he had already met, Madra, brought him his meal. In answer to his questions, she explained that caravans crossed the steppe several times a month, linking the cities of Dandimer to the north and Thurys to the south.

"And what lies to the west?" asked Adelrune.

"The empty steppe, and at the end of the steppe a town by the sea; its name is Corrado."

"Does anyone travel the steppe alone?"

"No one I've heard of, sir. There are great beasts of prey roaming the steppe: savage pardels and wolves with the minds of men, not to mention the Manticore. Lone travelers go to their death."

Pardels, so Adelrune had learned, usually dwelled in warm forests. Madra's claim of them seemed unlikely. Wolves were more to be believed, though; and what Madra called pardels might well be some other form of predator. Spotted lions, or even plains feroces. Definitely an unattractive prospect.

"I've never heard of the Manticore," he said. "What sort of beast is it?"

"Tall as three men, sir, and with a head that breathes fire from the nose and ears. Just seeing her face makes you die of fright, they say."

Adelrune restrained a skeptical grin. Madra might be letting imagination or credulity get the best of her, but her warning might still be reckoned to hold a core of truth. He had run enough risks for the nonce, he felt. Prudence was often the better part of valor; he would choose the safe course.

"I assume people do travel from Dandimer or Thurys to Corrado; so when might the next caravan be?"

"Perhaps four or five days, sir."

Adelrune mentally evaluated his finances: the Inn of the Five Winds' rates were reasonable, but still he was barely able to afford a week's stay. He would not be able to pay for his passage to one of the cities, but perhaps he would manage to be hired as a guard. No better strategy offered itself.

"I guess I will await the next caravan here, then."

Berthold Weer had come unnoticed into the common room. He now nodded pleasantly to Adelrune, and indicated Madra with a restrained flourish.

"Our Madra is a charming girl, is she not, sir?"

Adelrune politely agreed.

"When the caravan stops by, there is much demand for my girls' services, and prices are high. But I am in a generous mood tonight, and I will loan you her services for a trifling sum."

Adelrune, taken aback, gaped at him.

"If you do not quite fancy her, perhaps you would like to have a look at the others? Chloe works the kitchen and is more on the plump side; you might have glimpsed Ylionne already, coming down; a lovely wisp of a girl, but in all honesty she cannot compare to Madra here."

"No; thank you, but no," Adelrune managed to say. He felt a blush rising to his skin and fought to master it. The innkeeper shrugged in some annoyance and stalked off. Madra gave Adelrune a sad grimace and returned to the kitchen.

Adelrune returned to his room. Berthold Weer's proposal had both appalled and infuriated him. But how could he deal with the man? It was pointless to attempt to convince him to reform his ways; unthinkable to challenge him to combat to settle the affair. Should Adelrune then let events go on without protest? Probably so, despite that the whole matter stuck in his craw. Even should he somehow compel Berthold Weer to release the girls from their servitude, the situation would no doubt return to its previous state as soon as he left.

With sunset all color bled from the sky; the room grew dark. Presently, despite his brooding, Adelrune fell asleep, lulled by the comfort of the bed; a luxury indeed these days to sleep on a mattress! Hours passed as he slept.

There came a crack of wood. Adelrune started awake, flung himself to his feet, seized his lance.

"It's Madra," came a whisper from the darkness.

"Please," he said, "I did not ask for you—"

"I know. That's why I came; I wanted to ask you a question."

The door creaked as it swung shut and now Madra ignited a stub of candle in a cracked dish. Adelrune had somehow expected her to appear clothed in a nightgown, but she was still fully dressed.

"When the master thought you might have come from the witches, he checked that you were a man, and that settled it in his mind. But even if you're a man, it doesn't mean you didn't visit the Vlae Dhras, does it?"

After a pause Adelrune admitted: "No, it does not."

"The witches let men live if they're yet pure; that's what the women say. You refused me because you're chaste."

"I have sworn no vow of chastity," said Adelrune. "I did not ask for your services in bed because it is improper to sell the flesh of others, as Berthold Weer does. Or are you telling me you do this work willingly?"

"Everyone has to eat," said Madra bitterly.

There was an uncomfortable silence. Then Adelrune asked

her softly, "What do you want to know about the Vlae Dhras?"

"You were there? You saw the witches? What did you see?"

"Most of them are not witches, but warriors: good trackers and hunters. They live in tents and sing together; they speak a language of their own which they say men cannot learn. From what I saw, they seemed rather happy. I am lucky they did not shoot me dead on sight, and yet they were mostly kind and generous once we reached an understanding. . . ."

Madra listened to his story in silence, her face in the fluttering candlelight appearing agitated by a hundred emotions.

"Tell me one thing," said Adelrune when he was finished. "Master Weer's story, about the witch and the caravan; was that true?"

"I wasn't here then. They did burn a woman for being a witch five years ago: the caravans brought word of it to Thurys. But I'm sure she did nothing to deserve it."

"Most probably," agreed Adelrune. Madra seemed about to speak again, but kept her silence, and moved to his door. She blew out the candle before slipping out.

Adelrune lay back, troubled. Berthold Weer's offer rang again in his mind, and this time it was not solely outrage he felt, but a stirring of desire. His body shivered and he felt energies moving through him he had not known before. A treacherous part of his mind whispered to him of what he had missed, and a hundred images of lust passed before his eyes in the darkness. Riander had warned him: "The black cup aged your body by six years; but not only did it steal from your life span, it also gifted you with an engine of flesh you have not yet had time to master. I can teach you to control your limbs and your breathing, but there are aspects you will have to master on your own, once you go out into the world."

With difficulty, summoning one of the disciplines Riander had taught him, Adelrune compelled his mind to empty itself of thought. After a long, long time he fell asleep.

* * *

The next day passed slowly. Adelrune's legs itched to travel westward, but Berthold Weer had confirmed the dangers of the
steppe, and so he stayed with his earlier plan. Toward sunset, as
he strolled south of the inn, hoping to see a sign of the caravan,
Madra came up to him.

"I wanted to thank you," she said.

"For what?"

"For telling me about the Vlae Dhras. I've made my resolve;
I leave for the forest tonight. I've stolen some food and a pair of
the master's old boots. I won't see you again, so I wanted to give
you my thanks."

"That is five days' journey at the least!" objected Adelrune.
"Across the steppe, and through the outlying forest. I did not
meet with anything coming here, but that might have been sheer
luck. You may well be risking your life in the journey."

"I'm going anyway. I've always been a witch inside, but it's
only now I've understood it. I'll go, whatever happens."

"In that case," declared Adelrune, "I will accompany you. I
am responsible for your decision, and therefore honor-bound
to protect you."

Madra looked annoyed and relieved in equal parts. She told
Adelrune she would be waiting for him in the stable, behind the
house, at sunset. Sighing fatalistically, Adelrune left to pack.

An hour and a half later, as the sun's rim brushed the horizon, Adelrune made his way unobserved to the stable, having left
money in his room to cover his stay.

Madra was waiting for him, looking like a child in an old
pair of boots of Weer's, carrying a thin gunnysack bulging with
food. "Come along," said Adelrune, and the pair of them made
their way eastward, traveling along the shadow the Inn of the
Five Winds cast upon the steppe.

The sun set completely; only a wash of old rose remained on
the western sky. Adelrune, who had been glancing worriedly at
their backs, began to relax. Then he saw something move against
the darkening eastern sky. He put his arm on Madra's to stop
her, while he focused his eyes.

It flew high, so high that its feathers caught the last rays from the sun, and glittered coppery orange. It wheeled, and it dived at them.

"Down!" Adelrune screamed at Madra, and he shoved her flat against the ground. "Do not move, on any account!"

He bounded away from her, screaming at the top of his lungs and waving his lance to attract the attention of the cuprous owl. The bird altered its angle of descent and came straight at him. Its vast golden eyes shimmered with a light of their own. Adelrune stood his ground and pointed his lance, knowing that his effort was futile. The cuprous owl was so huge it could have lifted off a horse without effort.

The owl shrieked, a sound so terrible that Adelrune's mind reverted to the animal state. Blinded by panic, he dropped his lance, fell prone, and scrabbled against the grass as if to bury himself.

He felt a rush of wind, heard the beating of the vast wings, but the expected shock of the claws into his body did not come.

A measure of rationality returned to him. He had abandoned Madra! Sick with horror, Adelrune forced himself to his feet and looked back.

Only a few heartbeats had elapsed. Twenty yards distant, the cuprous owl hovered above Madra, and gently picked her up in one of its talons. It briefly turned its head all the way around, to fix its gaze on Adelrune one last time, then flew off upward and eastward, carrying Madra.

Adelrune went to retrieve his lance, and gazed to the east for a long while. Then he said aloud: "Fear, Oula. And madness, I suppose. The house, of course, being the mind. The lesson is appreciated, but I confess I find your methods a trifle heavy-handed."

Adelrune returned to the inn, to find it in an uproar. It appeared Madra had left a note to Berthold Weer apprising him of her intentions. When Adelrune entered the common room, Ylionne shrieked and went to fetch the innkeeper.

Berthold Weer, ginger mustache bristling, shouted abuse at Adelrune until the knight-aspirant swung his lance forward, rapping its heel loudly upon the stone floor.

"Enough," declared Adelrune. "Madra is gone, I can assure you she will not be coming back, and that will be the end of it."

"The little bitch was still indentured to me! I have lost at least three years' revenue! You will compensate me for my loss, or else . . ."

Adelrune took a step forward, anger finally uncoiling in him. Berthold Weer's composure fell and he retreated.

"Or else what? I owe you nothing," said Adelrune in an icy voice. "I have paid for my stay here, and you will not get a groat more. If you wish compensation, I suggest you petition the witches of the Vlae Dhras."

Adelrune turned on his heel and strode out of the Inn of the Five Winds, Berthold Weer's muttered curses at his back.

Westward, the Oula had said. He would not wait for the caravan. Under the emerging stars, Adelrune set out across the steppe.

Dawn found him a good distance from the Inn of the Five Winds. All around him spread the steppe, punctuated by small clumps of brush, the occasional tiny pond surrounded by rushes. Adelrune oriented himself by the sun and continued straight to the west.

As the day passed, he crossed the tracks of several hooved animals, which he assumed to be wild cattle of some sort, traveling in packs of five to ten individuals. Judging by the depth of the tracks, they were fairly small and should pose no danger if he should encounter them. Following the tracks briefly, he came upon something disquieting: three very distinct prints of a different nature: deep indentations made by a six-toed paw, with clear evidence of claws. The prints were nearly as large across as his own palm. A feroce? Whatever it was, feroce, spotted lion, or pardel, he had no wish to meet it.

He continued on his way, even more alert for any sign of presence. Yet, apart from the occasional bird wheeling in the distance, and insects buzzing among the grass, the steppe seemed empty.

In early afternoon he came to a dip in the land, at the bottom of which lay stone ruins. Reflecting that these might provide shelter, Adelrune went down to them.

The ruins were not extensive, and appeared to be the remains of a villa. Parts of a tiled floor were extant, and three pillars still stood upright, looking forlorn. The rest of the hollow was filled with a tumble of weathered stones. Adelrune poked carefully among them, wary of snakes' nests and other hidden dangers, but discovered nothing more terrifying than a colony of sow bugs.

It was preferable to travel during the day rather than at night; Adelrune decided to rest here until the next morning. There was plenty of dry grass to build himself a half-comfortable bed, and once this was done he sat with his back to one of the columns and ate.

The hollow was sun-warmed; Adelrune let his eyes close for a second. He felt his limbs go leaden and his breathing slow. With a vast effort of will he opened his eyes. The sun had set, the moon had risen, and the hollow now lay in silvered shadow. Adelrune raised his head—it seemed to weigh a ton—and looked upward.

Against the ink-blue sky, two forms now occupied the top of the other pillars. They were man-sized, and had large wings, whose ragged pinions drooped low. Their heads, deep within the hollow of their shoulders, grew great hooked beaks, and their eyes were set below, not above, their beaks.

One of them tilted its head and slouched forward on its perch to peer at Adelrune. The limbs by which it grasped the pillar looked uncomfortably like long-fingered human hands.

"See, Brother," it remarked, "it does not sleep."

"Not quite, Brother," said its companion. "It does not quite sleep, no, but it is not far from sleep."

"If it does not sleep, it is premature to feed, surely."

"But if it almost sleeps, it is unlikely to defend itself properly, even when the pain comes."

Adelrune knew he must be dreaming; the dream was unpleasant enough that he tried to wake, but he failed.

"But, Brother," continued the first being in its whining, hoarse voice, "when the pain comes, if it does defend itself, it can do us much harm. Look at the lance it bears, look at the armor it wears. Surely it is not an easy prey."

"I maintain that we should feed now. It has been too many days since we ate; I say let us feed upon it."

"Then you must go first, and alone, Brother, for I will not bear the risk of its attack. Go first, Brother, and eat its eyes and tear out its throat, and then it will be safe for all of us."

The second beast fidgeted on its perch, its fingers clenching the rotting stone. "Perhaps," it said after a while, "it would indeed be more prudent not to eat it, since it may be awake enough to defend itself."

"You are cowards, Brother, as well as idiots," came a voice directly above Adelrune's head, and at the revelation that a third creature stood perched not six feet above his head a thrill of fear shot through him, but it was dulled and slowed and did not suffice to free him from his torpor.

"It is not quite asleep," continued the third beast, "and so we should not risk ourselves attacking it."

"So you agree with me, Brother," said the first.

"I do not. You are ready to abandon so much meat, simply because the spell laid on this place has become too weak to hold it! Folly!"

"Then what shall we do?" inquired the second, plaintively.

"Did you not see Herself this morning, Brother, as you flew to the pond?"

"Yes I did, Brother. Herself hunted after a pack of antelopes and could not properly reply to my greeting."

"Then in all probability Herself will not lair far from here tonight. This is what we shall do: we shall fly outward and seek Herself, and once we have found her bring her back to this place. Herself will slay the prey for us, and we shall get half of the meat—at no risk."

The other two croaked assent at the plan and all three beasts flew off into the night. Adelrune, now thoroughly convinced that he did not sleep, exerted his will to the fullest but could not bring himself to move more than a fraction. Fear gripped him and he felt sweat forming on his brow. Was he doomed to remain here until whatever the flying beasts had gone to fetch returned to tear him apart?

When the pain comes, the beasts had said. When the pain came, he might defend himself. Adelrune focused his mind, setting aside his fear and anguish; he exerted his will again, and his right hand crept slowly upward, to his belt and the sheath at his side. Time was abolished; he could not tell if minutes had passed or hours. His fingers closed upon the hilt of his dagger and now he pulled it out of the sheath.

Careful to maintain his grip, Adelrune made his fingers crawl forward along the hilt, past the crosspiece and onto the blade. In the shadows still he could see the strange yellow-green luster of the blade, that had never faded away. He closed his fingers on the blade, setting the tip of his middle finger against the point. And then he squeezed with what pitiful strength was left to him.

The point of the dagger broke his skin and dug into the flesh of his finger. For a long time all Adelrune felt was a dull, dreamy ache, and then suddenly pain blossomed in his finger, and along the cuts the rest of the blade had made in his hand. A wave of burning heat traveled up his arm, reached his heart, and spread outward to his entire body. With a moan of effort Adelrune stood up and freed himself from the spell.

His limbs were sluggish still and he felt as if he floated in some impalpable fluid thicker than water, but he was master of his movements. He picked up his lance and made to leave, but now he heard the flapping of the ragged wings and the rasping voices of the three beasts. "There, there it is, catch it and rend it before it flees!" they cried.

Adelrune knew he could not fight in his present state; and whatever it was that now hunted him at the behest of the winged creatures, he knew that if he tried to flee he would be easily caught and brought down.

Adelrune threw down his lance, and dug into his pack with one hand while he grabbed a handful of the dry grass of his bedding with the other. As quickly as he could, he scattered the grass all around him in a rough circle. Then he wrapped Redeyes' scytale around the bone and for the second time read the five words of the cantrip.

A great ring of fire shot forth from the scattered grass; the flames were near-silver, fringed with blue. The winged beasts called in amazed dread and now Herself stood revealed. She walked on four six-toed paws; her long, lean body was marked in short stripes of black on tan; a dark curly mane grew at her shoulders and throat, and the long neck bore the head of a hag. The Manticore gnashed her crooked teeth and whipped her barbed tail about.

"You, you, you," she wailed, "you promised easy meat!" The three winged beasts stuttered incoherent protests. "Now, now, now, it protects itself with the burning flames!"

The Manticore danced in rage and screamed abuse at her three guides. While two of them flapped high above her, one descended to perch upon one of the pillars and tried to appease Herself.

"Hungry, hungry, hungry am I!" she wailed, and suddenly bunched her legs beneath her and launched herself at the top of the pillar. The winged beast tried to jump away, but the Manticore caught it with a forepaw and bore it to the ground, where she clawed and rent it into bloody gobbets, her screams mixing with those of her victim.

The two surviving winged beasts flew away, exclaiming mournfully upon the sad fate of their brother.

The Manticore rose from the corpse and turned toward Adelrune. Her face was drenched in gore.

"You, you, you," she keened, "I will not forget. One day I will feast upon your heart and your entrails."

She turned away and bounded off. Adelrune watched throughout the rest of the night, but she did not return.

With dawn his fire collapsed as abruptly as it had the first time. Adelrune climbed cautiously out of the hollow, but the Manticore was nowhere in sight. He forced himself to travel as fast as humanly possible, breaking into a ground-eating lope whenever the terrain seemed favorable. Desperate for rest, he allowed himself sleep from late afternoon until nightfall, when he once more made a ring of fire to protect himself. As he stood contemplating the flames, trying to prevent himself from sleeping, an idea crossed his mind.

"Sleep?" he said aloud. "Sleep, and death?" Another solution to the Oula's riddle, arguably better than the first. If he had been meant to discover it before his mishap in the ruins, he had badly failed the test.

Four more days of travel brought him out of the steppe. Throughout that time, while he often felt he must be hunted, he saw no sign of any pursuer. Finally, he smelled salt upon the wind, and came to the shore. Far to the north, his right, he now saw a dim huddle of buildings that must be Corrado. But this destination was not what the Oula had foreseen.

Impelled by his memory of the witch's prediction, Adelrune climbed down to the beach. He stepped up to the edge of the water and gazed at a mass of white clouds on the horizon. He heaved a sigh. He had once more reached the eastern shore of an expanse of water: logic dictated that he had been traveling in the wrong direction. Faudace must lie far to the east, and perhaps far northward as well. What was he to do now? Follow this coast to the north, until he came to the river Jayre, and then go up the river back to Faudace, and thence to Riander's house?

And what if Faudace lay in fact to the south instead of the north? This was also a possibility. He did not even know in which direction to follow the shore!

Adelrune blinked, distracted from his pondering. The clouds he had been looking at had developed an odd dark extrusion while he watched. The extrusion now widened and grew more complex in shape. A line of mushroom-shaped cloudlets? How could they grow at such an extraordinary pace?

But no, not clouds: trees: a forest. A floating island? But there were no such things. Was this a trick of the light, some distant coastline revealed by a spontaneous lensing of the air?

And then he understood. He had taken the sails for clouds, so huge were they. And he had thought that close-packed trees meant a forest and a forest meant land. He had been wrong.

It was no island that traveled the sea toward this shore.

It was the Ship of Yeldred.

9 THE SHIP OF YELDRED

FOR A LONG TIME ADELRUNE WATCHED THE SHIP HEAVE into view. It was so vast that he could not even attempt to estimate its dimensions. As he watched, he saw the immense sails wrinkle and then furl, like clouds thinning away into the air. The Ship grew nearer to the shore. Adelrune could see flocks of birds flying above the hundreds of trees that grew on the deck of the Ship.

When the Ship was still distant, a dozen slim lines were dropped from its side—anchors, no doubt. And indeed the Ship of Yeldred presently stopped its movement. Still staring in fascination, Adelrune noted a tiny craft detaching itself from the Ship the way a dory is launched from a fishing vessel. This craft raised its own sail and came toward the coast. Adelrune sat down upon the sand and waited for it.

When it did reach the shore he was astounded by its size: what he had thought was a tiny craft measured fully fourscore feet from stem to stern. It carried a dozen sailors and perhaps fifteen soldiers in armor. They had seen him early on, and Adelrune was careful to leave his hand away from his lance, which he had ground into the sand in such a way as to be able to snatch it up quickly should the need arise.

The boat reached the shore and the soldiers leaped off it

with fine panache. Their armor was burnished bronze, and their helmets supported extravagant plumes dyed green or blue. The emblem of Yeldred was blazoned on their shields: a golden ship on a field of azure, and above a curlicued Y rune, silver and sable.

"Greeting, stranger," said the leader; Adelrune was surprised to hear a woman's voice. "I am Sawyd, commanding the *Kestrel*. We are envoys from the Ship of Yeldred. You are from the town northward?"

Although her words were clearly recognizable, she had an odd accent, and her intonations had a singsong quality. Adelrune took pains to enunciate his answer clearly.

"No, I am not. I am merely a traveler through this place. I have come directly from the east, and I know nothing about the town to the north, except that it is called Corrado."

"And who are you, with your armor and your strange lance?"

"I am Adelrune of Faudace, knight-aspirant."

"Indeed?" The woman smiled. "You remind me of my brother when he trained for entry into the ranks of the Guards. When do you undergo your trial of certification?"

"To be honest, I believe I have already passed through a number of adequate trials. I have been trying to return to my teacher so that he may dub me."

"If you have been through trials, His Majesty might like to hear of them. Why not come for a visit at court? Maybe His Majesty will be willing to confer your title upon you."

Adelrune hesitated, but the thought of visiting the Ship was irresistible.

"I believe I would enjoy such a visit."

"Very well. Now we must do tedious business: every time we put ashore, we must carefully scout the nearest city and assure ourselves of its peaceful intentions. Not that this little town seems much of a danger, but His Majesty is exceedingly cautious. If you know nothing about the town, please await us aboard the craft. I delegate Urfil, here, to keep you company."

The company of soldiers left for the town. Urfil, a large man, motioned Adelrune to precede him aboard the craft. Adelrune climbed the gangplank and went to sit on a coil of rope; Urfil propped one leg up on a wooden beam, keeping his weapon loose in its sheath. Sawyd had evidently not blindly trusted Adelrune; he could not fault her caution, though Urfil's grin seemed none too companionable. Still, Adelrune had not thought to feel any villainy on Sawyd's part; as a soldier scouting unknown territory, her strategy necessarily depended upon caution. He might well have been a spy sent from the town or some such. Time would prove him out.

He asked Urfil: "Your Ship comes from Yeldred, the kingdom at World's End?"

"Aye. We've been sailing near fifty years on her now. I'm Third Generation, myself."

"I had heard of the Ship, but I would never have guessed how large it really was."

Urfil snorted appreciatively. "From land, even I can't believe it. Some cities, they think we're about to overrun them, and they send war fleets after us, or shoot iron balls at us from big metal tubes that belch flame. But what would we want with hurting cities? We live on the seas, and all we want is trade. Some things we can't make ourselves, and we're willing to pay well. Seems anyone would understand this when they see us, but often they don't."

"What happens when they misunderstand?"

"We sail away, mostly. No point in waging war on the landbound. That's why we anchored far from the town, and why we're sending soldiers by land, so they don't feel threatened. Sawyd's gone to see if these people will fight or trade. Are they reasonable hereabouts?"

"I do not know. As I said before, I come directly from the steppe to the east and have not met the local people."

"Hmm. Where're you from, then?"

"A town called Faudace. Rather far to the east of here, although I have become somewhat lost and do not know the exact direction."

"If you get an audience with the king, ask him to show you

his map. I seen it once, at a pageant. Wider than a man's tall, and half as high. It shows the whole world, and maybe Faudace is on it. Then you could find your way back home."

Adelrune smiled. "Thank you for the suggestion. I would really like to see that map." A weight had lifted from him. This was the key; he would soon know how to return home. He chatted with Urfil some more, trying to learn more about the Ship, but Urfil insisted that what he would see for himself would answer all his questions.

After a time the soldiers returned from Corrado. Sawyd announced that the town magisters had agreed to trade with the Ship and that there was no evidence of any ill-will on their part. The soldiers boarded the craft, which raised anchor and set out for the Ship of Yeldred.

The Ship continued to grow in Adelrune's sight as they drew near, and soon could no longer be encompassed by the eye. As they drew nearer still its side began to seem like a tall chalk cliff and it appeared to him once more that they traveled to an island, on which a dense forest had taken root.

The *Kestrel* finally drew next to the Ship of Yeldred, snuggling up to a wide mass of spongy substance floating at the waterline and designed to cushion any impact against the vast hull. From small balconies three man-lengths overhead sailors threw down ropes to the *Kestrel;* the ropes were then securely fastened to various steel rings set here and there about the hull. The sailors then tied their end of the ropes to stout cables of braided metal descending from the gunwales, still twenty-five yards above them. The cables tautened, and the *Kestrel* was gently lifted from the water, ascending slowly to a berth set ten feet below the gunwales, where it was pulled into place and fastened by another gang of sailors. Adelrune watched all this with wonder, while Sawyd and the crew of the *Kestrel* waited impatiently for the process to finish.

As soon as procedure allowed, Sawyd and her soldiers debarked, taking Adelrune with them. They ascended a stairway that emerged onto the main deck. They were met at a landing halfway up by a florid man in military uniform, wearing no armor. Sawyd made her report in deferential tones, and the florid man nodded in approval. Sawyd then added: "And see here a young man identifying himself as Adelrune, a knight-aspirant traveling from the east, who chanced to reach the shore at about the time we disembarked. At first I thought he might be spying upon us, but the folk of Corrado seem to lack the craft and the forethought to send this kind of spy, so I accept his tale. I felt also His Majesty might enjoy hearing him recount his adventures."

The florid man squinted at Adelrune and gauged his entire character, so it seemed, from an inspection of his outer person. "Ah well, and why not. King Joyell is in a mood to be entertained, these days. This . . . Adelrune, is it? will do. Assign him a visitor's cabin, and let him understand he is expected at the banquet at sundown sharp."

The florid man went up the stairs. Sawyd and her soldiers followed him, Adelrune one of the last of the group.

They emerged at the level of the main deck. Adelrune glanced about and was seized for an instant by a terrible vertigo. Along the gunwale the deck was free of encumbrance: the view was clear all the way to the prow. Without a frame of reference, this would have seemed merely like a large vessel; but people dotted the deck, and the little specks they became toward the prow conveyed a sense of its incredible distance.

As he reeled, arms outspread for balance, though the deck tilted not a whit, Adelrune told himself: *This is not so horrible. Just view it as an island, or a great city. Or think of the house of Riander, then. Remember the rooms extending into forever. This Ship is much shorter than Riander's house ever was.* By dint of such mental effort he regained his composure. Sawyd and the soldiers, who had been watching him grinning, seemed to appreciate the speed of his adaptation. Then they led him toward the interior

of the Ship, which rose in a big untidy sprawl of wooden con-
struction, behind which the forest of trees rose in turn. Standing tall behind the trees, dwarfing them, one of the Ship's masts
rose sky-high. It caused Adelrune such unease to look at it that
he began to abstract it from his thoughts, much as one gazes absently at the night sky, without reflecting upon the awesomeness
of scale it implies.

Sawyd and the soldiers parted. They went toward the stern,
and Sawyd continued alone with Adelrune toward the center of
the Ship.

"How big is this stand of trees?" Adelrune asked.

Sawyd answered: "Three full miles in width, and half of the
Ship in length."

"How do you manage to make it grow?"

"Like trees grow everywhere else: with sun and rain." Sawyd
chuckled. "And of course, a bit of earth. The center of the main
deck is packed with soil twenty yards deep. The soil doesn't perceptibly alter from year to year, but it seems we must constantly
fertilize it, or else the trees suffer. Every year we cut down a few
and replant seedlings in their place. In fifty more years the
forest will be at its climax and we will actually produce more
wood than we need . . . though of course, this time might not
arrive. . . ." She stopped talking all at once and drew Adelrune
somewhat brusquely toward a small house two stories high,
standing some hundred yards distant on the outskirts of the
Ship's central core.

"Within what we call the Town," she informed him, "we use
a simple system of orientation: your dwelling, as its door says, is
Starboard Fifty Astern Three In."

" 'Fifty' what, 'astern' of what?"

"Fifty squares astern of the main mast, and three squares in
from the gunwale," Sawyd patiently explained. "See the design
of the planks on the deck? These darker strips separate the
'squares' of the Ship, as we call them. Remember your address;
if you get lost, anyone can help you find your way home."

So saying, she opened the door of the building and showed him to a cozy little room on the ground floor. "We have no other guests lodged here at present: you have the run of this house, if you want. But all the rooms are alike in any event. You'll be served a light lunch at twelve bells and a collation at four bells, and the evening banquet will come at sundown. You may wander about the Ship as you will, but do be on hand at the banqueting hall before sundown; His Majesty dislikes tardiness."

"Where is the banqueting hall?"

"Just forward of the aft-mast, at the palace itself. It is now . . ." And Sawyd pulled back the sleeve of her bronze mail-coat to reveal a tiny little clock bound to her wrist by a leather strap, ". . . midway between ten and eleven bells. I will leave you, unless you have more questions. No? Well then, I shall see you at the banquet. One last word: our king cares little for outward appearances, but his most dreaded affliction is ennui. Don't waste time making yourself look brave and dashing, but do make sure the adventures you recount are interesting; embroider if you know how. Entertain His Majesty, he may reward you extravagantly; bore him, you risk his displeasure."

Adelrune sat down in a comfortable armchair of withe and shook his head in wonder. He put down his backpack next to the bed and stretched. Wandering about the house he found a bathroom with a small tub full of cold seawater. A sphere of hard soap fragrant with seaweed and spices rested on a shelf next to the tub. Adelrune undressed and washed himself, shivering from the touch of the water. He dared not wash his clothes in the tub and so put them back on, rumpled and stale though they might be. As he dressed, he heard a bell pealing eleven times, a deep sound that seemed to echo from the walls.

He went out of the house, leaving his weapons behind, save for his dagger. Again the scale of the Ship staggered him. People in their hundreds walked everywhere he turned. Some of them eyed him curiously. Adelrune, possessed of a sudden shyness, smiled at them but did not speak. He wandered here and there, crossed the Town and came to the stand of trees. He made his way inward a few hundred yards and it was as if he walked once more within a forest. He saw a russet squirrel perched on an oak limb, heard the twitter of small birds. In a small clearing, a fairy ring of mushrooms grew from underneath a carpet of ancient fallen leaves. Trees surrounded him in every direction, as if this forest were limitless.

Seized by an emotion that was not dread so much as a sense of psychic suffocation, Adelrune found himself running toward the Town, to stand suddenly gasping at the edge of the false forest, where the planking of the Ship's main deck became visible.

He returned subduedly to his room and found a meal waiting for him. He ate in solitude, and afterward went out on deck and sauntered over to the gunwale, and stood gazing out at the land. From the town of Corrado a few small boats—like toys from his vantage—laden with merchandise came to the Ship, and returned shortly after, carrying bales of cloth and other trade goods.

The sun neared the western horizon. Adelrune returned to his room to pick up his lance and made his way to the aft-mast.

The palace was a large edifice of wood and stone, with tall towers and sweeping wings, and windows of colored glass. The wooden walls were carved to show scenes from myth and legends, half-human gods and nameless heroes fighting, loving, dying. Adelrune asked an old man where he might find the banqueting hall. Following his directions, Adelrune entered the palace and soon reached a grand hall at the end of which a pair of massive doors stood closed. A small crowd of people had gathered there, and awaited the opening of the doors. Aware of the unusual figure he cut, Adelrune stood to one side, eyes downcast. After a while Sawyd found him. She had taken off her armor and now wore a smart tobacco-colored vest over a gray shirt and dark breeches, with well-polished boots of whaleskin. Her hair was curly and brown, gathered at the back like a horse's tail.

"I've arranged for you to sit next to me," she said. "When His Majesty asks you to tell your tale, rise from your seat, speak loud and clear, and look only at him. If he waves at you, he is bored: stop talking and sit down. If he nods, go on. Don't stop until he tells you to."

The doors opened shortly thereafter, and the people filed into the banqueting hall. Its walls and floor were stone, and a large fire roared in a hearth. Everyone found their assigned seats. The head table, at which three places were set, remained empty.

Sawyd had taken Adelrune to a table near the head of the hall, perhaps fifteen feet from the king's table. "Bringing the lance was a good idea. Is it a narwhale tusk? His Majesty likes sea beasts."

"No, not from a narwhale." Adelrune paused. "Sawyd, my tale has much death and pain in it, and I fear as a knight-aspirant I cannot distort it. Will it still please the king?"

Sawyd nodded. "Oh yes, I expect it will. Silence now, he's coming! Rise to your feet and bow your head until he's sat."

King Joyell made his entrance. He was a man in late middle-age, with a great dust-gray forked beard. His face was unlined, the face of a younger man. His eyes were a startling blue, gleaming like a child's. His crown, a small circlet of gold, was nearly lost in the waves of his hair.

With him walked a young woman who resembled him too much not to be his daughter. She had her father's blue eyes; her hair was a dark yellow mane, more disciplined than his. While her father wore long robes in purple and scarlet, woven with gold threads, she was dressed in a simple black short-sleeved tunic and skirt, belted at the waist, tawny-yellow hose and black slippers. At her left wrist she wore a small clock like Sawyd's, tied with a silk ribbon. The king sat at the head table, then his daughter sat at his left hand, leaving the third place empty. Everyone else sat in turn, and servants arrived with the first course.

A low buzz of conversation rose, and Adelrune whispered a question to Sawyd. "Why is the third place empty?"

Sawyd quirked a smile. "I would have expected you to ask her name first. She is Princess Jarellene, who recently celebrated her seventeenth birthday, and the place is her dead mother's. By royal decree always set, though no one sits there."

The meal progressed. The food was rich and well-prepared; however, there was no meat, only fish, until the next-to-last course: slivers of roast quail in a delicate sauce, which everyone attacked with relish. Adelrune had been discreetly observing the king's table. His Majesty sat eating with an abstracted air, his gleaming eyes fixed on some invisible vantage. At his left side, the princess Jarellene sampled her food one small bite at a time. Adelrune found himself fascinated by the movements of her delicate wrist, set off by the ribbon of silk and the tiny clock.

"Wasting the quail meat would be impolite," said Sawyd in his ear. "If you don't want yours, will you let me take care of it?" Adelrune shrugged assent and Sawyd slid off the small pieces of meat from his plate onto hers, then leisurely savored them.

The last course was a selection of sherbets, which Adelrune at first mistook for colored snow. Sawyd explained that blocks of ice were stored in stone chests down in the holds, and somehow kept from melting. "The ice is shaved off very fine, then fruit juice is added. We learned to do that from a city far to the east. It has become His Majesty's favorite food."

The sherbets had all been consumed; servants took away the last plates, and set small flasks of blood-red wine upon the tables. Sawyd frowned at her glass when she poured the wine. "Is something wrong?" said Adelrune.

"No matter," she replied, but still she frowned.

The king now signaled to someone outside the banqueting hall; a group of tumblers burst forth, turning somersaults, juggling with daggers and small steel balls. The king fixed his attention upon the tumblers and smiled broadly throughout their performance. Adelrune noticed that Sawyd was still frowning, and toying nervously with her wineglass; but a good part of his attention centered upon the Princess Jarellene, who gazed at the tumblers listlessly, sometimes letting her eyes wander, and once, for a thrilling instant, looking full at Adelrune. Had that half-smile been meant for him, or was it some sort of mask, covering up the ennui beneath? Adelrune hoped it was the first, but some part of his mind, speaking somehow with Riander's voice, was commenting sardonically that this was unlikely.

The tumblers finished their performance and whisked themselves away, to applause from the tables — applause that to Adelrune's ear felt somewhat forced. Now the king gestured to an old man who sat at the table to his left, directly across from Adelrune's table. The old man, bewhiskered and wearing an ornamental collar, cleared his throat and began to recite a tale from the ancient times. Adelrune was immediately fascinated by the tale, which recounted the travails of a dwarfish man who had vowed to kill five giants to avenge the death of his family, but after a minute or two the king waved at the old man, who instantly fell silent and sat down.

A tension made itself felt in the hall; the king's expression was now sour. At his left hand, Princess Jarellene distinctly blushed, eyes lowered, to evoke a sudden lump in Adelrune's throat.

The king turned his attention in Adelrune's direction. "I've been told," he said, "that a young man here has some *new* stories to tell. Where is he?" The king's voice was hoarse, almost grating, the voice of a bitter, aging man.

Adelrune rose to his feet, inclined his head. "I am here, Your Majesty," he said. "If it please Your Majesty, I will recount my adventures as a knight-aspirant." Remembering Sawyd's injunction, he raised his eyes and looked at King Joyell, and incidentally at the Princess Jarellene. The king nodded curtly. "Well then, tell your tale," he said.

Adelrune began, somewhat intimidated. "My name is Adelrune. As a child, I lived in the town of Faudace, far to the east of here. In my foster parents' house I had found a book, the *Book of Knights*, and so I resolved I would one day be a knight. . . ."

As he told his tale, Adelrune saw that the king's face expressed interest and presently enjoyment, and he relaxed and grew more assured in his telling. Once he noted that Princess Jarellene's mouth was downturned, and thinking he was perhaps speaking too softly, he made an effort to raise his voice, but the princess still seemed somewhat displeased.

So he told of his journey through the forest to the house of Riander, of his training, of his journey toward the ocean and his encounter with the Offspring of Kuzar, and thereafter with Melcoreon and the Gray Magician. He recounted his travels through the Vlae Dhras and his meeting with the Oula.

"The next morning, Challed and two of her comrades escorted me out of the Vlae Dhras. I traveled on for three more days until I reached a steppe. On that steppe stood an inn, the Inn of the Five Winds. . . ."

A broad smile had now formed on King Joyell's features. When Adelrune told of his misadventure with the three winged beasts, the king's eyes widened in amazement; as Adelrune described the Manticore and how he had protected himself from her, the king's face appeared suffused with excitement.

Adelrune now finished his tale. "And so I reached the shore of this sea, just to the south of Corrado, and I looked out to the horizon, and thought to see a bank of clouds; but it was your sails I saw, and I stood and stared at Your Majesty's Ship as it hove into view, and waited until the *Kestrel* reached the shore and I met with its crew, who took me here."

Adelrune fell silent, unsure how to indicate his tale was ended and whether he should sit down. It was King Joyell who rose from his seat, his face pink and his eyes gleaming. "Marvelous!" the king crowed, and now from every table rose applause as people struggled hurriedly to their feet. "Take a bow," said Sawyd in Adelrune's ear, and he complied.

"Ah, Adelrune, my dear young friend! Such a tale stirs the blood like nothing else!" exclaimed the king. His voice had become powerful and melodious; it rang like the voice of a young man. "I am more fully myself now than ever. I will retire to the

Octagon, and I invite you to meet me there when it suits you. The rest of you, go to your friends, tell them great things are in the offing! The winds have risen, and our sails belly!" A ragged cheer rose up from the tables, as the king spun on his heel and marched out of the room. The Princess Jarellene, striding out at his side, looked over her shoulder at Adelrune, on her face a mixture of grief and compassion he could not explain.

"Oh, by Dagon," moaned Sawyd, "what have you done?" People were filing out of the banqueting hall, most of them giving Adelrune ambiguous looks, though a few beamed and a few smoldered with anger.

"I did what you told me to do," replied Adelrune, bewildered. "What is going on? What is the Octagon, and what is it that I am supposed to have done?"

"Come with me," said Sawyd grimly, and she dragged him out of the banqueting hall, pushing people out of her way. Once outside, they went through a door guarded by a soldier in ceremonial livery, who obeyed Sawyd's curt order to let them pass.

They stood in a small antechamber, its floor tiled with thin panes of marble. Sawyd took a deep breath, let it out. Adelrune, more confused than alarmed, nevertheless struggled with a sense of impending chaos.

Sawyd bit her lips, then spoke. "You must understand King Joyell is a man given to sudden changes of mood. Sometimes he is melancholy, and all he does is ponder his old maps and play the viola. Sometimes his energy boils up, and then the Ship changes its course toward new horizons, and we must trawl the sea to find new and strange animals, and the army drills and we must forge what little spare metal we have into swords. . . .

"His moods alternate; usually they last no more than a few weeks each, and they are not too deep. But for over half a year now, His Majesty has been growing more and more despondent. Most people feared he would grow so sad he would waste away and die, but those of us in the inner circle knew what would happen: he would shift into his fervid mood, and it might be proportionately violent. I hoped that your story would ease His Majesty's mind, help bring about a smooth change of mood.

"As it happens, he was already shifting before the meal. I could tell because of the wine—he only favors that vintage when he feels aggressive—and the juggling. Telling him your tale no longer seemed such a good idea. I would have taken you away from the hall if I had been able, but I feared it would have angered him out of all proportion.

"If I had known, I would have taken you out still, and risked his anger. . . . You should have warned me." Her tone was bitter.

"Warned you of what?"

"That you did not need to embroider. Your story was better than any we've heard aboard the Ship in years, and it was *true*. It rang with truth, the whole hall could feel it. If it had been lies, His Majesty would have known: he would have been entertained, but not inflamed the way he was. You've fired him up with the passions of his youth, and now he waits for you in the Octagon, and . . ." Sawyd heaved a sigh. "Forgive me. My fault, not yours. Brush off your sleeve, you have bread crumbs on it. The Octagon is the Ship's war room, and His Majesty is waiting for you there, doubtless with his war chiefs, Gerard the Hound and old Possuyl, and most probably he has now decided to return us home and avenge the outrages of generations."

"You return home? To the end of the world?"

"Yes. Someone told you where we first set sail from?"

"My mentor Riander spoke of it. He told me of Yeldred and Ossué, of the tribute your kingdom paid while the Ship was being built. . . ."

"Exactly. And now we are going to get revenge for this tribute. You and I will drown in blood ere this madness is over."

" 'You and I'?"

"You will not leave this Ship for a long time, my friend." Sawyd shook her head sadly. "Now I must take you to the Octagon. Come along, His Majesty does not like to wait when he is in this mood."

Sawyd took Adelrune through narrow, richly decorated corridors, to a tall door of hardwood bound with iron. "Try if you can to be soothing, cautious, calm. His Majesty will be by now looking for any excuse to undertake wild schemes. If you could make your suggestions timid . . . it might be for the best."

"Sawyd—why do you not want to get revenge on Ossué?"

"Only the older people on this Ship ever lived on land. The king himself was a boy of five when we set sail. Most of us care nothing for the landbound; we've set our roots in the ocean. It's insanity to attack Ossué: they had ten times our numbers when we left and must have increased proportionately since. This Ship may look like a terrible force, but it is in fact hideously fragile. If we come too near the shore, we will ground on the shallows and snap our keel. We can defend ourselves, but we would be feeble in an attack." She made an angry gesture. "Enough. The Hound would say I am speaking treason. Perhaps I am only a coward. I command the *Kestrel,* yet I have no wish to die at her helm. Go through the door, Adelrune, and forget I said anything." She left, taking long, mechanical strides. Adelrune knocked softly at the door, then, when no reply was forthcoming, pulled it open.

Beyond the door opened a room of eight sides, paneled in dark wood. Most of the space was filled by a great low table on which were spread a multitude of maps. In one corner of the room a large grandfather clock clanged softly. Three men were bent over the table, scrutinizing a map. One of them was the king, now wearing a light corselet of shining mail; at his left hand stood a sandy-haired man with large ears, who sniffled constantly; at his right hand was a very old man in black robes, his brown skull mottled with dark spots.

The old man now raised his head, glared in Adelrune's direction. "Who is it who enters?"

King Joyell raised his head in turn and welcomed Adelrune expansively. "Come here, lad, and tell us what you think of the situation. Gerard, make room for the young knight."

"Ah . . . not yet a knight, Your Majesty. I have not been pronounced as such yet."

"And I say, young man, that you *are* a knight. I will dub you as soon as possible, to make it official for small minds, but in this room, a knight is what you are!"

Gerard the Hound indicated the map with a grunt. Adelrune bent over it, trying to make sense of the indications. Gerard pointed out the Ships' current position, symbolized by a small metal figurine. Adelrune let his gaze travel eastward and somewhat south on the map, and with a sudden tightening of the throat found a small dot labeled "Foddys" next to a blue line called the "Jar river." On the map, the distance was nothing more than three thumb-lengths. "What is the scale of this map, please?" he asked, and it was Possuyl who answered "Thirty leagues to the inch, more or less."

"Here is the course we have agreed upon, Adelrune," said the king, putting the tip of his finger next to the Ship and sweeping it in a vast arc, north and east, across two seas. "We will make a stopover at the Isles of Chakk, here. Possuyl advised that we should train our forces in debarkation maneuvers at that time. When we depart, we will follow this path—" the king's finger swept on, south by east, then curving sharply northward once more, "avoiding the Quiet Sea, as you suggested, Gerard, and so reach Ossué from the west. We will attack some hours before dawn, and then—" The king's voice rose to a peak and cracked with emotion. He tried in vain to speak on, then simply sank in an armchair, overwrought.

Possuyl nodded sagaciously. "Yes, my King," he said in a husky voice. "And then, indeed. We will do what we have waited so long to do. Ossué will fall, as it was always destined to." Gerard the Hound sniffled loudly. King Joyell looked with glee at Adelrune, who smiled back though he felt chilled inside.

"What does Your Majesty expect from me?" he asked.

The king had recovered the ability to speak. "As the one who woke me to the imminence of action, I will keep you by my side. We will go to battle together, brave Adelrune, and when we stand in Ossué's capital I will make you a baron, or whatever your heart desires."

"Your Majesty is too kind," said Adelrune. For a heartbeat he contemplated asking to be let go now, free to return home, but he knew the king would not grant that request. "How long does Your Majesty expect the voyage will take?" he asked.

"How long, Gerard?" asked the king. The Hound said, "At full sail, with favorable winds, four or five months." Adelrune's heart sank. Nearly a year before he could hope to be back anywhere near his home—if he ever did return.

Remembering Sawyd's advice to express caution, he asked, trying to sound innocent, "Sir Gerard, what do you feel our chances are against Ossué in battle?"

Gerard the Hound fixed him with a dangerous glare and said, "We will win."

"Of course we will win!" cried the king, who stood up once more and grasped Adelrune's arm like an affectionate grandfather. "Fear not, Adelrune! With these two men to advise me, with all of my fine subjects, and with you by my side, we cannot fail! I will show you. Possuyl, let us look at the rosters now. . . ."

For two or three hours the king and his war-chiefs analyzed the situation of their army, evaluated their needs in food, computed various logistical scenarios for the long trip ahead. King Joyell insisted that not an instant be wasted and brushed aside questions of navigational risks, so that Gerard's suggestion of a longer, but less costly and somewhat safer voyage was quashed. "I cannot wait that long. And moreover, Ossué must not suspect that we are in any way near them. Not even a rumor must reach them that the Ship is within half a thousand miles! No, we will proceed as I have outlined before." After this exchange Adelrune abandoned all hope of making some case for caution.

Finally, the meeting ended, not by King Joyell's decision, but at the request of Possuyl, who complained of incipient exhaustion and begged an adjournment till the morrow. The king assented with some ill grace. Possuyl retired. Gerard declared himself somewhat fatigued as well, and pointed to the clock which stated the time was now near to midnight. Adelrune murmured assent; he did not feel tired so much as dizzied by the talk and the figures. "Bah, suit yourselves!" said the king with equal parts bad temper and good humor. "I will go out on the deck and speak with the navigator on duty. I expect us to set forth with the dawn." He strode out of the Octagon.

Adelrune was left alone with Gerard the Hound. There was a moment of silence. "I do not wish to quarrel with you, sir," Adelrune said. "But I beg you to answer my earlier question frankly—I swear I will keep your words to myself."

The Hound sniffled. "I follow my king wherever he goes. If he goes to war, I serve him and advise him, but what he cannot hear I will not bother to tell him. I have no idea what our chances are against Ossué, but I will fight for my king until I can fight no more."

"You are not a man who changes his mind readily," said Adelrune.

"I resent that imputation," said the Hound. "When my king's mood changes, I change with it, without complaint. On the days he feels no use for anything but poetry, I sit by his bed and recite sonnets until I lose my voice. It is Possuyl who never changes his mind. He was a young man in his twenties when the Ship set sail. His sweetheart was taken away, paid over to Ossué for the last cargo of timber needed to finish the Ship. His hate for Ossué is the only thing that has kept him alive all this time. Often I have wondered if I ought to kill him, but my king values his counsel and Possuyl is canny enough not to seek his ear when my king's mood is inappropriate. And I must warn you: if you attempt to impose your will upon my king, I shall slay you without compunction."

And Gerard the Hound went out of the room without further words.

Adelrune found his way out of the Palace with some difficulty and returned to his quarters, only to discover a young servant asleep in his chair. When woken, the boy explained that he was to conduct Adelrune to his new quarters, which were in one of the wings of the palace. Adelrune shrugged and retraced his way, following the boy.

He had been assigned a suite of three rooms on the third floor of the west wing. The vastness almost offended him; he recalled his cramped room on the last floor of his foster parents' house with a bittersweet pang.

The boy set Adelrune's pack on a stool and started to point out the various amenities. Adelrune cut him short, thanked him, and motioned him out the door. Then he went to sit on the edge of the bed, held a hand over his eyes; his body ached for sleep but his mind spun and sparked.

There came a knock at the door. Adelrune groaned in annoyance; what had the boy forgotten? He rose, opened the door, a brusque phrase ready on his tongue. The Princess Jarellene stood at his threshold.

"May I come in?" she asked. Adelrune retreated from the doorway. She stepped inside and only then did he recover his manners and execute the semi-formal bow Riander had taught him one winter's afternoon, "for use when in private conversation with lesser royalty."

"Your Highness," he said.

"Please, do not dance for me. I hate it." She had a voice as soft and mellow as her hair. "Sit down, Sir Adelrune. I must speak with you."

He sat down; so did Princess Jarellene, in the seat next to his. She was close enough that he could smell her perfume, a delicate blend of fragrances in which flowers from the palace gardens mingled with a marine tang. He was aware that his heart beat with an almost painful intensity.

"It seems you have cured my father's despondency. I heard him say he would keep you by his side until we reach Ossué and bring that kingdom down. It is a great honor. Perhaps he will offer you my hand as well."

Adelrune was too stunned to speak. Jarellene looked at the floor. "Not that I am casting aspersions. You are a man of virtue, and not ill-favored. In all frankness, I prefer you to Gerard, if only because your age matches mine."

" . . .More or less," breathed Adelrune. Jarellene paid no attention; perhaps she had not heard.

"I tore out my mother's womb when I was born," she said, "and she bled to death. I almost died then myself. I am told five nurses kept watch by my bed throughout my first night, to blow softly into my mouth whenever I forgot to breathe. They say I wanted to follow my mother into the realm of the dead—but in the end I was persuaded otherwise.

"I will tell you a great secret. I do not like the sea. I have no wish to rule over the Ship when my father dies. Ever since I was a small girl, I have wanted to live on land. Does that shock you? It would appall everyone else on the Ship. If my father had remarried, he would have had other heirs, and I could have freed myself from the ocean, somehow. Now that we are returning at long last to Yeldred and Ossué, there might be a chance for me to escape. When we have cast down Ossué, he will regain his equilibrium. He may well remarry—there is no shortage of available ladies at the court. If this happens I will ask my father to let me rule over the land of our ancestors, and leave the Ship to his other heirs. I have been thinking that if I marry a landbound knight, I will be able to make a stronger case."

"I . . . I do not know what to say, Your Highness."

"When you told of your visit with the witches, you explained that they had allowed you entry by special consideration, and then you glanced at me and stammered, although you did not blush the way you are doing now. You have never had a woman, have you? That was why the witches let you into their forest."

"It is true I am chaste," said Adelrune with what little aplomb he could muster.

"There is no reason for embarrassment. I am a virgin myself. The Ship has visited many lands; in some, women are kept behind veils and not even their husbands see their naked face until their wedding day; in others, women choose their mates and undergo trial marriages, so that an inexperienced girl of seventeen is a rarity. Aboard the Ship of Yeldred, fathers traditionally choose their daughters' husbands, although it is considered archaic not to take the woman's wishes into consideration. But if a woman commits an indiscretion with a man, she is usually compelled to marry him. In this way, I might be able to force my father's hand if he proves recalcitrant."

Adelrune made an inchoate protest in strangled tones.

Jarellene's voice grew breathy. "I know I am callous. I am not an ordinary person. I am a princess of the blood of Yeldred, and my own life does not belong to me. Once I let a page kiss me. We were caught and my father had the boy flogged half to death. No one aboard this Ship is worthy of me in his eyes, save perhaps Gerard the Hound. He will throw me to him as he would a bone." Her face was flushed. She stood up from her seat, grabbed Adelrune's shoulders before he had a chance to react, kissed him on the mouth with an intensity that bordered on violence, pulled back her head; there were tears in her eyes. "I am not insane!" she cried. "I am his daughter, but I do not share his moods! And besides, he is not insane, he is only sad, no matter what you may think! If he knew what we have just done, he would . . ." She let go of him abruptly and fled the room. For a long time, Adelrune sat and waited, but Jarellene did not return. He closed the door, lay down on the bed, and presently slept.

*   *   *

The Ship of Yeldred sailed with the dawn. Its huge sails bellied with the breeze, and after a time its immense bulk began to move. Adelrune woke to find the Ship already well underway. He washed himself in a tub of heated water, put on the splendid clothes he found inside his wardrobe. He felt as if he were wearing a costume.

For a time he sat mournfully by the small ornately framed window of his bedroom, gazing out over the Ship's main deck and beyond that to the sea. Every instant took him farther and farther away from his destination. Had this been a trap set by the Oula? Or had he been foreordained to travel on the Ship of Yeldred; perhaps to die on the shores of a foreign land? Adelrune heaved a bitter sigh. This line of thought clove too close to the Precepts of the Rule for him to accept it. He did not believe the future was fixed and immutable—but this, alas, did not mean one could easily control one's destiny.

At eleven bells, a servant came to fetch him to the midday meal, at which King Joyell was present, though not his daughter. The locale was a small dining room, not the grand hall of the day before; the king sat Adelrune at his right hand, with Gerard the Hound at his left and various other personages of the court at the single long table. King Joyell was in better humor than ever and joked with everyone present. Gerard the Hound guffawed heartily at the king's jests and was at last prevailed upon to sing a bawdy song while strumming a lute. Adelrune watched him with a mix of emotions he did not try to label.

Over the next few weeks a routine began to congeal about him. Midday meals with King Joyell, afternoon conferences in the Octagon, copious repasts in the evening, with entertainments of a vigorous nature: the tumblers and acrobats were supplemented by mock sword fights, which grew more and more frenzied. Princess Jarellene was absent more often than not at the evening meal.

Throughout this time, King Joyell maintained an unflagging good cheer and energy. Whispered reports from his chamber staff had it that he slept barely three hours a night. Ship procedures began to change, on direct orders from the king. Long-established traditions were overthrown, an entirely new set of signals between the Ship and its outriding vessels was devised. The *Kestrel,* along with the nineteen other outriders, was set upon the ocean and various patterns of deployment were tested.

The king's mood had infected the entire Ship, so that most of its inhabitants became restless, infused with an energy they did not know how to dissipate. Fights became much more frequent, and constabulary forces incarcerated several dozen offenders in an appropriate area of the lowest deck, just above the bilge.

Adelrune grew acquainted with the knights of Yeldred, who numbered six. He supposed it was unkind to think this, but they did not impress him as he had hoped they would. They were fine men, skilled at arms and in various arts (though not, of course, riding; there were no mounts on the Ship of Yeldred), and they followed a code of honor. But something seemed to be missing. These men had not had to undergo trials to prove their worth; they had inherited their position from their fathers. Still, Adelrune could not fault their virtue or kindness. And he grew guardedly friendly with Sir Heeth and young Sir Blume. Of the other knights, only Sir Childern was cool toward him.

One evening, Princess Jarellene visited Adelrune in his quarters. She was accompanied by a maid, and spent an hour or two chatting of inconsequential matters. As she left, she thanked Adelrune for his hospitality, and this time obviously expected a bow, which Adelrune tendered. Was this a form of apology, or a new angle of attack? She had proved charming and quick-witted, for all the simplicity of their conversation. When he tried to imagine himself in her place, Adelrune could not really fault her for her despair. Had he not sought escape himself, from the suffocation of the Rule? The face of Didactor Moncure rose up in his mind and he made a grimace of distaste. Could he blame Jarel-

lene for wanting to subvert her destiny? The plans she had con-
fided to him might have been no more than wild schemes entertained solely for relief of the spirit. . . .

She visited him again two days later, and they met by acci-
dent—or so it seemed—in the gardens of the palace the next
week. On that occasion no maid accompanied Jarellene. She invited Adelrune to sit next to her on a delicate bench that over-
looked a pond full of gray-green fish.

"You should disregard what I said to you in our first conversation," she said.

Adelrune recognized this as a royal apology and answered in
the correct way. "Those words have fled my recollection, Your
Highness."

She inclined her head gravely. Then she added: "But I still
hold by my first assessment of you, Sir Adelrune. You are a good
man, and I enjoy your company more than that of Gerard the
Hound. I will tell my father this if circumstances so dictate.
Meanwhile, you may expect to be dubbed before too long. My
father has the servants all in a tizzy preparing the Grand Hall for
the occasion."

"I am grateful to your father and to yourself, Your Highness."

"Perhaps I will see you again soon."

"I would be delighted."

Princess Jarellene rose to her feet and sauntered away, leaving Adelrune astir with various emotions.

Two days later came the ceremony. In the Grand Hall, surrounded by the other six knights of Yeldred, Adelrune kneeled
before King Joyell, who dubbed him lightly on both shoulders
with a ceremonial sword and pronounced him a knight of Yeldred, now and forever. Adelrune rose to his feet amid cheers.
Sawyd came up to him and kissed him on both cheeks. Gerard
the Hound and old Possuyl were on hand to congratulate him

formally, while Jarellene offered him a smile and a delicate nod of the head which seemed charged with meaning.

Adelrune was dispensed from the war council that day; in a dreamy mood he found himself strolling into the forest that grew at the center of the Ship. For a time he wandered the well-tended paths near the palace, but soon he found himself leaving them, to make his way among trees ever more dense. After a time it was as if he traveled a forest of the land. Unlike his first trip into the forest, this time he was not overcome with unease.

He found a pretty little glade among oaks and sat down upon the ground. He should be swelling with pride, his heart leaping for joy; yet for a fact, he felt strangely empty. For so long he had waited to become a knight, and now he was one. Yet it seemed he could not believe it. It was as if something were missing. What could it be?

Riander's presence, perhaps. Adelrune missed his mentor; it was wrong that he should not have been there to attend the ceremony. Perhaps it was something else as well. In the midst of the celebration, he had felt guilt needling at his subconscious, then the memory of the doll in Keokle's shop had floated abruptly to his consciousness. Once more he had felt unease, a sense of shame at the delayed duty. Guilt had come to spoil his joy.

And yet there was nothing he could do. He must be steadfast and serene, remember all the knights before him who had spent weeks, months, years unable to fulfill promises, yet had persevered. He could no more plunge into the sea and swim to Faudace than he could order the Ship of Yeldred turned around. . . .

He saw the doll's pain-twisted face in his mind's eye, felt a rush of pity. "I will come, I swear it," he murmured, and felt some easement of his guilt. He passed a hand across his face. The dubbing ceremony had unnerved him; no doubt his turmoil would abate presently; he would regain perspective and be able to rejoice. . . .

Out from among the trees came Princess Jarellene, in a gown of brown and green like a huntress. She sat down next to him in silence, and now she leaned against his shoulder, extended her face for a kiss. Adelrune could not make himself think; he took her in his arms. His body's urgency would not be denied. Jarellene made no protest and soon her garments lay strewn about.

10 THE WAR WITH OSSUÉ

THE SHIP REACHED THE ISLES OF CHAKK AFTER TWO months of voyaging. It anchored in a deep bay not far from shore and the outriding vessels were all deployed, both for protection in case of hostile presence and to ferry scouting parties to the islands. The Isles of Chakk were too wind-scoured and too distant from the continent to harbor any permanent human population. The scouting parties located sources of fresh water and were able to gather a small quantity of fruit and edible tubers. At the king's insistence, a hunting party was formed and they set off on foot, to try to shoot some of the small game which was to be found—mostly hares and various species of birds. After three hours' exertion, the hunting party returned empty-handed; no one aboard the Ship was trained in hunting on the land.

Sawyd offered to take Adelrune ashore on the *Kestrel* and he gratefully accepted. Even though the Ship of Yeldred was so huge that it neither rolled nor pitched perceptibly, Adelrune felt a keen desire to set his feet on firm ground once more.

"How goes it with you?" asked Sawyd when they stood together at the wheel of the *Kestrel*.

"Well enough," said Adelrune. He did not elaborate, though he knew that Sawyd was probably aware of his liaison with Princess Jarellene.

He and she had met eight times now, always in secluded places, where they would couple with intense physical passion. They spoke little, either during the act or afterward, and when they did speak it was of inconsequential matters. Adelrune wondered about his feelings and hers. A part of him loved her, while another part remained afraid and distant. For this reason as well as because of Jarellene's own silence, he could not bring himself to speak his feelings out loud.

He sought in vain among the stories he knew for help with his situation. Generally, such liaisons as theirs came to a bad end, if only when the lovers were abruptly parted. Thus it had been with Sir Julver and Diamosine, the daughter of the Iron Duke, who disfigured herself in torment at his exile from her father's realm. But then, Jarellene was no timorous, wan Diamosine. Was she then more like the proud and tormented Loraille, who had taken Sir Tachaloch to her bed out of sheer boredom and defiance of established law? Perhaps, but how to know for certain?

For all the energy she brought to their trysting, Adelrune felt Jarellene was fragile, "with an eggshell heart," as the *Book of Knights* put it. When he held her in his arms afterward, she would lay her head on his shoulder and sob gently. In those moments, he could not bring himself to believe that she did not love him; his mouth would open to tell her how he felt, and then she would mutter that she was expected in the music room in ten minutes, and she must leave at once. Adelrune would find himself alone, half-dressed, more bewildered than ever.

The part of him that feared would raise its inner voice then, warn him about the consequences of their trysting. Even if all went for the best, even if they were not doomed to mutual disgrace as Sir Quendrad and Albatte of Wyest had been, he could neither remain aboard the Ship of Yeldred, nor dwell in a land at the end of the world for the rest of his life. He would not let himself forget his quest again. . . . Yet when he brought the doll's image to his mind's eye, all too often he would next behold Jarellene's nakedness as he had first seen it, and his lust would rise up in him, leaving him at once driven and enervated, bold and dejected.

"Have you practiced with your lance of late?" asked Sawyd, snapping him out of his reverie.

Adelrune gave Sawyd a startled look, but she stared placidly ahead; he interpreted her question at the literal level. "Not much, no. Truth to tell, I have spent very little time training with weapons since I came aboard the Ship."

"Then this is the occasion. We will stop over at the Isles for a week or two, at most, and during this time we shall have to train ourselves to our peak. No need to tell you that ceremonial shield His Majesty burdened you with is unsuitable for combat. Do you want one of mine? There are three in my cabin."

Adelrune thanked Sawyd and went to look at the shields. After some thought he picked the heaviest of the three, a well-constructed round wooden shield with a steel rim. On it the Ship of Yeldred had been painted in some detail, floating on vividly rendered foam-crested waves.

The *Kestrel* reached the shore and her passengers debarked, including Sawyd and Adelrune. For a while Adelrune wandered the island, enjoying the utterly stable ground under his feet. Long grasses covered the sandy soil; further inland they gave way to shorter plants; tiny flowers starred the ground, and a few dwarfed, twisted trees stood against the wind. This was a lonely place, but not without its melancholic charm.

He returned to the shore, where Sawyd was engaging in practice battle against Urfil and Choor, two of her men. At sight of him she left Urfil and Choor to engage each other and took herself somewhat apart, in a posture of challenge. Adelrune grinned and hefted his lance in his grip, adjusting the shield on his arm. Then he rushed at Sawyd, lance held dangerously forward. She caught it on her shield, thrust at him with the wavy-edged sword she favored. Adelrune parried with his shield, executed a classical feint followed by a shield-thrust, and Sawyd's sword left her grasp. Adelrune stood back to break the combat, but Sawyd drew a short hatchet from her belt and charged him with a blood-curdling shriek. Surprised, Adelrune was late in reacting; had Sawyd's attack been genuine, it would have shattered his wrist.

As it was, she stopped her thrust at the last instant and fell to laughing. "Pah, what a knight you are! If I fought with a broom, we might be on equal terms."

"Pick up your sword and we will try it again."

They tried it again, and this time Adelrune had the advantage. Sawyd retreated, adjusted her weapons. "A third pass, Adelrune." And now they fell into an exhausting dance which prolonged itself for several minutes, to end with Sawyd's surrender.

"Enough, enough! I am winded." With a grunt Sawyd let herself fall to the sand; she stripped off her plumed helmet and unbound her curly hair, then ran her fingers through it, panting.

Adelrune seated himself in turn. "I may not be much of a knight," he said maliciously, "but I could still fight for a while, whereas I doubt you could hold up even a broom."

Sawyd chuckled. "Have mercy, Sir Adelrune. You are still young, while I will be thirty in a few months. Old women are allowed to be tired, you know."

She fell silent then, but in her eyes Adelrune could read her thoughts. *I may never see thirty. In a few months we will probably be dead, you and I.*

"Let us walk around the island," said Sawyd in a subdued voice, and they did so. After a silent time, she asked, "What is it like, to live landbound? It must be strange always to see the same country surround you, year after year."

"Well . . . When I was young my horizons were very narrow. Faudace is smaller by far in extent than your Ship, but I never saw more than half of it. To me it always seemed like a vast country; even now, when I have seen many places, there are mysteries about Faudace that seem deeper than any I have seen outside of it. . . . Perhaps I only look at it through a child's eyes still."

"What did your parents do? Your story didn't tell."

Adelrune sighed, ill at ease yet unwilling to forgo an answer.

"My true parents I never knew, as I believe I mentioned. My foster father, Harkle, used to be a mason before he and Eddrin adopted me."

"And what were her functions?"

"She was his wife; back in Faudace, few women are anything but wives and mothers."

"Both of my parents work with the Ship's supplies," said Sawyd. "My father is a porter and my mother a storage clerk. They were very surprised when I told them I wanted to join the ranks of the army. How did your parents feel when you chose to become a knight?"

Adelrune let out a strained exhalation. "They never knew. I can barely conceive of their outrage if I had been foolish enough to inform them of my decision. In my house, the most important thing was to obey the Rule. As a child, I memorized all one hundred of its Precepts and most of the *Commentaries*. I could quote it all to you for hours: pages and pages of hateful drivel."

Sawyd had put her arm on his, to make him fall silent.

"Forgive me," she said. "I have been prying where I had no right. I was merely curious, but now I'm making you speak of things that hurt you."

Adelrune shrugged. "There is nothing to forgive. It was a natural question. I am the one who should apologize, for remaining bitter long after the matter has lost all importance. In fact, it is good to have a friend to confide in. You are the second friend I have had, after my mentor, Riander."

He linked arms with her then, and in companionable silence they finished their walk around the island. When they returned aboard the *Kestrel*, Adelrune handed Sawyd back her shield, but she said, "No, no. I meant it as a gift, not just for practice. Take it."

"Oh . . . Then I thank you greatly, Sawyd. This means more to me than you realize."

Adelrune returned aboard the Ship of Yeldred, in the grip of a vague euphoria. A lack he had felt for the longest time had finally been filled. It occurred to him that he had experienced similar bliss not long before, after his latest dalliance with Jarellene; but *that* lack was never filled for long, and indeed now made itself felt anew. Boldly, as if he imagined himself invulnerable, he went to the princess's apartments, and asked for an audience. She received him with grave courtesy, presently sent her maid away on an errand. They went into her bedchamber and for the first time coupled on her bed.

When they were done Adelrune felt languid and stretched out on the fragrant coverlet. Jarellene was already dressing and motioned for him to do the same. "Aline will be back shortly. In fact, I think I hear her in the outer room. . . ."

Adelrune sighed and laced up his clothes. Jarellene cautiously opened the door, but Aline was in fact nowhere to be seen. By the time she returned, Adelrune and Jarellene were once more demurely seated around a low table and discussing the weather.

After some time Adelrune took his leave. As he left, Aline gave him a broad grin and a wink; he nodded politely in return. If this kept up, reflected Adelrune, the whole Ship would soon be in the know.

The Ship stayed at the Isles of Chakk for twelve days. Then, early one morning, not long before midsummer's day, it drew up its anchor and offered its sails to the breeze. Gathering speed, it traveled east by north, on its way toward the kingdom of Ossué.

Excitement aboard the Ship reached a new pitch. The standing army of two thousand had doubled in size with the addition of reserves and volunteers. Metal for weapons was in short supply: everywhere aboard the Ship, people gave up utensils, drinking cups, cauldrons, to be melted into spearheads and swords in the small forges at the stern.

War-councils in the Octagon became less frequent, as every detail had long ago been hammered out, and King Joyell found planning tedious after the third repetition. Adelrune found a little more time to himself; as he could not spend all of it with Jarellene, he busied himself in an exploration of the Ship, and sometimes in combat training with Sawyd or some of her crew. When night came, he would gratefully sink into sleep from sheer exhaustion, without any bothersome thoughts crossing his mind.

And then came the end of their voyage. From the crow's nests at the top of the masts, swaying an unthinkable height above the deck, came word that land had been sighted. The Ship immediately furled most of its sails, swung about to the north, and detached two outriding vessels, the *Harpoon* and *Fair Issia*, to scout ahead. The outriders returned not long after dawn the next day: they had carefully investigated the coastline, and drawn up a detailed map. In the Octagon, King Joyell and his two war-chiefs, accompanied by Adelrune, compared, with the help of the Ship's master cartographer, the map to their records of Ossué's coastlines.

"There." The cartographer pointed to the section of coastline that best matched the approximate map compiled by the scouts. "See that cape? It must be the Hag's Head. And those outthrusts of rock would be the Hag's Teeth."

Gerard the Hound was cautious. "We cannot afford to be wrong," he intoned, but the woman insisted. "No place else matches the map this well. This puts us within half a dozen leagues of Kwayne. Why doubt the work of the navigators, sir?"

"Have faith, Gerard," said the king. "This is all as it should be. We now sail due north. By nightfall we shall be at the proper place. Everyone, begin your ultimate preparations! Sir Adelrune, you shall be by my side from this moment onward, until we stand together in Kwayne's central square!"

The Ship raised anchor and traveled northward. The wind was perfect in both direction and intensity, and King Joyell saw this as a favorable omen. He had retired to his private chambers and paced the floor like a caged animal. For a time he sat down and engaged Adelrune in a game of chess; Adelrune knew the game rather well, having played it often with Riander, but his mind was preoccupied and the king trounced him like a beginner.

The sun set, and shortly thereafter the navigators had the Ship halt its northward movement and swing carefully toward land. All lights aboard had been extinguished so that the Ship would not be visible from shore in the darkness. The twenty outriders were ready to be deployed, each crammed with two hundred soldiers.

The king had gone to the Octagon with Adelrune in tow, for the ultimate conference with his war-chiefs. Gerard would accompany him and Adelrune aboard the flagship, while Possuyl would be aboard another vessel, acting as second-in-command. Not long before midnight Adelrune begged leave from the king for an instant; he exited the Octagon, strode down a seldom-used corridor, opened a door leading to a small closet. In the closet waited Princess Jarellene, as she had promised in the note she had had delivered to him not long before. Adelrune and she embraced with desperate energy.

Her flesh was warm, her skin tangy with both perfume and sweat. The stifling atmosphere within the closet might be responsible in part, but clearly anxiety was the main culprit. Jarellene ground herself against Adelrune, knotted her fingers at the back of his neck as she pressed her mouth to his with bruising force. There were tears in her eyes when she drew back.

"You must be careful," she said. "I do not want you hurt."

"No one knows what awaits us. I promise to be prudent, but I must follow your father."

"That is not good enough," she insisted. "You must promise me you will not be injured. You must promise!"

"Jarellene, I cannot. I have no such control over the future."

"Yes you do. My father does. He is the king, and even Destiny obeys him. You are his favorite; why can it not obey you as well?"

The gleam in her eyes was not only from tears; there was a dose of madness there. Perhaps, Adelrune told himself, she was simply irrational from anxiety. Uneasily, he tried to reason with her.

"I will take all reasonable precautions, I swear. I will not risk my life pointlessly. I am a skilled knight, better-trained in fact than any of the other knights of Yeldred, though I would not say this publicly. I will be safe, Jarellene: your father will keep me by his side. If you believe he commands Destiny, then surely his power will protect me as well."

"You mock me," she accused. "You speak to me the way my father spoke when I was a tiny child and threw tantrums."

"I know you are scared for me; I am trying to reassure you, that is all."

"You must not mock me," she said, her mouth twisting in anguish. "I am not insane, and neither is he. Adelrune, I love you!"

It was the first time she had said it. And, standing within the stuffy confines of the closet, lit only by the stub of a candle, smelling her sweat and his, while he felt his manhood painfully engorged, still Adelrune could tell that she did not truly mean it. She clung to what she called love, but it was a fakery, a deliberate obsession which served her as a bulwark against her own fears, her dread of madness. His heart moved within him in a spasm of feeling, whether love or pity he couldn't tell.

"I . . . I know," he said, unsure whether it would be truthful to say he loved her back, hoping she would hear in his words what she wished to hear. But she could read his face, which he could not guard at such close quarters.

"You think I do not love you," she said, in a tragic tone.

Adelrune merely stammered in reply. What could he say? Riander's lessons on evasion lay in a heap at the back of his mind; he was too much in turmoil to resort to dissimulation.

"I do love you!" shouted Jarellene, and Adelrune hushed her with two fingers on her mouth, fearful that her shouts would be heard. She kissed his fingers, bit at his palm, half the love-bite she favored, half in anger.

"I do love you," she repeated, crying freely. "Oh, how can you doubt it?"

"Please, Jarellene . . . Your Highness . . . You must not put yourself in such a state. I know you feel strongly for me. . . . This is not the time to discuss it. When I return from Ossué, we will talk. You will be feeling better then. . . ."

"Go away," wailed Jarellene, her face undone, "go away!"

Adelrune opened the door of the closet and staggered out. Not knowing what to do, he started to shut it on Jarellene, then left it open a crack and fled down the corridor.

He made his way to the deck of the Ship, stood breathing in the evening air, waiting for Jarellene to appear, screaming at him, for the king to stride out with either a bared sword or a pair of wedding bands in his hand. . . . Nothing happened. Eventually, when he felt that he might successfully conceal his turmoil, he made his way back to the Octagon and the war-conference. Gerard the Hound sniffled inquisitively at him, but Adelrune said nothing to explain his long absence.

Presently the Ship of Yeldred began to travel eastward; two hours later it had reached its planned position and the twenty outriding vessels were deployed. The six knights of Yeldred were each assigned to a ship. King Joyell, Gerard the Hound, and Adelrune were aboard the *Lightning,* the finest of the small fleet. Possuyl was commanding the *Gray Cloud,* to their left.

Not far lay the coast of Ossué and the mouth of the river Liane. Kwayne lay some miles inland, on the banks of the Liane. The Ship could not have sailed up the river by any stretch of the imagination; but the outriders were sufficiently small and maneuverable, and so the plan was to travel straight to the capital and attack before the dawn. Kwayne had no real fortifications, so there would be no significant obstacles to the assault.

A smudge of pink still remained on the western horizon, but the rest of the sky was dark. The outriders traveled swiftly toward shore.

Adelrune was standing by the king's side at the prow of the

Lightning. Suddenly voices were raised behind them; an instant later Princess Jarellene strode to the prow, followed by an angry Gerard.

"My King! Her Highness does not belong here!"

King Joyell frowned at his daughter. "I thought you were to stay aboard the Ship."

Jarellene looked at him with defiance, but in all she spared him little more than a glance; it was Adelrune whom she regarded, once more a gleam of insanity in her eyes.

"I promised no such thing, Father," she said, still looking at Adelrune, who felt his heart sink. "You merely assumed I had. Would you deprive me of seeing our triumph over Ossué? It is my right to be with you now."

Gerard began a protestation, but King Joyell cut him short.

"Come, Gerard! You should be delighted that my daughter has inherited her father's spirit! It is too late now in any event. Jarellene, I am angry with you but I shall forgive you—on the condition that you allow Sir Adelrune to be your protector in this venture. Agreed?"

Jarellene smiled and inclined her head. "Agreed, My Father." She moved close to Adelrune, close enough to whisper in his ear: "I told you I loved you, and now here is the proof. I would not let you go off without me; now I shall never leave you again."

Adelrune, for all his hatred of the beatings he had taken from adults, still wished at that instant to strike her. He kept a tight lid on his emotions and said in a smooth voice, "I shall guard you most carefully, Your Highness."

"Let us have an end to this babbling," grumbled Gerard. "There might be guard posts at the mouth of the river. We agreed on silence and discretion, my King."

But now from the crow's nest of the *Lightning* came a hiss of alarm. Gerard cursed. "Someone has broken alignment, we may run into each other. What fool was it?"

Then a chorus of war-screams rose from up ahead, and a pale yellow flower bloomed on the water. By its light a small galley stood revealed, less than half the size of Yeldred's vessels. The flower was shot upward, and swelled as it came toward the *Lightning*. Shouts of alarm echoed from one vessel to the next. The flower splashed into the water less than three yards from the hull, and vanished in a hiss of steam.

"Take cover!" screamed Gerard the Hound. Other flowers bloomed: flaming balls of tar, held in the arms of catapults. Adelrune counted seven of them. One after the other, in quick succession, they were shot at the forces of Yeldred. Four missed, one struck *Fair Issia* a glancing blow, and two landed on the main decks of the *Stargleam* and the *Fist*. The attack was so unexpected as to slow everyone's reaction, and the enemy ships took advantage of the confusion to close in.

Aboard the *Stargleam*, the fire was rapidly contained, but the other fireball had hit the *Fist* squarely and shattered itself into a hundred burning fragments, setting aflame both the mainsail and part of the deck, and seriously wounding a dozen of the crew.

Gerard bayed orders, and now the vessels of Yeldred regained their cohesion and executed a turn to distance themselves from their antagonists. The latter, however, had been rowing frenetically toward them and now were within range of their lighter weapons. Bowmen shot arrow after arrow toward the vessels of Yeldred.

Aboard the *Lightning*, after the initial surprise, Adelrune had reacted as promptly as he might. Grabbing Jarellene's arm with a painful intensity, he dragged her toward the hold, shoved her down a ladder so that she almost fell. Jarellene protested. "Be silent!" ordered Adelrune. He noted that King Joyell had not followed them. Adelrune had no doubt that in his current mood, he would be oblivious to the danger. Adelrune's duty extended to his safety as well as Jarellene's. "Stay here," he told the princess. "I must get your father to shelter as well." And he ran back up the ladder.

When he came out on deck, King Joyell still stood at the prow, shouting defiance at his enemies. A ball of flaming tar shattered itself against a nearby vessel's hull, eliciting a chorus of cries. Adelrune called to Joyell to take cover, but the king seemed not to hear. Gerard was giving orders at a frantic pace and could not spare any time for the king. Adelrune rushed to Joyell's side, seized his arm, tried to pull him away. The king fought him, bellowing in rage.

Adelrune heard Jarellene's voice behind him. He turned, saw that she had followed him out on deck. "Get back!" he shouted. "Get back inside!" And he pulled on the king's arm roughly, dragging him along through sheer force.

He would never know why Jarellene ran toward them at that instant. He preferred to think that she was coming to his aid, that she feared for her father's safety and wished to see him taken down to the hold quickly.

Whatever the reason, she ran, straight into the path of enemy arrows. As a hail of missiles drummed onto the deck, Jarellene was struck and fell.

Adelrune screamed her name. Letting go of the king's arm, he bolted to her. Joyell ran after him.

The princess lay on her side, surrounded by spent shafts, some of them sunk into the deck and standing vertically, like strange markers. She had taken an arrow through the neck. Adelrune saw no intelligence left in her eyes as he reached out to her. His hand touched her shoulder; and though her flesh was warm, he knew she had died.

Adelrune gathered Jarellene's body in his arms. As he straightened up, another flight of arrows hit the ship, nearer the prow. He hurried down into the hold, King Joyell on his heels.

Yeldred now fought back. Archers returned fire, the vessels assumed a defensive position. Aboard the *Kestrel*, Sawyd saw a tactical opportunity and slewed the ship toward an enemy galley. The *Kestrel* overran the galley and snapped off all the oars on its port side. The galley floundered, and now a score of Yeldred's soldiers swarmed aboard. Another fireball bloomed to life, but the catapult's arm was smashed before the missile could be shot;

the fireball fell onto the galley's deck, and the flames began to spread.

The tide of battle turned; under Gerard and Possuyl's leadership, Yeldred's forces rallied and turned on the enemy galleys. The galleys, deprived of the advantage of surprise, were not able to oppose sufficient resistance. Three were quickly boarded and their crews killed. The remaining four attempted to flee; three of Yeldred's vessels caught up to them and presently the enemy captain had been captured. Three of the four galleys surrendered; the fourth tried to flee close to shore, hoping to deter Yeldred's vessels from following. It fell victim to its own gamble, tore its hull upon reefs, and sank.

Gerard the Hound came below decks to speak with the king. With him was a tall dark man, his wrists bound with chains. Gerard sniffed and coughed. "This is the captain of the fleet," he said softly. The king had been looking only at his daughter's corpse; now with enormous slowness he turned his gaze away and focused upon Gerard and the captive.

"Who are you?" breathed the king in a hollow voice.

"Galwain of Thiroy," said the dark man. "Captain of Ossué's defense fleet."

King Joyell's face grew scarlet; his hands made claws at his side. Adelrune had remained silently by him since Jarellene had been killed, his own emotions a confused swirl which left him capable of little action. But as he looked at Galwain of Thiroy and at the king, something burst inside him and filled him with a clarity of vision and of purpose that had been absent ever since he had stepped aboard the Ship of Yeldred.

The king had half-raised his arms toward Galwain, who glared at him with defiance. Adelrune spoke up in a mocking tone.

"Oh yes, my King, by all means attack him, claw him, make him bleed. You've already killed your daughter, now it is time to kill your son."

King Joyell turned toward Adelrune, taken aback. Gerard the Hound drew a vast breath, but Adelrune spoke again, before Gerard could roar out in protest.

"Your *son,* my King. This man is of your blood; of the blood of Yeldred. He is kin to everyone on this vessel, everyone on the Ship. How can it be otherwise? The people of Ossué were never seafarers. Whom could they have pressed into service aboard their fleet, but those of the blood of Yeldred? For a hundred years you gave the flower of your youth to pay for the building of your Ship. Galwain! Was it your mother that was from Yeldred? Your father? I see it was your father. Why did you wage battle against your kin?"

"I am of Ossué," said Galwain coldly. "All my adult life I have served the defense of the realm. We have maintained the fleet ever since the Ship left Yeldred, in preparation against just such an attack. I feel no loyalty for those who betrayed my father and sold him like a head of cattle."

Gerard shouted in outrage. Adelrune shouted him down. "He is right, Gerard! The youth of Yeldred were sold, like cattle. This is the sin that weighs upon all your souls. It should make you crawl under a rock in shame! Instead, you bring violence and death to Ossué, as if that could erase your fault. The two lands have shared in it, the sellers and the buyers both. And it has come to this. Your daughter is dead, Joyell. Nothing you can do will change it. And the guilt is yours, o my King. You vowed to avenge yourself on Ossué, when the fault was yours, yours all along! *You* killed her, my King, her blood is on your hands! Look at yourself! Look at this madness you have wrought!"

King Joyell's gaze returned to his dead daughter, lying pitiful and frail on a stretch of planking, her face twisted with the pain of her death, blood clotted around the tear in her neck. Adelrune saw the glow of rage in the king's eyes waver, and drove home his point.

"How many more must die to satisfy you, my King? Has

there not been enough death, enough pain and tears? In the name of your dead daughter, who could never live her own life as she had wished it, end this now. It is all pointless, all worthless. There is no meaning to this. None."

His voice had grown steadily softer, down to a whisper. He drew a breath, but he felt drained of words. King Joyell's head drooped, he kneeled by his daughter's side, and began to weep silently. There would be no more need for words. Adelrune had managed to drive him back into despair. He staggered out onto the main deck and leaned against a mast, desperate for fresh air.

Gerard the Hound had followed him. In the light that leaked from below decks Adelrune met his gaze. "I remember your warning, Hound. Will you kill me now?" But Gerard the Hound dropped his gaze and shook his head as if to clear it of some senseless thought.

He turned away, gave a series of orders. The fleet veered in its course and rejoined the Ship of Yeldred.

With the dawn the Ship sailed away to the northwest, into the near reaches of the limitless ocean at the end of the world.

All through the night after the battle, Adelrune wandered the main deck of the Ship. Eventually the sun rose; still Adelrune wandered the vast Ship. The forest rose to his left; he stayed well away from its trees. By pure chance he met Sawyd. She asked him, "Do you know what happened? We received strict orders to retreat. I have sought out the Hound for explanations, but no one knows where he is. Will we attack tomorrow night?"

"Most probably not," said Adelrune. "I believe I have stopped the war." Speaking the last word, his throat constricted and he nearly choked.

Sawyd took his arm, concerned. "Have you been wounded? You need to sit down. I think you're suffering from battle shock. Here, sit."

Numbly Adelrune allowed his body to fold at the waist and

sat down upon a crate. Sawyd loosened his armor then probed skillfully for wounds.

"There is not a scratch," said Adelrune. Then: "Jarellene is dead." It had come out far more easily than he had thought it would. "She was struck down by an arrow. I still cannot believe how fragile people are. Riander tried to teach me, but one does not really understand until one has seen someone die."

Sawyd was stunned. "The princess dead? Why was she aboard the fleet? Wasn't she supposed to stay aboard the Ship?"

"So she was," answered Adelrune in a strained voice. "But she slipped aboard the *Lightning*. She meant to prove . . . to prove something, or so she said. When the surprise attack came, I got her down to the hold. . . . I told her to stay there, but she followed me back up. . . . I fought with the king to get him to cover, and Jarellene came to help me. . . . Then she fell."

He clutched at Sawyd's arm as he told the story, feeling dizzied. After taking a huge breath, he went on.

"I used her death," he said. "The king was ready to drown Ossué in blood to avenge her. But I spoke to him. I accused him, in front of everyone, of being responsible for her death. I drove him down into despair. That is why we retreated: because I convinced him that it was all meaningless."

Adelrune fell silent. The clarity he had felt while delivering his speech aboard the *Lightning* had long since dissolved away. Now he knew not where the correct path lay, if indeed it existed.

"Do you think you can walk a short distance?" asked Sawyd gently. "You should be abed. I could take you to my suite, I have a little guest room you would like."

Adelrune nodded absently and came to his feet. As he walked leaning on Sawyd's arm, he said "There is one thing that frightens me: when I spoke to the king, I found myself using words from the Rule. At one point, I was parroting Didactor Moncure word for word, even to his tone of voice. As if he were speaking through me. I renounced the Rule and its absurdities when I was still a child. I freed myself of its influence when I left home and became Riander's pupil. And now, after all these years, I find myself mouthing it. What am I, Sawyd? I betrayed the king; I failed to protect Jarellene and now she is dead. Riander did not say being a knight would be like this. Somewhere, somewhere I must have failed. . . ."

Sawyd made no reply; she took him to her guest room and gave him a draught of somnifer. Presently he fell into an agitated doze full of inchoate nightmares.

He awoke toward sundown. Sawyd was sitting in the parlor, and rose to her feet when he appeared.

"Are you better?"

"Somewhat, yes. What happened while I slept?"

"The Ship is headed for the open ocean. No explanation given. Possuyl reportedly is in a blue fury and went to the palace this morning to demand the attack be pushed forward. He has not been heard from since."

"How many casualties did we take?"

"All told, less than fivescore people. Only nine dead. The *Fist* was severely damaged but she made it back to the Ship and can be repaired. There . . . there has been no word about Princess Jarellene. Those who saw her death haven't been talking."

"I should probably leave you now. I feel Gerard the Hound may well accuse me of treason, and I would not have you implicated for a kindness you have done me."

"Stay here," said Sawyd. "You are my friend and I'll stand by you. Do you know how many people owe you their lives?"

"I beg you, do not say that."

"It's no more than the truth. Do you recall when I told you how I feared the outcome of the king's venture? Adelrune, whether you will admit it or not, you have saved hundreds of lives."

"Not Jarellene's."

"No. Not Jarellene's. I do grieve for her, but I have seen death before; I can still rejoice because many live who might not have otherwise. I understand that this makes you angry."

"No, I am not angry. Just so . . . *tired,* Sawyd. I feel old. Is that not extraordinary? In Riander's house, I grew years older in the space of a night, but I feel I have aged much more in the time I have been away."

"I felt much the same after I had first witnessed death. It will pass." And Sawyd squeezed his hand, trying to impart a small measure of comfort. But Adelrune only shook his head, like an aged, palsied man.

Later that day the news of Princess Jarellene's death was made public. All through the Ship there was consternation. No details were given as to the circumstances, beyond the fact that she had chosen to accompany her father aboard the *Lightning* and had been slain during the battle. By the next morning, Sawyd had overheard half a dozen rumors, all of them speculating on Jarellene's means of death, the wildest asserting that the princess had in fact committed suicide in protest at the attack on Ossué. Though these stories continued to circulate, it seemed not even their most ardent propagators gave them much credence; perhaps they were mostly a way to distract shock and grief.

Two days later, at sundown, Princess Jarellene's body was given to the waters. She was dressed not in robes of state, but in the simple dark tunic and skirt she had favored. The tiny clock on its silk ribbon was tied around her left wrist. She was sealed in a jeweled casket with a crystal window in the lid, that the light of the deeps not be kept from her face. The casket was launched from the sterncastle and fell a long distance before hitting the water, disappearing in a splash of foam.

King Joyell was present at the ceremony, but his gaze was dull and lifeless. When it was all over, he went away, looking puzzledly right and left as if he wondered what he had been doing there.

Adelrune stood to one side, with Sawyd. He had not returned to his apartments at the castle, staying instead, at her insistence, in her guest room. She had helped him shed some of his gloom, and though his grief for Jarellene was still keen he no longer felt guilty to be alive.

Officially, the Ship was no longer in a state of war; with the king too distraught to give any orders and Gerard as mute as Joyell, Possuyl had attempted to assert authority but could not sustain it. Following a chain of blood relations, command now fell to the king's cousin, Lord Melborne, a quiet man of middle age with not a shred of decisiveness in him. For a week the Ship stayed on its course, until the navigators advised that they turn south, as they were headed into poorly charted regions.

The Ship of Yeldred perforce turned southward, and stayed on that course until it neared land. More by reflex than by conscious design, Lord Melborne ordered the Ship follow the coast at a wide distance. King Joyell meanwhile remained deeply affected and kept to his rooms. Once he was prevailed upon to come out on deck; Adelrune, observing from a distance, was shocked to see the king's decrepitude: he looked a hundred years old.

By this time, the fashion of Jarellene's death had become generally known. Witnesses to her death had spoken up and though no official acknowledgement was made, it was understood that the palace accepted their accounts as factual. As well, some of the soldiers who had witnessed Adelrune's confrontation with the king had also revealed what they knew. This caused much turmoil among the people of Yeldred: while many were openly grateful that the king's eyes had been opened, many others saw Adelrune's intervention as a mark of disloyalty if not outright treason.

Matters came finally to a head one morning. Adelrune was accosted by Sir Childern, who took hold of his arm and spoke in a venomous tone.

"Sir Adelrune! It has come to my ears that you deliberately poured poison into our king's soul; that you are responsible for the stillbirth of our attack on Ossué; that you gloat about these ill deeds. I demand to hear confirmation or denial from your lips."

"I have not boasted of anything I have done. I was with King Joyell, as you were not, when his daughter was killed. I revealed to the king that the leader of Ossué's fleet was a descendant of Yeldred's people. I prevailed upon the king to abandon his attack, as it would have brought about the death of hundreds, if not thousands. I do not know if I acted with wisdom or not, but I followed the dictates of my conscience."

"You *do* boast of it! This is infamy! I challenge you, Sir Adelrune, though you are unworthy of a title that the king bestowed upon you in a moment of weakness. Fight me, sir!"

Adelrune, pale and shivering, said: "I refuse. You do not have the authority to instigate a duel between us, only the king would. As fellow knights bound to the same sovereign, we may not fight."

Sir Childern, enraged, began to strike him bare-handed. Adelrune tried to walk away, while blows thudded on his face. One of Sir Childern's rings cut into the flesh of his cheek and blood flowed. At this Adelrune seized the other man's arm with both hands.

"Enough! I have refused your challenge, Sir Childern! You demean yourself by persisting."

"You have no lessons in deportment to give me, young fool. I name you traitor to the king and the Ship, to Yeldred! I accuse you formally!"

People had gathered about them both. At Sir Childern's accusation, shouts of protest were made. People came to Adelrune's defense, many of them, to his surprise, soldiers who had been aboard the *Lightning*. But others echoed Sir Childern's cries of "Traitor!"; someone struck someone else, and suddenly a screaming melee had begun. Adelrune, appalled, tried to disengage the combatants, but there were too many people. Constables of the law arrived on the scene and eventually managed to quell the riot.

All participants, Adelrune and Sir Childern included, were incarcerated until the evening. At that time Adelrune was released and brought to Lord Melborne's chambers.

The Ship's de facto master appeared ill at ease. He sat on a large chair in the middle of the room. In one corner stood Sir Childern, glowering. In the other were Sawyd and Sir Heeth.

"Sir Adelrune," said Lord Melborne, "I have heard Sir Childern's accusations in regards to you. Possuyl the war-chief was here earlier and amplified them. Exemplary punishment was demanded. However, Commander Sawyd and Sir Heeth made extraordinary appeals on your behalf, and I could not disregard them.

"I am therefore in an ambivalent state. Are you a traitor to the king, as Sir Childern asserts, or are you the courageous knight who loved his king so well that he felt honor-bound to awaken his conscience to the horrors of war, as Commander Sawyd counters? What have you to say, sir?"

Adelrune had had a long time to reflect upon that same question. He now said: "My Lord Melborne, I must speak the truth; and I will tell you that I myself do not know. What I did, I believe I did with a clear conscience, but I am not exempt from doubt about that belief. I was overcome with grief at Princess Jarellene's death; perhaps I let anger speak, instead of loyalty. Still, I have reflected long upon Sir Childern's accusation, and I do reject the label of traitor.

"But I have come to understand that I can stay aboard this Ship no longer. Whether I am traitor or hero, I do not belong here any longer. I suggest, my lord, that you exile me. Thus Sir Childern and those who side with him will no longer have to endure my presence, and there will cease to be division aboard the Ship."

Lord Melborne smiled with obvious relief, then caught himself and tried to look stern.

"It is so ordered. Sir Adelrune, henceforth you are exiled from the Ship of Yeldred. You will be conveyed ashore tomorrow morning. In the meanwhile . . ."

Sawyd made a discreet gesture.

". . . you are remanded into the custody of Commander Sawyd."

Sawyd took Adelrune to her apartments. Once there, she wept with frustration. Adelrune attempted to console her.

"Sawyd, please. I chose the doom myself. It is time that I was gone. Would you rather have me tried, found guilty of treason, and sentenced to die?"

"Of course not. But you would not have been. Too many people would have risen in your defense."

"And the Ship would have been further divided. Sawyd, I have brought too much evil amongst you. It is better for everyone if I go now. Tomorrow morning I will take an old dory and row ashore. Or someone can come with me and row back."

"No. You will go, because you must. But I will take you ashore myself, and it shall be aboard the *Kestrel*."

In the morning the *Kestrel* left the side of the Ship of Yeldred and sailed toward the shore. It dropped anchor in a sandy cove. Adelrune went ashore; Sawyd followed him.

"I wish you had been able to stay."

"So do I. There are many things I wish for; too many. I must go on and stop wishing."

"Goodbye, then, my friend." Sawyd put her hands on his shoulders and kissed him warmly. "I am glad to have known you. I will think of you often, and with love."

"So will I," said Adelrune, his throat tight. "I thank you for everything you have done."

"May you reach home safely." They stood awkwardly in silence for a few moments, then Sawyd went up the gangplank, and the *Kestrel* raised anchor and sailed back to the Ship of Yeldred.

Adelrune waved good-bye, then watched the *Kestrel* shrink slowly, making its way to what once more appeared as a floating island, crowned with trees, under a covey of white clouds.

11 A DREAM IN HARKOVAR

DURING HIS LAST DAYS ABOARD THE SHIP OF YELDRED Adelrune's grief had begun to ease. He mourned Jarellene still, but his youth and his life burned strong in him, and with every breath he exhaled, a tiny measure of pain left him. On some days, upon waking, he had felt as if he had harbored this pain since birth, not knowing for whom he grieved. Now that he knew at last whose death he mourned, the hurt was easier to bear.

And he would now at long last travel toward home; the prospect gave him a small measure of, if not joy, then certainly pleasure, which mixed at times strangely with the ebbing pain.

Sawyd had filled his pack with food and drink, and many useful implements, the most important of which was a map of the surrounding lands. A small purse at his belt held some coins, with several more hidden amongst his clothing, as a measure against thieves. He wore the Oula's armor and Sawyd's shield, and carried Kadul's lance. He inspected his reflection in a tide-pool and had to admit that he did not cut a bad figure.

He took out the map and studied it. Sawyd had pointed out their position before they reached the shore. This was a land known as Aurann; it was thinly peopled, with many small villages but no major town or city unless one traveled far eastward. Faudace lay to the southwest: according to the map, the coast of the sea ran more west than south for a long distance. Adelrune had no desire to visit a city, and indeed would have preferred to avoid human habitations altogether, for he felt the need to be alone for a while. But traveling to Faudace on foot held little appeal; he resolved to purchase a mount if he could find one. The money Sawyd had pressed upon him should be more than sufficient to the purpose.

He traveled southwestward along the shore until sundown, bedded down in the shelter of a small bush. It was the height of summer, and the air stayed warm about him throughout the night.

The next day he came to a small village by the shore, called Alraba. The people, at first suspicious, proved guardedly friendly after he had established his good intentions. They had no riding animals, but Adelrune was promised that the next village inland would have horses. He paid a copper coin to rent a small shack belonging to a local fisherwoman for the night. While he prepared a bed from a pile of old burlap sacks that smelled of brine and seaweed, the fisherwoman's youngest son came to watch him. The lad was no more than six, brown-skinned from running half-naked in the sun all day long, his hair a tangled mess and his fingernails filthy.

"Ayuh reelly a wurrior?"

"I am a knight."

"Wassat?"

Adelrune pondered the question and to his surprise found himself unable to think of a clear answer. The small boy watched him expectantly. Finally, oddly embarrassed, Adelrune said "A knight is a warrior who has shown his valor . . . and who has pledged to respect a code. . . . Do you understand?"

The boy shook his head no.

"Well . . . I am a knight because a king dubbed me one."

"Yuh seen a king?"

"Yes, I knew a king."

"Whuwus the king like?"

"He was an old man, with a long gray beard, and long gray hair, and bright blue eyes like yours. He wore a big coat with many pictures drawn on it, with shiny thread."

"Ana crown?"

"Yes, he had a crown. A small circle of gold, very thin."

"Ahn. Thasnot a crown!"

And the little boy went away. Adelrune watched him go back inside his house. For a moment, shaken by the child's disbelief, it seemed to him that, had he claimed to be a great king himself, or a magician, he would have been no more of a liar than when he had stated he was a knight.

With morning he left the village and went eastward. By mid-afternoon he reached the next village inland, where the people farmed and raised livestock. They were less impressed by his garb, but less friendly also than the people of Alraba. Adelrune made inquiries about mounts and was directed to a surly man who had a gelding for sale. The animal, to Adelrune's untrained eye, appeared sound and of a calm disposition, which he considered essential. He had much theoretical knowledge of horses, having read several treatises on the subject, but Riander kept no horses and while still living in Faudace he had rarely come close to one. A placid mount would suit him just fine.

The owner stood watching Adelrune with a sneer, and presently asked brusquely if he wished to buy or not. Adelrune asked for a price. The man named a large sum, which Adelrune was able to bargain down somewhat, though he knew the man was getting the better of the deal by far. Still, Sawyd's funds would cover the purchase. After paying a supplement for the harness, Adelrune led his purchase out of its stall, buckled on saddle and straps with much effort and wasted motion, and attempted to climb upon the animal.

The former owner guffawed as Adelrune slipped and slid, but in the end Adelrune was able to gain the saddle. The horse snorted noisily, as if to comment on his skills, but remained otherwise quiet.

"Does the horse have a name?" asked Adelrune, who had forgotten that aspect until then.

The surly man merely shrugged and turned away, no longer interested.

Adelrune clicked his heels against the horse's flanks and the animal moved forward at a gentle pace. With growing assurance, he led it outside the bounds of the village and turned south, following a trail that snaked across the fields.

"What name would you like?" Adelrune asked the horse after a time. He pretended to expect an answer, then when nothing was forthcoming, made various suggestions. For a time he almost settled on Bruno, but sunset brought out the reddish tinge of the horse's coat, and in the end he chose Griffin.

He made camp in a copse of oaks, carefully hobbling his horse, and soon fell asleep. In the morning, as he had expected from the various books he had read, his legs were so sore he could barely walk. He forced himself through a series of exercises that reduced the ache to something bearable, then climbed back up on the saddle, with some difficulty.

With the passage of days he grew more accustomed to this mode of travel. Griffin was a good mount, not particularly swift, but dependable and tolerant. The land of Aurann was mostly flat, grassy country, and they were able to cover much ground. From time to time Adelrune stopped at an inn for the night, more out of concern for Griffin than for himself. Always he saw to it that the horse was well fed. His care of it was inexpert at best and he strove to learn by example from the stablehands.

After two weeks they crossed the Aurannese border and ventured into a hilly region claimed by no one. Adelrune constantly checked their progress on his map and tried to discover the best way through the hills. The going was now rougher, but Griffin managed well. The hills were said to be inhabited by wild tribes of men, if not worse, but Adelrune saw nothing to that effect save, once, a solitary fire burning in a distant valley.

Eventually mount and rider came out of the hills and, according to Sawyd's map, into the westernmost spur of the duchy of Donpei. This land was too far from the coast to be anything more than a blank area on the map. Adelrune pondered the merits of seeking out a village, but remained unsure of what to do. His decision was taken for him when, having dismounted at a stream to refill his gourd and let Griffin slake its thirst, three men stepped out from cover on the other side of the stream and pointed their halberds at him.

All three were dressed in dark browns and grays, and wore leather skirts over loose trousers. On each man's head was set an enormous conical felt hat nearly two feet tall, with a wide brim that shadowed its owner's face.

Adelrune gauged them with a glance. They held their weapons inexpertly, but they had assumed an efficient defensive formation. These were far from professional soldiers; they were more intent on protecting themselves from him than on attacking. Probably they were part of some militia. In any case, if he took care not to seem threatening, he should defuse the situation; and even should it come to fighting he could defend himself or simply flee.

"Good afternoon," he said courteously. "I am Adelrune of Faudace, a traveler."

Griffin had pulled up its head at the appearance of the three men. Now it took a few steps toward Adelrune, snorting in nervousness.

"Aye, the beast is real," muttered one of the men.

"Means naught. No iron's on him," replied another.

"What about the armor? That's got iron, no?" said the third.

Adelrune could not understand the tenor of their discussion. He decided to ignore their words and continued: "I am traveling to the southwest; can you tell me what lies in that direction?"

The man who had not yet spoken spat on the ground. "You know most well what lies over there. You got caught on this side, and now you want to return. I tell you we won't let you."

"I regret I cannot understand what you are talking about."

"Well, if you want to understand, cross the stream and grasp this blade. I'll tell you then." The third man held out his halberd, blade horizontal, in a gesture half-threatening, half-mocking.

Adelrune hesitated, then crossed the brook in two strides and seized the halberd's blade. The three men exclaimed in surprise and he who had spoken first said, "I told you he wasn't a spandule!"

Adelrune raised an eyebrow. "Well? I am waiting for my explanation, sir."

"Ah . . . Begging your pardon, then. We thought you'd be a shade, see? Especially with your lance here, that's not metal. And you haven't a witch-hat on your head."

"I am no ghost," said Adelrune, letting go of the halberd. The three men had relaxed and now held their weapons loosely. Still fearing some ruse, Adelrune kept a tight hold on his.

"Yes, we see that now you've crossed the stream and touched the iron. So you're really a traveler? We get none in these parts, most years."

"Yes, I am. I am traveling to the town of Faudace, which is a long distance to the southwest. You implied danger lies that way."

"Yes, it does. But it's ill luck to speak of it outside where one can be heard. We'll take you to Harkovar and tell you about it there."

Adelrune would rather have pursued his journey, but caution seemed to dictate that he accompany the men; whatever lay to the southwest, it seemed a source of evil influences. He went back for Griffin, and followed the men for a few miles, until they reached a small village huddled inside a heavy stone wall.

There was a gate in the wall, made of timbers bound with thin strips of metal in a complicated geometric pattern. Guards were posted both before it and on the top of the wall; the gate swung open only after the three men had vouched for Adelrune.

Once inside, the men relinquished their halberds to an older woman who watched over a small arsenal. They also took off their hats and wiped their sweaty foreheads. Deprived of the obscuring hats, their faces now took on startling character. They had been three nearly identical strangers; now they were a blond man barely adult; an ugly, middle-aged man who had to be his father; and a taller, dark man in the full force of youth, whose broken nose marred an otherwise flawless visage.

The dark man, who had spoken last of the three, said: "I'm Thran. This is Lovell and his da, Preiton."

"I am Adelrune."

"Will you come and drink with us, Adelrune? Now we're inside we can speak without too much worry."

"Very well."

The houses of the village were also built of stone. Their narrow windows had heavy shutters, set inside the walls instead of outside; the doors were likewise narrow and appeared quite heavy. The villagers, one-fifth of whom wore the tall conical hats, gave Adelrune wide-eyed looks. One such behatted woman, crossing his path, made a ritual gesture and hurried away.

"May I ask why some people wear their hats, while you have taken yours off?"

Lovell, the blond youth, said "They're the more cautious folk, the ones who fear the queen even within Harkovar and in daylight."

"So the hat protects against adversity?"

"Certainly! You must really come from afar if you don't know that. They have no witch-hats in your country?"

"None."

"Fancy that."

"Tell me," asked Adelrune, "what is it that guides your conduct then, in general? Do you have a council of elders, priests, prophets, or didactors? A Rule?"

"None of those," answered Preiton. "In the past we had the duke's man dwelling in the castle over there, telling us what to do—" so saying, he pointed to a house slightly larger than the others, hardly deserving of its title, "but he went back to the capital long ago and we're on our own now. The old ones know how to act and they teach the brats how to behave. How do they do it in your parts, then?"

Adelrune perceived Preiton was annoyed at what must have seemed to him implicit condescension. He tried to smooth the man's ruffled feathers. "In the city I come from, we have people to teach the Rule to children. There are Didactors, churches, and rectories, but the difference with Harkovar is not so great."

Preiton nodded, somewhat mollified.

They came to a large building—larger in fact than the "castle"—whose door stood open. Steps were revealed, descending to a room from which came the immemorial sounds of people drinking. Adelrune tied Griffin's lead to a nearby stone post.

"Will it be any problem if I leave my mount here?"

"None. There's no thieves in Harkovar," said Thran, answering the unspoken question, to Adelrune's embarrassment.

The four went down the steps to a large, shadowy common room, where they were given seats at a corner table. Over mugs of thin beer, Thran, Lovell, and Preiton provided explanations.

"We're most far from the capital here, and most close to the forest, less'n a day's walk away. The duke won't come here unless there's a war on, or when he's a new duke that's just gained the seat, you see? So we're left to ourselves for years on end. We have to defend ourselves, and that's why we have the wall and the patrols to find any wandering shades."

"What are you defending yourselves against, precisely?"

"The forest, what else?" said Lovell.

"He means what's *in* the forest, boy," said Preiton. "It's very old, that forest, see? Once it reached all over the land up to the sea far away, but now it's much smaller, all broken up into little bits. The forest here is the most large part that's left, but it's said all the parts, even although they're separated, they still touch one another, somehow. No one here understands how, but that's what Ulrick said when he came by with the young duke five years back."

"Ulrick, he's the duke's wizard," interjected Lovell.

"Yes, that's right. So the old forest, it's full of dark, strange things. Once in a while some idiot goes for a stroll in the margins while it's still daylight, to prove he's no coward. They always come back white as sheets; sometimes they don't come back, like Thracia's son didn't. They'll tell you they heard voices speaking in tongues no one understands. One lad said he looked through the trees and he saw a bear with a man's face growing out of its shoulder. The man's face, its eyes were closed but its mouth was working, like someone trying to wake up from a nightmare. . . ."

Thran now spoke. "And then the forest sends out shades, spandules Ulrick called them. Mostly they walk about at dusk or in the night, but the harder ones can stand the light of day. We can tell them because they can't touch iron, and they burn when they cross running water. They can maim you just by a touch, and make you go blind if they look into your eyes. Or sometimes they touch you and look at you and naught happens, and you spend days waiting for it to come, and in the end you go mad."

"And you believed I was such a being."

"*I* thought you had to be real because of the horse, because the shades don't have horses," said Lovell. Preiton shrugged.

"Can you tell me who is this queen some people fear so much?"

Preiton made a warding gesture and Thran's voice lowered as he answered. "The queen rules the forest. She's the one who sends her evil out. She's a great sorceress, she can do anything with her spells. For many years, things were quieter than usual; some people thought the queen was gone away, or maybe she was dead. But about two years ago things went bad again so we knew she was back. One morning everyone found a painting of the queen on their doorstep, just like that. She sent her magic into the village, to put all those pictures at everybody's door. It still makes me shiver when I think of it."

There was a long silence. Adelrune pondered what he would do. Bringing to his inner eye what he recalled of Sawyd's map, he judged he would probably have to travel westward toward the coast, then go due south for many leagues.

He took a sip of beer, then broke the silence, asking if there was an inn at which he could stay the night.

"No inn here," said Preiton. "You'll have to stay with someone. I can put you up for the night, and I won't ask for much."

They agreed on a sum. Adelrune paid for the beer, and departed with Preiton and Lovell. They made a stop by the village stables, which sheltered the half-dozen plowing horses various families possessed, and left Griffin in the company of its fellows. When they reached Preiton's house, they were greeted by a sixteen-year-old girl who turned out to be Lovell's wife. She studied Adelrune and remarked, "So that's the stranger," the only words she would say all evening.

The four of them ate a modest supper. Afterward, Preiton sat down by the fire and brooded into the flames. Lovell played a few games of morris with Adelrune, then rose to show him his room, a curtained-off little nook obviously meant for future children.

Lovell nudged Adelrune's arm and leaned his head close. "I got something to show you, if you're not afraid," he whispered.

"I am not easily frightened."

Lovell kneeled down and pulled something from a narrow crack in the wall.

"What Thran said, about the pictures of the queen? Well, when we got them, we all put them on a fire and burned them. Except I kept mine. I'm not afraid like the old men. Want to look at it?"

Adelrune looked—and he shuddered. He had seen Lovell's picture before: it was the Queen of Cups, the playing card he had given to Redeyes long ago.

Lovell let him take the card in his hand, examine it. It was not the very same card he had given to Redeyes, of course. The back, instead of a red-and-white diaper, displayed a strange pattern of interlaced vines, dark green on black. The pattern shimmered unpleasantly in his vision when he peered closely at it; he turned the card over. The picture was the same as the one his playing card had borne: the dark-haired Queen of Cups, sitting on her throne, holding a silver chalice in one hand and a scepter in the other. Adelrune had often played cards with Riander; never had the court cards seemed anything other than conventional symbols. But in isolation, somehow, the representation of the Queen of Cups had acquired a load of undeniable malice.

Adelrune returned the card to Lovell with relief. Grinning, Lovell thrust it back into its hiding place. A wonder, thought Adelrune, that Lovell was unaffected by the card's aura. Either he was thoroughly unperceptive, or his courage was a match for Sir Actavaron's. . . . Lovell bade Adelrune good night and left for his own room. Adelrune went beyond the curtain and undressed for the night.

Adelrune's bed was so small he had to sleep tightly curled in order to fit. The night air was warm and stuffy; he woke up again and again, feeling as if he couldn't breathe, his upper body drenched in clammy sweat. He dreamed of a darkness punctured with dozens of red stars, and of a black-haired woman peering into a basin filled with ink, where trembled a ghostly image, black on black.

He woke once more, and heard a distant cry of alarm. He rose from the bed, stepped to the house's heavy door. Had he dreamed the cry? It was repeated. It was not a human cry, but the neighing of a panicked horse. Griffin's. Adelrune loped back to his room, seized his lance and shield, unbarred and opened the door, and ran out into the night.

The ground tilted under him, then swung the other way, as if he stood on the deck of the *Kestrel* in heavy seas. The night sky was full of stars and many of them flickered red. He heard Griffin's neighing again. For a moment Jarellene ran beside him and he smiled at her with all his love, but then he remembered that she was dead, and she faded away. The night was full of the scent of cloves. Turning the corner of the last house, he found himself inside a garden of shadows, a garden of black-leaved ferns and ivies, of mossy tumbled walls and still pools reflecting the stars.

At the center of the garden stood a woman, draped in jewel-encrusted velvet, holding a metal goblet. She saw him and smiled, beckoned with her free hand. Adelrune's eyes kept crossing and losing their focus. He could not see the woman's face clearly, only a pale blur, framed by dark tresses. His throat was dry, his flesh burned with fever. He took a step closer to the woman, then another.

Something touched his left wrist, like a huge, soft insect. He tried to shake it loose but it clung tightly. He tried to bat it away but his right hand was holding his lance and his movements were clumsy.

Then something else scratched painfully at his left eye; his head snapped back and his arms rose to protect his face. A blow thudded hard into his belly and winded him. He fell to the ground and awoke.

He was in the middle of Harkovar, not far from the stables; Preiton stood in front of him, shouting, his arm drawn back, ready to strike again. Adelrune dropped his lance and shield, shook his head. "I am awake, Preiton, I am awake now!"

"What in the Divine's name happened, man? You rush out of the house in darkness, you can't see me or hear me. . . ."

Adelrune licked his dry lips. He felt a feverish thirst, almost strong enough to mask the coldness of fear. "I think I saw the— I saw *her*. In a dream . . . it might have been a spell."

Preiton made the same warding gesture as the day before. His gaze hardened. Adelrune could almost read his thoughts. He said: "Thank you for awakening me, Preiton. Something ill might have happened to me had I continued to dream. To forestall any more such problems, I suggest that we both keep awake until dawn, after which I will leave Harkovar."

Preiton's face showed some embarrassment, but he nodded. He led Adelrune back to his house, where Lovell and his wife were now awake. Preiton brusquely told them to get back to bed, and they obeyed.

Preiton and Adelrune sat at the table. Preiton, after adjusting his witch-hat solidly on his head, laid a short-bladed axe in front of him and stared stonily at Adelrune. Both maintained an uneasy silence. Adelrune, used by now to depriving himself of sleep, waited out the hours in relative comfort. Once, when Preiton began to nod off, he coughed lightly to wake him.

Finally, the sun's light began to stain the sky and Preiton rose from the table with a grunt. Adelrune stood up, went to gather his possessions. He put on his armor, shouldered his pack.

"Shall we go fetch my horse?"

Soon after Adelrune found himself at the gates of Harkovar. The sentries on duty inched them open wide enough for him and his horse to pass.

"I'm most sorry," said Preiton.

Adelrune shrugged. "It is nothing. I could not have stayed, anyway."

"Where will ye be going then?"

Knights did not lie; in this instance Adelrune did not even feel like evading the truth. He said: "To meet with the queen."

Preiton gaped at him wordlessly, his face looking tiny beneath the huge hat.

"I feel the dream was a summons of sorts," Adelrune explained. "I do not believe I could escape the queen in the end, no matter what I tried. So I will confront her now. Once before I faced down a magician; it was not easy, but I won free. Perhaps I shall have luck today as well."

Preiton's mouth worked and he frowned in indecision. Then he gave a curt jerk of the head, pulled off his witch-hat, and held it out to Adelrune.

"You should have some protection," he said. "Wear the hat."

"Thank you," said Adelrune, touched, "but I would not deprive you of it."

Preiton proved insistent, while the sentries grew annoyed at the loitering; in the end Adelrune had to put the hat squarely on his head, before waving good-bye to Preiton and passing out of Harkovar.

12 THE QUEEN OF THE FOREST

He had felt a dim intimation of his future as soon as he had seen Lovell's card and held it in his hand. He had known it with certainty at the moment he had awoken from the spell's net last night. He must go into the forest.

He stopped at noon for a brief nap, overcome both with the heat and his previous sleepless night. After clambering down from the saddle, he pulled the witch-hat off his head, considered it ruefully. It was a sincere gift and so held real value, but Adelrune simply could not bring himself to believe the cone of felt held any power to protect him. For a fact it made him feel utterly ridiculous as long as he wore it, and it hampered his vision. He folded it carefully and put into his backpack, reasoning that as long as he wore the pack, he would be wearing the hat as well, in a manner of speaking.

He did not urge his mount to any great amount of speed; it took him till mid-afternoon to reach the border. Here he experienced a chill of déjà vu, for the perspective seemed nearly the same as when he had set out of Faudace, so long ago it seemed now. He took Griffin to the extreme edge and dismounted. The horse began to crop the wild grasses placidly. Adelrune decided to follow its example and ate some of the food stored in his pack. Then he rummaged inside and pulled out a folded square of dirty pink cloth: the old tablecloth he had taken from a cupboard in his foster parents' home. He opened the cloth and looked at its contents: ten sheets of blank paper, a quill and inkpot, a white bone with a scytale loosely wound about it, and the three cards that remained of the four Stepfather had given him so long ago.

The first was the Master of Suns, a serene old man in a robe of gold, a dozen flaming spheres spinning around his hands. In Triple-Bid, whoever played the Master won the hand immediately. In solitaire, he was supposed to be paired with the Mistress of Stars. The second card was the Duchess of Wheels, one of the lesser trumps, that matched either Swords or Hearts. The Duchess was depicted as a maiden dressed in white and red, with braids in her long malt-brown hair. She strummed a lute marked with the wheel symbol, and if one looked closely at the card one could notice her fingertips were bleeding. The third card was the Prince of Cups. Adelrune studied the portrait intently, as if it might hold some information. The Prince had the same dark hair as the Queen, though in fact his face resembled hers very little. His pose was also dissimilar, for he was depicted with one knee raised, his green-booted foot resting on what must be a stone dais or perhaps a natural shelf of rock. There was a bow on his shoulder, a quiver strapped to his back. In his right hand he held a cup from which he was about to drink; his full-lipped mouth was half-open in anticipation, and the glint of teeth thus revealed combined with the thin, curling mustache to give him a dynamic, almost dangerous air.

Adelrune examined all three of the cards once more, but they said nothing to him. Idly, he turned them face-down, shuffled them, dealt them out, chose one at random, flipped it over. The Prince of Cups. He repeated the procedure, once more turned over the Prince. Five more times he shuffled and dealt the cards and every time the result was the same.

Unnerved, he rose to his feet. He felt like a magician's apprentice suddenly come upon deep mysteries through a chance gesture and a random string of syllables. He considered the cards, the Prince face up between the two others, lying on the grass, and wanted to leave them there, yet in the end he bent down and scooped them up, putting them back into his pack. Where the cards had lain, in three precise rectangles, the grass and plants were now sere, the ground gone ash-gray, as if blasted by the heat of a hundred summers.

He did not remount, but instead walked with Griffin at his side. Under the shade of the trees, despite the summer's heat, it was quite cool. The forest was strangely silent, and Adelrune saw no flickers of animal life. He advanced further in, and the sunlight dimmed very fast, so that soon he walked in a sub-aqueous gloom. Then he began to hear noises; drawn-out hisses, faraway metallic tinkles, once disjointed notes, like an idiot child singing. Griffin's ears were pulled back, but the horse remained at his side, from time to time snorting softly. Adelrune rubbed its neck and patted its head, more to calm himself than his beast.

There were no paths visible here, and keeping to a fixed direction would have been difficult. But Adelrune did not feel concerned. He knew that in such places, it seldom mattered how carefully or recklessly one traveled. This forest was like the Old Waste which Sir Judryn had explored in his quest for the Hollow Man's mislaid soul: no matter in what direction, it was enough that one travel within it. Adelrune felt content with putting one foot in front of the other, knowing that he would wind his way deeper and deeper in, regardless.

Some time later Griffin stopped short and whickered. It took Adelrune nearly half a minute to discern what had upset his horse. The snake looked like a thread of green metal, coiled around the trunk of a sapling elm. It raised a triangular head toward them and its tongue flickered in and out of its mouth, almost invisible in the gloom.

"Let me help you," said the snake, although its mouth did not move. Its voice was a woman's voice, dry and flat; it was as if it impressed itself directly upon the eardrum.

Adelrune felt warmth flood into his muscles and his heart

start to pound. He recognized the beast from descriptions; in fact, there had even been a picture in one of Riander's bestiaries, though the faded watercolors did little justice to the liar-snake's vivid metallic sheen.

He could have tried to stab the liar-snake with his lance, but he forbore. Killing it would net him nothing. Its kind were not dangerous in and of themselves, as all sources agreed. Their fangs were sharp but fragile and bore no venom. The poison lay in their words, as Sir Hultelve had learned too late. The best strategy therefore was to take no notice whatsoever of what a liar-snake said.

"I do not think I want your help," declared Adelrune.

The liar-snake spoke again. "Without it, you cannot hope to reach your goal. I offer it freely, mind you. I am motivated only by my great affection for your kind."

Liar-snakes never told the truth, and there was no hope of second-guessing them. They could read one's mind and their answers always confused, misled, and deceived. It was said that at the dawn of time it was they who had taught humanity to lie.

"I see you think you know about us," said the liar-snake. "In fact, it was your kind that taught mine the art of untruth, and for it we were punished by the Eld, being sentenced to lose our limbs."

"You know that I cannot believe anything you say—and so I will leave now."

"Please do not."

There was a loud sound from behind him. Adelrune spun on his heel, saw a boar emerge from behind a tree. Its forelimbs were human arms, covered in coarse reddish hair; the nails of the hands were broken and filthy, and the hands pawed and scrabbled blindly at the ground.

"You do not need to fear it," said the liar-snake. Adelrune grew tense with indecision. If he did need to fear the boar, should he attack it, or not?

To his left he heard more movement in the undergrowth,

and then a child's voice, a little girl's voice, quite clear. "Don't hurt me. Please, don't hurt me!" The boar stared at him with rheumy eyes. Its hands dug into the soil.

Griffin shivered, took a step sideways. Adelrune thought he could smell the horse's fear. Loudly, he said "I wish to see the queen."

"But will she agree to see you?"

There were more rustles and vague ominous shapes now became visible all around him. Adelrune quoted the *Book of Knights,* the passage rising almost unbidden to his mind: "One night in the middle of Jorkys Fen, Sir Gharod found himself besieged by a legion of spirits, who poured forth a multitude of horrible visions to unnerve him. He sang battle songs and told jokes to himself until the dawn, and when the sun arose he found that the apparitions had ceased. With a sigh of relief he rose up, only to find he had been sitting in a pool of his own blood, leached away from him through the hours of the night. He felt such terror his heart almost stopped, but he had been well trained. His fright turned to rage; he drew his sword and slapped it on his breastplate in defiance, yelling his war cry. The metal sparked, and the spirits fled back from the cold light. Their last illusion dissolved; and Sir Gharod saw that he was unharmed, that it was still night, that no more than an hour had passed in the thrall of the spirits' visions."

Adelrune stepped toward his left, pulling Griffin's lead. The horse followed him, trembling. From very close now came the little girl's voice. "No . . . Oh no, please, no! Oh please!" There was a sound Adelrune could not identify. Then the girl gasped in pain, and started to sob. Adelrune felt a sheen of sweat cloak him. He could see nothing but bushes where he walked, yet the little girl's voice was very close. She whispered "Oh please, oh please . . ." almost in his ear. He did not turn his head, but walked forward one step at a time. Behind him were the liar-snake and the boar with man's arms and who knew what else. He bit his lip and stepped forward.

Silence fell, suddenly. The gloom deepened; the sun was already sinking. He had stood for hours in the net of the liar-snake's illusions. Night would come in a matter of minutes.

Griffin pulled on his lead. Adelrune turned to it. It was not Griffin he led. At his side walked a young woman, on her hands and knees. Her pale body was naked, and grotesquely deformed into the shape of a horse. Her head lolled at the end of a foot-long neck down which grew a straggly mane of blond hair. The bit was driven through her cheeks, on which blood mingled with tears.

"No." Adelrune forced the word out. His teeth were clenched painfully and he felt about to vomit.

Against his eardrum came the voice of the liar-snake, fainter with distance. "She never left your thoughts, of course. And you always felt her rescue was of paramount importance. It was in no way or fashion an excuse to petition your tutor to train you as a knight."

"Damn you!" It was more a wail than a shout of defiance. Adelrune found he was weeping. His legs trembled under him. The deformed girl still walked at his side, blood oozing from the wounds in her cheeks. She turned her head to look him full in the face and opened her mouth as if to speak.

"I did forget about her," said Adelrune. "I vowed I would not let her stray far from my thoughts again, but I did not keep my promise. I let myself be distracted by Jarellene and my own misery." His rib cage pained him, as if it were about to snap in two with the pounding of his heart. The young woman's face neared his. "Her plight was an excuse in some way," he admitted, "but had I not believed then that she was worth rescuing, Riander would never have accepted me. I still believe in the rightness of my quest. She might be only a doll, but I must and I will rescue her." He brought his hand up to the distorted face, and with this the illusion finally broke.

He touched Griffin's flank, felt the play of muscles under the warm skin. His horse neighed and walked forward, pulling him along, their roles reversed.

The sun was still many hours from setting. Illusions within illusions, like a dream of waking up. The eldritch noises faded away, the forest thinned, and man and horse emerged into a clearing. A still pool occupied its center. Adelrune reached it on trembling legs, knelt by the edge, smelt then tasted the water, and in the end allowed Griffin to drink. The pool was remarkably transparent, and empty of the smallest living thing.

Adelrune drank what remained in his water-bottle and re-filled it in the pool. Then he sat down on the grass and compelled himself to relax. He went through the many exercises Riander had taught him to soothe the nerves in the middle of a long battle, and others to focus his mind and offer less purchase to spells directed at the psyche.

The face of the doll rose again in his sight, and he heard once more the liar-snake's reassuring words, more painful than any accusation could be. Standing up suddenly, in a gesture of defiance, he leaned on his lance for support and let the shame wash over and through him, crest and ebb. Slowly it receded; Adelrune felt the sweat that had drenched him dry off. His pulse and breathing slowed. His mind was clear once more. Perhaps the liar-snake had intended to further unnerve him by making him fear he would never be able to rescue the doll, that he would be slain or forever imprisoned within the forest. But in that respect it had failed. Adelrune's resolve was now stronger than it had been.

The sun had declined to the level of the treetops and now half of the clearing lay in shadow. Adelrune felt dirty and rank. He wondered how much time was left before nightfall, and then shrugged and laughed harshly. He stripped off his clothes, and washed himself with the water of the pool, letting the wind dry him until he shivered. Then he dressed again, the armor warm and close-fitting around his body, a second skin almost. Sunlight had quit the whole clearing; the sky was turning pink. Taking Griffin with him, Adelrune walked across the clearing and entered the forest again.

The going was more difficult here: large tree roots criss-crossing on the ground, numerous thorny bushes blocking the way, stretches of sharp rock emerging from the earth. Through it Adelrune and his horse passed, and now the light failed rapidly. Trees became lost in the gloom. After an hour Adelrune stopped still. He could barely see ahead. With something approaching calmness he waited for a further manifestation of the forest's will. Soon he perceived whitish flickers at the edge of his sight, somewhat to his left. He moved off in that direction. Griffin protested, but yielded to his authority.

The light became clearer, and now acquired color: a cold blue, with overtones of violet. The tree trunks grew more distinct, and man and mount walked more easily.

Finally they reached the source of the light: a swarm of insects, not fireflies but something much larger, wingless, immobile on the flanks of a pair of huge boulders. Between the boulders the first steps of a stair going down could be seen. There was the sense of a vast space beyond, open to the night sky, through which moved a chill breeze.

Adelrune approached the steps, retreated. He held Griffin's head between his hands, spoke to the horse with all seriousness. "I do not know how much you can understand me. I have come to suspect you of being more than you seem. Whatever the case, I ask you to wait for me here until the dawn. If I am not returned by morning, go where you will. . . . And if you can, forgive me for taking you into danger."

Griffin blinked its eyes and snorted softly. Adelrune returned to the stair and descended.

The light improved once he had passed from beneath the trees. The night sky was cloudless and stars by the hundreds twinkled. Strangely, there was no moon. Looking at the patch of sky where it should have been visible, Adelrune could with difficulty make out a soot-black, featureless disk. He turned his attention back downward and descended the stair. He was going down into a very large depression in the ground, a bowl maybe two or three hundred yards in diameter and a good fifty feet deep at its center. The forest surrounded its rim, tall crowded trees growing up to the edge, but then disappearing.

It felt as if this place had been carefully landscaped over a period of many, many years. Low bushes and plants grew along the sides of the bowl. Night-blooming flowers, great pale corollas open to the starlight, stood at either hand. The steps of the stair were worn, their edges rounded and sometimes cracked with the passage of years.

He was near to the foot of the stair when he saw a dark mass below him, moving and shifting, too enshadowed to be seen clearly. Within the folds of it a dozen red pinpoints gleamed. As he descended the last twenty steps he heard its voice, like dry leaves rubbed together.

"Welcome, my friend."

He stood in front of Redeyes, closer than he had been at their first meeting. He felt a touch of the old terror, but he had grown nearly a foot since that time, and to that extent he felt vaguely reassured.

"It has been many days since our last encounter," said Redeyes. "I perceive that in the interim you have bargained away much of your youth."

Adelrune found nothing to answer.

"Will you rest, take refreshment? The queen is a gracious host and can offer you whatever you require to that effect."

"No, thank you."

"Your voice has matured also. What it gained in power it has lost in musicality."

Adelrune, his tension flaring almost to anger, said: "What importance does this have?"

"Perhaps none. I was merely making conversation, which is one of the duties of a good host."

"I have come here to meet with the queen."

"It might be more accurate to say that the queen wished to see you and summoned you here."

"Why then did she put liar-snakes and horrors in my path?"

"To test your mettle? As a delicate jest? For some reason unfathomable to fleshbound minds? Perhaps none of these. I am not in her confidence to that extent."

"You are worse than the liar-snake."

"Harsh words for one who saved you from death not that long ago."

"Because he had found hope when I gave him the portrait of the queen."

"Quite. It is regarding that matter, in fact, that the queen wishes to speak with you. Since you desire no refreshment, perhaps you will proceed along the path to her arbor?"

Not with you at my back, Adelrune wanted to say, but he remained polite: "Lead the way, if you will."

"I have business elsewhere, and the queen wishes to see you alone in any event."

"Do not let me keep you, then. I will go along the path in a moment." Adelrune allowed his lance to tip forward a trifle. Redeyes stayed motionless a moment, then withdrew silently into the darkness, the ruby glints winking out one by one.

Adelrune sighed, started along the path, which was made of crushed whitish gravel, faintly luminous in the starlight.

The path curved and detoured around obstructions: masses of rough stone like unfinished statues, tall trees of species Adelrune had never seen, once a fountain from which bubbled sulfur-scented water. There were walls now around him, though no roof over his head. Adelrune, struck by a sudden inspiration, paused briefly, withdrew something from his pack and put it inside his armor, in a fold of his shirt, next to his heart. Then he went on.

He could smell the scent of cloves; he took the last turn of the path and stood in the garden of shadows he had seen before in his dream. Black-leaved ferns and ivies, mossy tumbled walls, still pools in which the stars were reflected. At the center stood the queen, and this time her face was perfectly clear to his sight.

It was the face of the playing card: a broad, fleshy face, with full red lips, heavy lashes, a snub-chin, a straight and wide nose. The queen's black hair was braided and coiled on either side of her face. She wore a heavy silver crown spangled with chips of colorless stone.

"Please, Sir Adelrune, approach." She had a rich, deep voice, exquisitely modulated, familiar and not. Adelrune stepped forward reluctantly, till he stood some five yards away from her.

"I have heard you wished to speak with me, madam."

"Yes, I did. It seems I owe you thanks for my rescue."

"I did not undertake that task."

"But you gave my portrait to my servant whom you met, and restored his hope in my fate. Not long thereafter he finally contrived a way to free me from durance. Without your intervention, it is likely he would have despaired—and I would still be imprisoned. For this reason I would reward you."

The queen gestured with both hands—this time, she held no goblet—and a coil of mist rose from the ground at Adelrune's feet, then solidified into a chest of ebony with silver hinges. The lid swung open.

"What would you have? The glass jar holds pure happiness, distilled and crystallized. One grain, when dissolved under the tongue, brings a week of joy. The cloth band, when tied across the eyes, gives sight into unknown realms. The brass glove with claws is a weapon that will tear steel plates as if they were silk. The two rings—"

"Thank you, madam, but I wish nothing of those."

The queen's voice sharpened. "You do not trust my gifts?"

"I have no desire for them. I did not knowingly attempt to have you freed, and I neither want nor deserve any boon from you—though if you insist upon one, I would ask that you turn your attentions away from the village of Harkovar. Its people live in perpetual dread of you."

"As well they should. As should you, Sir Adelrune, if you should fail to please me."

"I do fear you, madam."

"Then accept one of the gifts."

"Tell me, madam, who was it who imprisoned you, and how?"

"A knight named Gliovold. He tricked me and sealed me by magic into a loop of time without beginning or end. Choose one of the gifts; I say it for the last time."

"I regret that I must refuse."

The queen hissed in fury; she spoke three words whose syllables broke against Adelrune's sense of hearing like glass smashing against a wall. Instantly, from the darkness sprang a dozen spandules of all shapes. A young girl with fist-sized black eyes and a round lamprey's mouth reached a spidery hand, touched Adelrune, then pulled back her smoking flesh. "Au, he is wrapped in metal, the beast!" A bearlike man from whose shoulders a dozen tentacles sprouted lumbered forward, baying. Adelrune retreated a step, into the embrace of a homunculus jointed as a centipede; its insect's jaws closed on his calf, tore the fabric of his breeches, and began to rip at his skin.

Adelrune frantically pulled out the object he had put inside his armor. It was the playing card depicting the Prince of Cups. He grasped it with both hands and tore it.

"NO!"

The queen's shriek was deafening. The spandules froze into immobility; even Adelrune found his movements suspended. He had torn no more than a fraction of the width of the card. Blood flowed from the tear and stained his fingers. He had not known, could not have known, but he had guessed right.

"Call off your demons, madam," he shouted, his voice almost breaking. The queen spoke a word and the spandules faded. Her face was twisted in a rictus of agony.

"Give me the card," she said, almost pleading.

"You would kill me in the next instant."

"Have you no mercy for a mother's grief?"

"In your case, very little. So your son is imprisoned also?"

"Yes. I was pulled free, but I could only save myself, not him; he is still caught in the twist of non-time. Give me the card, I beg you."

"I will bargain with you. Swear on what you hold dearest that you will refrain from harming me, directly or through any of your creations; that you will allow me to leave your forest as I wish; and further, and most important, that you will cease forevermore to torment those who live by the forest, in particular the people of Harkovar. In exchange, I will swear not to tear the card."

"Hell take you, manling! Give me the card, or I will destroy you!"

Adelrune tore some more of the card. There was a further spurt of blood, warm on his hands.

"Stop! Or I will call back the spandules!"

"I can tear this card in two before any of your spandules have time to kill me. And if your son is half the horror you are, my life is a small price to pay for his destruction. I will not hesitate."

The queen of the forest shrieked again, a cry of purest rage, which melded into words.

"Yes! Yes, I swear, I swear to your conditions, by all that I have ever held dear, by my son, by all the powers that are mine, by tree, by leaf, by the vault of the night!"

Adelrune returned the card to his bosom. He could feel blood still seeping from it, and a pulse that was not his heartbeat stuttered against his chest. The queen was kneeling in the center of the garden, her face still twisted in pain. He stepped toward the entrance, turning as he did so to keep her in his sight.

As he passed out of the garden a vast shape rose and engulfed him. A year's training asserted itself in him: without thought, Adelrune pivoted his lance and jabbed. There was a tearing sound, like heavy draperies being ripped apart, and then a dry shout of pain like a thousand crickets stridulating. Dust filled Adelrune's lungs. Suffocating, he jabbed again, spread his arms apart, burst free of the enclosing mass. He whirled on one foot, coughing violently, the indrawing of his breath so long delayed it seemed it would never come. Scraps of darkness, winking with a dozen red pinpoints, withdrew into the shadows. A voice of dried leaves spoke with some difficulty. "I will . . . My Queen . . . I will . . ." And then another identical voice joined it, and they spoke in chorus, yet their words were slurred into unintelligibility, leaves rubbed together, flaking to nothingness.

Adelrune coughed again, spat out a clot of sooty phlegm, drew in a shuddering breath, exhaled, inhaled. There was a dark cloud in his sight, like a bruise, but it presently dissipated.

The queen had not broken her oath: Redeyes was not one of her creations, but a willing servant. Adelrune had not even killed it, only divided it into two halves, it seemed. They were probably too confused and hurt to attack him again, but other servants of the queen might lurk about.

Adelrune walked along the path, as rapidly as he dared. No attack came. He reached the stair and started up. He was gasping when he attained the summit. Griffin had waited for him and now whinnied in welcome. Adelrune led it through the trees, trying to keep to the same direction. Eventually they came to a stretch of forest that was sparser; Adelrune took the opportunity to mount and urged Griffin to a swifter pace. In the far distance hootings and shrieks could be heard, and bluish lights flickered among the tree trunks.

After an unmeasurable time horse and rider came out of the trees. The moon was now visible, almost setting. Adelrune pressed Griffin to continue, wanting to get as distant as he could from the forest. Perhaps half an hour later they passed close to a large building, which Adelrune identified as a farm. Furious, rough-voiced barks erupted from the yard. Blackdogs. Griffin broke into a trot. They passed by several other farms, and then, too numb by far to feel surprised, Adelrune beheld Faudace across the river Jayre.

13 THE TOYMAKER

WITH MORNING HE RODE INTO THE TOWN OF HIS BIRTH. He hadn't envisioned his return in this way. He had aimed to go by Riander's house first, to recount his travels, and to receive his mentor's confirmation of his knightly status, before setting out for Faudace in earnest. But he would not delay any further the rescue he had vowed to accomplish.

When the people of Faudace saw him ride into the town, there was some alarm. A flock of lesser Rectors emerged from a Canon House and eyed him with suspicion. One of them, a fat rubicund little man who carried his stomach in front of him like a prized possession, waddled forward and spoke in a huffy tone.

"Sir, I must demand to know your identity and your business in our town."

Adelrune had never met this particular man before; he was deprived of the satisfaction of addressing him by his name and unsettling him even more.

"My name is Adelrune. As to my business here, it is a private matter which does not concern you."

The little Rector pursed his lips and tilted his head even further back. "We seldom see strangers in armor and bearing weapons here; your appearance excites some unrest."

Adelrune smiled, showing his teeth. "The Fourteenth Precept of the Rule, first and second verses, states: 'One must show kindness to wanderers who come calling at one's door. It is the duty of all the faithful to give correct welcome and hospitality.' And while Didactor Roald commented that the 'correct' welcome for hoboes and reprobates should extend only to opening the gaol door for them, I do not believe that this applies to wandering knights."

The little Rector's mouth gaped. Adelrune clicked his heels against Griffin's flanks and the horse moved forward, out of the flock and into the main street.

Adelrune had seen such vastness in his travels that Faudace seemed absurdly small to him now. The houses hunched over the narrow streets; cramped dwellings built for dwarfs, despite their three or four stories. Shops and guildhalls, private residences, taverns and temples, grown close together like barnacles on the hull of a ship. Here and there were pockets of greenery, an ostentatious yard in front of a rich family's house, a little park where once he had played in the sand as a child, and found a buried wooden toy soldier, its red-and-blue uniform barely chipped. Ever the dutiful child, he had asked for permission to keep it; this had occasioned some debate at home, but in the end Didactor Hoddlestane's Commentaries had triumphed: "Let no one keep a possession not his own, for there is no small theft. In the eyes of the Divine they who steal a grain of rice not theirs are as damned as those who steal a king's ransom." The toy had vanished the next morning.

Oceanic rage rose in Adelrune then, blotting out his sight with a red veil. A detached part of his mind wondered that such a trivial thing could still, after so many years, affect him. But then he remembered that he had never protested originally, never allowed himself disappointment, much less grief, over his loss; that he had not, at some level, believed he could feel anything about it.

Adelrune's sight returned to him. He wiped his brow, adjusted his armor which chafed him at the shoulders. In so doing he felt the outline of the Prince of Cups inside his shirt; he drew it out to look at it, but it was only a half-torn playing card, with the barest red stain on the ragged fibers at the tear. The heart-beat that thrummed in his fingertips was his own.

He directed Griffin through the familiar streets, but instead of going straight toward the toymaker's shop, he guided his mount down other streets, to finally stop in front of the four-story house where he had spent the first part of his life.

He alighted. His heart pounded and his eyes felt seared. The liar-snake would have said that this was no real delay at all, that no one could fault him for diverting his aim away from his sworn quest, even when only a few minutes ago he had been filled with unswerving resolution. But quests had to be fulfilled in the proper manner. Sir Quendrad had shaved off his forelock before his bat-tle with the Ogre Gessangt, Sir Athebre had had his natal chart drawn up by the blind astrologer of Prince Mekthar's court before he dove down the Green Well; so now did Adelrune feel he could not confront Keokle before settling the matter of his parentage.

He strode up to the door, and rapped it with his closed fist. There were noises from inside the house. Adelrune knocked again, and Stepfather opened the door. For a moment Adelrune was disconcerted. Always these two people had been towering giants to him. Even at twelve he had still come up only to Step-father's shoulder. Not anymore. Now he was taller than Step-father, and Stepfather—Harkle, he must think of him as Harkle, there was no longer any reason to do otherwise—was obviously intimidated by him.

So strange, so unexpected, that. Harkle had always shown the same obstinate face to the world; he was unmovable, forever smugly disapproving of everything, buoyed by his standing within the Rule. And now he visibly cowered before a stranger come to his door, who was the same boy he would strike with a switch once a week, no matter what he had or hadn't done. Striking carefully, three times across the back, employing neither too much strength nor too little, as he followed Didactor Mafe-lin's Commentaries on the Thirty-fifth Precept.

"What do you want, young man?" From the back of the

house Stepmother's voice rose tremulously, in chorus: "What does he want?"

"I would like to speak with you and your wife, sir."

And without waiting to be invited in, Adelrune stepped inside. This was his house, after all.

Trying hard to retain some dignity, Harkle led him to the parlor. Eddrin followed in their wake. She seemed less scared than her husband; perhaps the event was too extraordinary for her to feel fear.

Adelrune sat down in the visitors' black armchair, for the first time in his life. He couldn't restrain a bitter smile. Alas, his armor was a stiff enough barrier that he couldn't truly enjoy the cushions intended for the comfort of Didactor Moncure's bony buttocks.

He grew aware that Harkle and Eddrin were waiting for him to say something. Adelrune focused his thoughts and spoke.

"I have come to ask about your foster son, Adelrune."

"Hmpf. If I'd known *that* was the matter . . ." began Harkle, but then he lost his bravado and the threat died unborn.

"What about him?" said Eddrin.

"He ran away two years ago, I understand."

Harkle snorted. "Yes, the little ingrate vanished one day, without even a good-bye note. After all we'd done for him!"

Eddrin was nodding in agreement. "It was a severe blow. We don't dare show our face in the Temple even now, we have to have private worship. We've wasted years of income on the boy, and all for nothing."

Adelrune was surprised at his own calm. He should have felt outrage, yet all that moved him was a vague, half-affectionate contempt. He'd known these people too long to expect anything better from them.

"I want to ask you about his parentage," he said.

Blank gazes in return. Adelrune rephrased his question.

"I mean: who are his real parents?"

"Only the Divine knows," said Harkle, with a sour expression.

"There must have been rumors," pressed Adelrune, his heart sinking. "Someone was pregnant for all of nine months before his birth; tongues must have wagged."

"The Eightieth Precept enjoins us to shun gossip, sir," said Harkle haughtily, "and even if we'd heard anything, which we never did, we wouldn't repeat it. By what right do you ask us these questions, anyway? Who are you?"

Adelrune leaned back in the chair and shut his eyes a moment, defeated. Should he go to the nearest temple? Pointless. The Didactors would never prove amenable to his requests, and probably none of them knew either. He would have to fulfill his quest without settling who he really was. Well, then, so be it. He had wasted far too much time already. He rose from the chair.

"You're his brother," said Eddrin suddenly. Perhaps she was more used to looking at the faces of children than her husband; whatever, she had at last noticed the resemblance between the face of the man in armor and that of the child she'd brought up. "Aren't you?"

"No, but you are not too far from the truth," answered Adelrune. He looked at her, made a last appeal. "You know *nothing*? Truly?"

"I'm sorry," said Eddrin. "We never knew who'd sired him. No one did."

"What business is it of yours anyway?" demanded Harkle, growing angry now that Adelrune had become subdued. "And if you are family of his, how about reimbursing us for all we did? When I think of the sacrifices we made—"

"Oh, will you quit your whining for once?" Adelrune was shouting, his voice having risen without his volition. Suddenly he felt imprisoned, constricted within these walls, far worse than when the gray magician's rope had held him bound. He glared at Harkle, and for a moment envisioned getting retribution for every methodical beating he'd endured at the uncaring hands of this man. He felt his hands rise, his fists clench; then he forced himself to relax and made for the door.

He strode out of the room, letting his rage bleed away. He

couldn't step back in time and subtract his younger self from the switch. Nothing he did now could change what had happened. It was unworthy of a knight to exact this kind of revenge.

His foster parents trailed behind him, both of them silenced by the fury he'd let show in his outburst. When he'd stepped outside, he turned back toward them.

"Though you never bothered to ask, I will tell you that your foster son is well; he could be happier, but certainly leaving this house was the best thing that ever happened to him."

He mounted his horse and rode down the street, imagining that he felt their gazes on him. Yet when he turned to look back, there was no one standing before the house, and its door was shut.

He passed through the marketplace, which was only sparsely occupied. A costermonger had set up in one corner. By one side a firewood-seller displayed bundles of kindling. Next to him a flower-woman offered some bedraggled blossoms. Adelrune could see his destination now; but he stopped Griffin, dismounted, went to the flower-seller. He recalled her face from his childhood. As the woman gaped at him, he looked through her stock, found a chrysanthemum, white mottled with red. He withdrew one of the last coins from his purse and put it in the woman's palm, then took the single flower and knotted the stalk into the metal weave of his armor.

"Sir . . . your balance."

"Keep the whole coin."

"It's too much, sir!"

"No; it is not enough." He did not remount, but crossed the rest of the market leading Griffin, then went up the street a short ways, until he reached Keokle's shop.

This side of the street was still in shadow; through the shop window only dimness could be seen. Adelrune went to the door and banged on it with his fist.

It opened almost instantly. In the doorway stood Keokle.

Dark shirt and trousers, white-shot black hair and beard. He looked almost exactly the same as he had the day of their first fateful encounter. Around his neck he had tied the black ribbon the especially devout wore on lesser holidays.

"Forgive me, but my shop is closed this morning," said Keokle. "I observe the feast day of St. Axinous."

"I am not a customer. I have come on an important errand."

Keokle considered him a moment then stepped back, allowing him inside. Adelrune pushed the door closed behind him; the latch bar fell into the groove with a loud clink.

Toys and dolls surrounded them. Soft dolls lying on shelves, string puppets hanging from their crossbars, hand puppets with felt bodies and sculpted wooden heads. Adelrune swept his gaze across them all, seeking for the doll he had come to rescue. He knew she would not be there, but proprieties must be observed; this was like the salute before a duel.

"Well, what might be your name, sir, and why have you come here?"

"You have no other stock on hand?" asked Adelrune.

"I thought you weren't a customer."

"Answer me: have you no other stock?"

"Nothing finished. What was it you wanted?"

"I am looking for a specific doll," said Adelrune, feeling as though he were incanting a subtle spell. "She would be about two feet tall, with dark blond hair. Wearing a blue dress, with lace at cuffs and collar, an indigo waist-cincher."

Keokle had gone pale. "I'm afraid I don't have anything of the sort. I could build one on special order—"

"Once before you gave me this lie," said Adelrune, his voice getting louder. "Now you repeat it."

"Once before . . ." breathed Keokle, then his eyes widened. "Adelrune?"

"Yes, though it is Sir Adelrune now. I have returned here to fulfill a knightly quest."

Keokle was shaking his head from side to side. "You've grown abnormally fast," he said in a soft, wondering tone. "I can barely recognize you. How did you manage to reach adulthood so swiftly?"

Adelrune shrugged. "I bargained away six years of my youth."

"I had no idea that could be done. You've been dealing with magicians, then. What was it like?"

"What concern is that of yours?" asked Adelrune, bewildered. Was Keokle foolish enough to try changing the subject? "I have not come here to chat about wizards. I have told you what I want; will you deny a third time that you have it?"

"All right," said Keokle in a placating tone of voice. "I admit it. I do have what you seek. But don't you want some explanations first? Or perhaps you already know the whole story. Did your wizardly friends show you the truth in a crystal ball?"

"I fail to understand you. What do you mean by 'the whole story'? What explanations?"

Keokle smiled wanly. "Tell me then," he asked, "why have you come for the doll? Why do you want her so much? If it's just a doll?"

"I have come to free her," said Adelrune. "It is my quest. Stop trying to confuse me!"

"I'm not. I just think I have to explain first. You must understand what happened; and that it wasn't my fault. Please, may I sit?"

Adelrune felt as though he were caught up in some net of words, tangling itself about him every time he tried to press forward. Was this a further part of the preliminaries, a dance of sentences he must follow, or some sort of a spell? Let Keokle ramble on, he decided. Remember Sir Vulkavar and the Council of the Elendiles: respect proprieties as long as it does not lead you astray—and when it does, cut speech short, with a length of steel if you must.

Keokle had perched himself on a tall stool; he was looking down at his hands, whose fingers clasped and unclasped nervously.

"When I made your mother," he began in a low voice,

"when I crafted her out of porcelain, of wood and cloth and baby's hair, I had no wrong intentions. The Fifty-eighth Precept warns us against sorcery in general, but there are exceptions. St. Pancratus, after all, did use a spell to shelter his household during the War of Flames, as Didactor Kottin informs us in his Commentaries. Likewise with Didactor Renuil, whom two independent accounts credit with sorcerous knowledge.

"And at first, besides, she was no more than a doll. The best doll, the prettiest doll I'd ever made. For weeks I just sat her on a shelf above my bed and looked at her. In the right light, she already seemed alive. There was nothing wrong with that, nothing wrong with imagining her alive, was there?"

Keokle swallowed noisily. Adelrune, stunned into immobility, stood listening to him, all other thoughts forgotten. The toymaker went on. "But then there were the jester's spells. He was a man who came through Faudace fifteen years ago. I went to see his show. He rode in this shabby wooden caravan painted white and blue, and his tricks—well, they were awful. He could barely juggle four balls at once, and when he tried to breathe fire he opened his mouth too wide; the naphtha dribbled down his cheeks and he almost ignited himself.

"I confess it was for the assistants I went. I expect that was true for many of the others as well. You see, he had two girls with him, beautiful, lithe and young. The way they pranced, and tumbled, and stood on each other's shoulders . . . It isn't wrong to admire women; Didactor Otterlene says healthful desire is the first foundation of a family.

"After the jester's performance, I went to talk to him. The girls—they stood next to him, and I could feel the heat from them, and smell their sweat. It dizzied me. He'd noticed me watching, he said. He made a joke about me and his girls, and all three of them laughed. I laughed too, even though the joke was cruel, because it felt so good to hear the girls laugh.

"He looked at me strangely then, and he said he might have something for me. If I was willing to pay the price. I thought he was offering to sell me one of the girls for a night. I told him I would have none of it; the Rule forbids women to sell their bodies and men to purchase them.

"The three of them laughed at me again. I remember . . . I remember one of the girls, the blonder one, said 'You silly man, I'd never bed you no matter how much you paid! I'm his, and his alone. He made me that way.' And she looked at the jester with a look on her face that was like devotion, and like ownership . . . I knew she was speaking the truth.

"He told me about what he had in the caravan. Pages torn out of a spellbook. There were six spells within, he said. Sympathetic magic. The sixth one he'd used himself, twice, to make the girls. Out of inert matter in human semblance. He'd made them from puppets, he said, and in truth they were puppets still."

Keokle mopped his forehead. The story was spilling out of him faster and faster; he stared into space as he told it.

"I wouldn't believe him, I thought he was making fun of me; but he *showed* me. He gathered us inside the caravan, and shut the door. Then he spoke words while he touched the blond girl. I saw her and I saw a doll, together, in the same space, and then there was only the doll. It wasn't even a pretty doll. I could do better. I remember thinking that all the while: *I could have done better.*

"He showed me the pages. They were as he'd said: thick old vellum, inked in purple and silver. He told me he was willing to let me copy them, if I paid. He named his price. It wasn't so much as I'd thought. He said he wanted to do me a favor. He said few people had any aptitude for the sorcerous arts, and he'd felt the talent in me. He talked some more, of the brotherhood of magicians, and many other things. I don't recall any of it. All through his speech, I kept touching the doll that had been a woman a minute before. When he was finished, when he knew he had me, he let me take up the doll, lay it on my knee. Then he spoke the spell in reverse, and the blond girl was back, sitting in my lap. She was warm and heavy, and the smell of her was in my nostrils. . . .

"I went home for the money and I returned to the caravan after nightfall. I never worried the jester might have set up an ambush, that he and his girls might intend to beat me and rob me blind—no, the only thing I feared was that they would be gone. They weren't. The jester led me inside his house on wheels and I gave him my silver. He took out the pages from a chest and put them on a tiny wooden desk. He lit a taper, told me I had one candle's worth of time to do the job. I didn't make any protest, just started on the work without a second's delay. I finished it just before the candle flame drowned in its own wax. He showed me out. My eyes were worn out from the copying and I had trouble seeing my way, it was still dark. Behind me I could hear the jester inside the caravan, talking to someone. I heard a girl laugh, with a catch in her breath. . . .

"I made my way home, with my copy of the magic pages hidden under my shirt. For weeks I let them lie inside a chest, unread. I was crafting a new doll, in between custom orders. I took my time, and used the best materials I could obtain. She was so beautiful. . . . I felt pride in my handiwork. I've always been very skilled.

"But eventually I couldn't keep on admiring her as she was. I had to try the jester's magic. I took the pages from the chest and started studying them. The spells weren't convenient to use and test. I memorized them and rehearsed the castings. I had no idea if I was doing things properly, but I felt power stirring within me when I spoke the words. Eventually, I felt confident enough to try the sixth spell, the animating spell the jester had used. I brought the doll down from her shelf, rested her on the bed, and cast the magic.

"She came to life as the jester had promised. Full-sized and warm, and so pretty, oh so pretty. I loved her then. Can you credit that?" Keokle's gaze lifted to meet Adelrune's. His voice grew louder, hoarse. Adelrune listened to him without outward reaction, though inside him was a tumult of feeling.

"Believe me, I loved her. I had never loved a woman before, but her I loved from the moment I saw her. And she looked back at me, with the same look in her eyes the jester's girl had had. She was mine.

"I took her; I couldn't wait. She was everything I'd ever imagined, and more. And when I was sated . . . I changed her back. Like the jester did with his girls. It was easier that way, you see. Much easier. I could concentrate on my work, and she didn't attract any attention. When I grew lonely, I brought her to life, and we dallied. Afterwards she became a doll again. She didn't mind. She told me so herself.

"I was very happy for a long time. But then something happened; one night, after our dalliance, when I tried to change her back, the spell failed to work. I thought I had forgotten a syllable, so I tried again, but it still didn't work. I began to fear that the magic had run out, or that I'd lost my ability to enchant. It was none of these things. It took me some months, until her belly started growing round, to understand what had happened. You see, the spell would change a single life back into its previous form, but not two. It had never occurred to me I might quicken her womb; after all, she was only a doll. But I had, and now she was heavy with child.

"Throughout her pregnancy, I had no choice but to hide her within my house. She became . . . most inconvenient. She ate in prodigious quantities, and constantly threw fits of temper. Nothing I did was right by her. She was no longer the sweet, pliant thing who'd shared my bed with a will. She'd shout at me, and start crying for no reason. I kept trying to make her understand no one must suspect she was in my house, because then there would be no end of trouble. She paid me no heed and shouted all the louder.

"Once Didactor Moncure came to visit me; he said it was just a dominical visit, but I knew he was trying to tell whether or not I harbored anyone within my house. Fortunately, by that time I'd managed to get a hold of some powdered sleeproot. I gave her a teaspoon in water every morning, and it kept her quiet most of the day. So Didactor Moncure never heard or saw anything suspicious, and he left reassured.

"At long last she gave birth. It was a brief affair, tidier than I'd feared. I had expected you not to be viable, or at the least severely distorted. But you appeared well-shaped and healthy enough. I cut the umbilicus myself, with a wood chisel, and tied it securely. I'd given your mother enough sleeproot that she fell asleep as soon as the afterbirth had been expelled.

"I couldn't stand to wait any longer: I cast the spell. She returned to doll form without a hitch. I wrapped you up in a nice warm bundle and went to the closest temple. The time was well past midnight; no one was abroad. I left you on the doorstep and rang the bell hard. I knew someone would come. I was watching in the shadows when a Rector came out and picked you up. Then I went back home."

Keokle suffered a brief coughing fit. He wiped his eyes and went on.

"I left her in doll-shape for a long time after that. Nearly a year. I needed peace and quiet, a house empty except for myself. I busied myself at my toys. I recovered slowly. At last I grew lonely again. So I turned her back into a girl.

"From her point of view, next to no time had passed. She asked after you. I told her what had become of you, that you'd been adopted by Harkle the mason and his wife. She wanted you brought to her. I explained to her that this wasn't possible, or even reasonable. I reminded her it was I who had made her, and that she was mine. She started crying. I begged her to stop. I told her how much I loved her. And then I showed her. It had been a long time for me, and I couldn't deny myself.

"When I was done she'd stopped crying. She stroked me and kissed me. She was being tender again. She asked to go to the kitchen, to eat and drink a bit. She promised she'd be quiet now. I felt such relief and joy, knowing that she was back to how she'd been before. I held her tightly and kissed her a dozen times.

"We went downstairs. Once we'd sat ourselves, she asked me to get her slippers. She'd forgotten them in my room, and her feet were cold. I went up to fetch them.

"While I was upstairs she took a knife from a drawer and slit her own throat. She'd promised she'd be quiet, and she was: I didn't even hear her fall. Perhaps she lay down on the floor before she killed herself.

"When I returned, I found her in a pool of blood. She was still thrashing about, but only a little. It was like a string puppet with its cords tangled. There was nothing I could do. Do you understand? Nothing. The gash was so deep her windpipe was gaping open. No one in Faudace could have done anything.

"I did the only thing I could. I returned her to the doll-shape. I mopped up all the blood, made sure everything was clean. I didn't notice at first that there were tears and blood on the doll's face. I tried wiping them clean, but it was as if they were a kind of varnish on the porcelain: nothing would remove then. The neck was cracked almost clean through, but I was careful and the head remained attached to the shoulders.

"I reformed after that. I understood the warning of the Fifty-eighth Precept now: 'Let not your path stray into sorcery, for by the wizardly arts you shall put your soul into peril.' I sealed the pages away in a trunk. I vowed never to use the animating magic again. The doll I kept, to remind me of my failure. I usually sit her down in the workroom, where she can watch me work. Sometimes I put her on a shelf here, so she can look out the window. I take pains that she won't be readily seen.

"I talk to her often, you know. I've had long conversations with her, and I believe I've learned much from them. Certainly, I know that what happened wasn't my fault. She was flawed, in some way. Likely my mastery of the magic wasn't strong enough; perhaps the Divine intervened in the enchantment, in order to teach me a lesson. She was flawed, and that's why she contravened the Ninetieth Precept and took her own life. . . ."

Keokle broke off. Adelrune had altered his grip on his lance, raising it slowly, as if preparing for a point-blank cast.

"Now, Adelrune," the toymaker warned him, "think on what you're doing. Don't be foolish."

"I have no need for thought," Adelrune said huskily, "this is the time for action."

"But you can take the doll now. She's in the workroom. Just open the door and get her."

This distracted Adelrune; he could not resist going to the door, opening it, and stepping inside the workroom. At the far end of the room, a tiny armchair had been installed. The doll sat in it, her face twisted with despair, bloodied and tear-stained. Adelrune took a few steps toward her, then whirled to face Keokle, who had entered the room after him.

"You killed her," he said, almost wonderingly. Keokle's story was still roiling through his mind. The feeling that gripped him was something other than rage; it was like a viscous acid, searing his very soul.

"I did not. She took her own life. I would have prevented her if I could. Adelrune, she tricked me: she sent me away on an errand so she could kill herself. It was not my fault!"

"Enough words," gasped Adelrune. He raised his lance slowly; Riander's training echoed inside his head in bits and snatches. *Pull back your arm further, Adelrune. Better. Remember, when you cast the weapon, you must put your weight behind it. No, not like that. Sight with the point. . . .* He saw the lance transpierce the toymaker's body again and again, in his mind's eye, until he felt surprise that the weapon was still in his hand, not yet cast, that Keokle still stood alive and unharmed. His movements were slowed; as if the release of killing were denying itself to him.

Keokle had raised his own arm, displaying a string puppet he had fetched from a shelf in the storefront. It was the knight puppet Adelrune had admired, so long ago, back when he was yet a child, when the shop front held only beautiful things whose sight filled his need for wonder. Keokle held the crossbar with one hand and the puppet's midsection with the other. His face was very pale as he looked at Adelrune.

"I made your mother, and thus I made you," he quavered. "In that sense I am both your father and your grandfather. I claim power over you by the principles of sympathy. *This* is you, Adelrune." He spat on the puppet and spoke a string of words.

Adelrune felt a warm shock inside his body: some spell had taken hold of him. This stoked his anger; he felt the hesitation in him dissolve.

"Enough words," he repeated, "and enough magic!" He pulled back his arm to its fullest extent, drawing in a breath to be released at the instant of the cast. Keokle plucked at one of the puppet's strings: its sword arm tilted upward and jerked sideways. Adelrune's arm instantly followed suit, the lance's haft rapping the floor loudly then shrieking against the flagstones.

Adelrune snarled as he fought the magic, trying to wrest his arm back into position. But Keokle had now grasped the puppet's weapon; he wrenched it out of the wooden hand and sent it across the room. Adelrune's lance was torn out of his grasp and landed clattering at the far end of the workroom. Keokle repeated the procedure with the puppet's shield. Adelrune's own was torn from him and flew after the lance.

"Please leave," said Keokle. "Take the doll with you and leave. I promise I won't hurt you. I didn't want to use magic anymore, but you've forced my hand. . . ."

Adelrune paid him no heed; with a growl of rage he advanced upon the toymaker, his hands shaping themselves into claws. Keokle twisted the puppet's strings; Adelrune was jerked about in all directions. A swing of the crossbar and Adelrune was slammed against some shelves. A half-dozen wooden animals mounted on wheels fell upon him then clattered onto the floor.

"Give it up, Adelrune, please. Take her if you must, then leave. Otherwise I must keep you bound here while I summon the constabulary. You can do nothing against me."

Adelrune strove to overcome the spell's influence. He could move his limbs sluggishly, but then Keokle would pull the strings tight and Adelrune's least movement would be negated. He began to feel he had truly lost. The toymaker might even kill him where he lay; who in Faudace would fault Keokle for defending himself against a murderous stranger? He sought for help in all the tales he had been told, came up with nothing except tragic ends. Sir Athebre crushed by the wyrm's jaws, Sir Judryn buried under mud at the bottom of the Yellow Pits. . . . But then the faces of those whom he had loved came to his sight, and at that moment he finally solved the riddle of the witch. "Doubt; and despair," he whispered.

He hung his head, made feeble motions of yielding with his arms. Keokle relaxed his hold on the strings. Adelrune, his limbs more free to move, struggled away from the shelves, let himself slump against a workbench. Keokle started to say something. In the instant that he was off-guard, Adelrune acted.

Scissors at best were awkward weapons, but a good knight knows to employ what is handy; so Riander had taught him. Adelrune grasped the pair that lay on the bench, with one fluid motion threw them, wide open, toward the puppet's strings. The blades cut through the strings and the puppet fell on the floor, where it shattered, wooden limbs, torso, and head skittering across the flagstones. Adelrune felt the hold of the sympathetic magic on him break.

Keokle gasped in dismay. As Adelrune straightened and flexed his limbs, the toymaker backed up against a wall. Adelrune pulled his dagger from its sheath and stepped toward his adversary.

"You can't do this," Keokle pleaded. "You said you were a knight. Aren't knights bound to act honorably? I am unarmed. The single spell I cast I used to protect myself. I have not harmed you. I am your true father. You can't kill me!"

For an instant Adelrune stopped, then he shook his head bitterly.

"When I came into your shop I still believed myself a knight," he said. "I had a quest to fulfill; I had been trained by Riander himself; King Joyell aboard the Ship of Yeldred had dubbed me. It has taken me a long, long time to wake up from that dream. The one I swore to rescue is dead; Joyell was mad; and for all Riander's training, I have failed him. I cannot possibly be a knight, since a knight would not be willing to commit murder."

His arm rose, the dagger's stained blade glinting at the end of his fist.

"No! Remember the First Precept of the Rule!" shouted Keokle. "Thou shalt not—"

Adelrune rammed the dagger into his throat.

There was very little blood. The toymaker, slammed against the wall by the force of the blow, stayed immobile for an instant, then collapsed forward. Adelrune turned him face up with his foot; only the dagger's hilt protruded from Keokle's flesh. The toymaker's eyes were rolled up; a red trickle crawled from his mouth into his hair.

Adelrune fell to his knees beside the corpse and let out a shuddering groan. For an instant he thought he would die as well, from sheer horror, and then that he would pull out the dagger and slash his own throat.

He remained prostrate instead, his head buried in his arms, hoping that the roil of his thoughts would decrease, that he could start making sense of things again. He riffled the *Book of Knights* in imagination. In the seventh chapter the tale of Sir Oldelin's first slaying was told. He had killed a reaver who'd terrorized the countryside, pillaging and raping. The reaver had come close to skewering Sir Oldelin on his poisoned blade, but in the end the knight had triumphed.

Sir Oldelin had dug a grave for the man, his cheeks awash with tears all the while. He was found thus by a party of woodcutters, who had thereafter told everyone of the knight's matchless nobility: while weeping in pain from the terrible wound he had received from the reaver's envenomed weapon, still he had performed more than proper funeral rites for him, digging a wide grave fit almost for a noble. The Book had held the truth of the story: that Sir Oldelin felt such overwhelming guilt over the death that he had been planning to lay his own corpse beside his enemy's within the ground, and would have gone forward with his plan had he not been surprised by the arrival of others.

Riander had touched upon the matter more than once—but

Adelrune could not stand to recall his mentor's teachings. He had failed him. What did it matter whether or not knights felt such terrible anguish the first time they killed? A true knight would not have killed Keokle in the first place.

After a long moment, Adelrune's pangs of guilt ebbed somewhat. He found the strength to uncurl and rise to his feet. His quest remained for him to complete, however meaningless it might be.

The doll still sat in her chair, her blind gaze seeming to accuse him. Adelrune staggered over to her and took her in his arms. She was surprisingly heavy, and taller than she had seemed. Her head lolled against his shoulder, her eyes now closed as if she were merely sleeping. The cut in her neck had begun seeping blood. The porcelain and wood of her were altering, turning into flesh. She grew taller and heavier by the second.

He carried her to the front of the store. "I am sorry," he whispered to her corpse, in a broken voice. "I am so sorry. I was too late."

"Don't be sorry," said a voice that came from his left.

Adelrune started, looked about for who had spoken. He noticed a doll on a shelf, with curly brown hair gathered at the back. She looked like Sawyd. And as a matter of fact it was Sawyd's voice he had heard.

The puppet spoke again. "You must not be sorry. What more could you have done?"

"What is this?" cried Adelrune, as shivers flowed through his flesh.

A string puppet spoke. It was dressed all in gray, and in its features Adelrune thought to recognize the gray magician. "There are several possible explanations. Perhaps, since Keokle is dead, the magic he once wielded has been released unformed throughout this house; and so apparent miracles can occur. This would account for your mother's transformation into human shape, although the contact of your flesh—which is also hers— might in theory be sufficient to trigger the metamorphosis through the principle of contagion. Another explanation, perhaps likelier, is that the experiences you have just passed through have unhinged your mind, so that you now see things that do not exist. Then again, perhaps it is something else altogether."

A puppet dressed in ermine robes sat up and spoke with King Joyell's voice. "Whatever the explanation, can you not see that it does not matter? You have at last achieved what you set out to do. Your quest is fulfilled."

"Or is it? I think he has ruined and destroyed everything." This was a dry, dry voice, and it came from a torn scrap of black velvet, with tiny paste rubies sewn into it, draped across a peg on the wall.

"Adelrune," said Jarellene, her wooden head and its tawny blond hair peeking out from a low shelf, "do not listen to any of us any longer. Go out, now, and finish it. You have freed her, now free yourself."

"Jarellene . . ."

"I am not Jarellene. If ever you loved the one who bore that name, go."

Adelrune walked out of the toy shop. The corpse in his arms weighed more by the second. In the street, people saw him, raised an outcry. He ignored them, walked down the street into the market square. He told the man who sold firewood to untie his bundles; the man looked at what Adelrune held in his arms and obeyed numbly.

Adelrune laid the body down on the fagots. He smoothed the blue dress with the lace at collar and wrists, straightened the limbs. The blood had seeped from her gashed throat and stained the neckline of her dress. Adelrune arranged the head so that the gaping wound was closed. Then, from the pink tablecloth he still carried tied to his belt, he took out the scytale, wrapped it onto the bone. The silver letters gleamed, formed five words. With a soft roar the kindling caught, vivid flames rising, clearly visible even in the sunlight. Then Adelrune threw the scytale and the bone into the fire, and with a terrible screech a column of flames rose twenty feet high. Onlookers screamed and ran.

Adelrune stayed motionless, though the supernatural heat

burned his flesh worse than the breath from an open forge, looking on with unblinking eyes though the light was almost brighter than the sun's, waiting until his mother's pyre had burned itself out.

Then he turned away. Behind him only ashes were left, silvergray, scattering already in the morning breeze. He pulled out his purse, let drop two coins to pay for the wood.

He returned to the toy shop, went back inside. The puppets in their ranks on the walls stayed silent and immobile. In the back room the dead man lay face upward, the flow of his blood now stopped. Adelrune gathered his shield and lance.

He would have left then, but he recalled Keokle's story and its mention of the spells. He climbed up the spiral staircase in the workroom that led to the upper floor. He sought for a trunk, eventually found it in the toymaker's bedroom, facing the bed. It wasn't even locked. Inside was a fine mess of paper: a battered copy of the Rule, three books of Commentaries, broadsheets announcing festivals both religious and secular, two treatises on wood carving, old sketchbooks filled with ideas and diagrams for toys. At the bottom, in an envelope sealed by a drop of colorless wax, Adelrune found Keokle's magic book, such as it was: a few parchment sheets sewn together at one corner.

He scanned a few lines of text. The letters were crabbed, the pen strokes uneven. Fanciful symbols had been clumsily reproduced in the margins. Despite the crudity of the transcription, Adelrune could feel the power of the words tingling in his fingers, singing in his brain. It would seem he had some native aptitude for magic after all; small wonder, for the offspring of a magician and an enspelled manikin. . . .

He hurriedly folded the manuscript in half and stuffed it into his pack. He should have fetched it before, burned it on the pyre. Too late now to think of burning it by some more mundane flame. He had already dallied too long in this house. He would take it to Riander; let him dispose of it as he saw fit.

Adelrune returned downstairs, strode out of the workroom.

His dagger he chose to leave in Keokle's throat, appreciating the bitter symmetry between the manner of his finding it, and his leaving it. When he came out of the shop, he saw Griffin not far, its mouth full of grass. The horse came at his call. Adelrune mounted and prepared to ride out of Faudace.

People were waiting for him, beyond the now-deserted market square: a half-dozen troopers with a captain on horseback, accompanied by a trio of Rectors and a Didactor. The foot soldiers appeared distinctly unhappy to be confronting him; their lieutenant bore a resolute expression, as did the servants of the Rule. Adelrune turned his horse to go back the way he came and find another exit from the market square; but six more soldiers blocked his way. He swung around again.

"Gentlemen, please let me pass," called out Adelrune. "My business here is done and my dearest wish is to leave, never to return."

The Didactor replied in a nasal, pedantic voice: "Stranger, you are disruptive; you wreak panic and use sorcery, in flagrant defiance of the Fifty-eighth Precept. Your behavior cannot be allowed to continue unpunished! You must now come with us to the carcery, where you will be appropriately disciplined."

"Is that you, Didactor Febule? I thought I recognized your red hair. It seems two decades dealing with small boys has robbed you of your perspective, Didactor. Did you really think I would be as amenable as a pupil of the Canon House who has just been caught napping in class? I will not accompany you anywhere. I am leaving Faudace and no one shall stop me."

The Didactor was taken aback at being recognized, but clearly chose not to pursue the matter further. He motioned to the lieutenant, who sent his half-dozen men forward. The foot soldiers, brandishing their maces, stepped forward hesitantly.

For all that these were professional soldiers, they were little more qualified than Lovell, Preiton, and Thran who had met him at the borders of Harkovar. Faudace was a peaceful place, and its constabulary's duties rarely extended beyond apprehending tipsy revelers on festival nights. Even though they were six against one, they would have been fairly easy to defeat—were it not that the very thought of even wounding one of them made Adelrune feel sick to his stomach. He feared even should he need to defend his life, he would be unable to risk taking another's.

Inspiration made him snatch the folded parchment from his pack. He waved the pages at the advancing foot soldiers.

"Did you enjoy the magic I wielded in the square?" he shouted, threateningly. "Would you like to see more? I carry a half-dozen spells on my person. Let me go, or I shall cast one on you!"

This was enough to halt the men's advance. Farther up the street, one of the Rectors quietly edged away. Adelrune glanced over his shoulder: the foot soldiers at his back were standing their ground. Didactor Febule's voice rose: "Ignore the miscreant's threats! Forward! Apprehend him!"

Adelrune brought the pages in front of him and picked a line of text at random. In a thunderous voice, he began to recite the words, meanwhile brandishing his lance at the foot soldiers.

The syllables burned his mouth and dizzied him; he felt strange energies stirring, though impotently. His invocation was random, and could not bring a proper spell into being. This distinction was lost on the foot soldiers, who beat a hasty retreat.

Adelrune stopped reading—it took an effort of will to tear himself from the page, as if the spell itself wanted to be completed. He wheeled Griffin around. The soldiers at his back lacked an officer's presence and were unnerved. With a shriek, he sent Griffin into a gallop toward the men.

They scattered before him; he had two clear opportunities to run a man through, and kept his lance well out of harm's way.

The rest of his escape was a mere formality: plunging through the narrow streets, evading a pair of mounted pursuers, galloping out of town. It felt like a boys' game of pretend made real. Though there was no more pursuit once he had exited the town,

Adelrune kept Griffin moving at a good pace. As long as he moved swiftly, he could imagine he was a noble knight leaving the scene of his vengeance, he could forget that he was a criminal fleeing a murder.

14 SIR ADELRUNE OF FAUDACE

IT TOOK HIM THREE DAYS, AS IT HAD THE FIRST TIME. HE might have tried to hurry, but travel through the forest was bound by laws of time more than distance. Once they had entered the trees, he let Griffin pick an easy pace, absorbed himself in his surroundings.

There were no sounds as he passed among the trees, and he saw nothing: the queen kept her promise. Yet he knew eyes watched him; he could feel the queen's hate and rage, almost palpable in the air. The nights were warm and he did not need to make a fire. He dimly feared Redeyes would return, but in fact he was not bothered.

Once he took out the Prince of Cups from his pack. Pressing his fingers against the card he felt a ghostly heartbeat, and a fat drop of blood oozed out from the tear. Lest he break his own promise, he put the card back and did not touch it again.

On the third day he reached the hills. He dismounted to reduce Griffin's burden. Man and beast zigzagged up the slopes, picking the easiest way. Adelrune had let his mind go almost blank, an echo of the first time he had come here. Now as then, he fled from the memory of something frightening. But this time the thing was inside himself, and do what he will, he could not escape it forever.

By sundown he reached the combe and saw at last Riander's house. He led Griffin down the small valley, up to the door of the house of pink bricks. Half of the building lay in shadow, half was turned to the color of peaches by the sun. Adelrune dismounted, went to knock, but the door recognized him and swung open of its own accord.

He walked into the house. It had remained the same, a still eddy in the flow of time. The rooms went on forever. Riander was not to be seen. Adelrune walked along the parlor, and presently reached the gallery, where he finally saw his mentor, working on a painting. He approached in silence, not because he did not want to be heard but because he dared not make a sound.

Then he saw it was himself Riander was painting. He breathed sharply; Riander started, saw him, dropped his brushes, shouted in welcome, and embraced him. In his mentor's arms Adelrune shivered violently, struggled. "Let me go!" he begged, and Riander released him.

Adelrune sat down on the floor, huddled and trembling. After a time he raised his head and considered the painting. Riander had crouched down next to him, concern plain on his face.

On the wall Adelrune was depicted against a dark background of tangled trees, wearing the Oula's armor, bearing Sawyd's shield, and holding Kadul's lance. The blue gem in the dagger's pommel gleamed at his belt.

"You knew, then," he said, turning to Riander. "You knew what would happen. . . ."

"No. Not in that sense. I could not know beforehand what would befall you. I truly believed you would return here after a week, or at most two. I could not foresee what did happen. I was able to paint this because I saw your travels in dreams; what I took from you links us to some degree." Riander was shaking his head, looking distraught. "I was very concerned. No other of my students was ever tested so."

"It would be more correct to say 'tested to destruction.' Riander, you must erase this painting immediately. I am not a knight. I am ashamed it took me so long to understand it."

Riander stood up, his face showing disbelief mixed with some other emotion. Adelrune felt too awkward sitting on the floor; he struggled to his feet, declined Riander's proffered hand.

"How can you not be a knight?" asked Riander when his student had risen to face him. "The king dubbed you, aboard the Ship of Yeldred."

"Joyell was mad! What did it mean for me to be knighted by such a man, a man whom I thereafter betrayed, whose dreams I destroyed? And besides—and besides, his knights were not of the quality they should have been. Yeldred's knighthood is not the true knighthood."

"So you judge King Joyell was not fit to pronounce you a knight. But then is there anyone who is?"

". . . You. But—"

"And what if I were to tell you that you are a knight?"

"Hah! My mentor could not be such a fool."

"Why is it such a foolish thing?"

Adelrune did not reply. He peered at the painting, and now he saw that the gnarled trees and the masses of foliage hid shapes in their depths. He could make out faces: he recognized King Joyell, and Madra, and Kodo. . . .

Riander spoke again. Gently, he asked, "Tell me, Adelrune, why is it so foolish for me to judge you a knight?"

"Did you not see what happened?"

"All of it. Including what took place in Faudace."

"And you still ask the question?"

Riander nodded.

"Shall we begin with the trivial reasons?" said Adelrune, his voice trembling. "If you must hear it all, very well. I am not a knight, I am not and never will be fit to be a knight, because I led Kodo into the clutches of the gray magician and we escaped through sheer luck. Because I chose to do nothing about Berthold Weer's exploitation of his serving girls. Because I betrayed King Joyell of Yeldred. Because I undid the work of Gliovold by freeing the queen. Because Jarellene died by my fault."

"You are Adelrune of Faudace, who released those Offspring

of Kuzar held in the gray magician's bondage. Who befriended the witches of the Vlae Dhras, and escaped the Manticore. Who averted the massacre of Ossué and thwarted the power of the queen of the forest. Of all my students, none has had such an immediate impact upon the world as you have. Can you not understand? Everything you touch is changed. You are a hero of whom songs will one day be sung. Your life is barely beginning, and already your deeds would be enough to satisfy many a seasoned knight."

"Very well, then," said Adelrune bitterly. "Very well, I am a hero worthy of song. What would you propose for the final verse, the one where I murder my own father? 'Sir Adelrune came a-wandering into the shop, his quest to complete. The toymaker he confronted, and slew with a blade through the throat. . . .' "

Adelrune's voice was rising in a scream. Riander grabbed his wrists and squeezed sharply. "Enough, Adelrune. Be silent!"

Adelrune found his mouth had shut of its own volition.

"Some would say," Riander continued, "that you avenged your mother's death. That you repaired the injustice that was the root cause of your birth."

"They would, but they would be wrong," said Adelrune, calmly now. "I tried telling myself this a dozen times during my trip here, but it will not hold up.

"I did not defeat a mighty enemy. I did not slay a wizard who threatened my own life. I killed an unarmed, scared man who had worked his twisted magic to fill the void in his life. Even then, if I had killed him with outrage foremost on my mind, if I had done it in my mother's name, then I might yet believe I had done rightly. But do you know why it is I killed him, in the end?"

"Tell me."

"I killed him because I could not forgive him for disappointing me. Here was the man who had destroyed my life and my mother's, and he had done it out of simple selfishness. He did not even hate me. He was petty and fearful, nothing more.

I think . . . I think I might have spared him in the end, had he begged for mercy. But he quoted the Rule at me, and I was so sick of Precepts and Commentaries . . . I wanted to silence him. In the very end it was to shut him up that I killed him."

Adelrune sobbed out a breath, wiped the sweat that had beaded on his forehead.

"I agree with you," said Riander. "That was indeed an ignoble slaying. Unworthy of a knight."

Adelrune looked at him, taken aback. He had expected Riander to patiently deny his self-directed accusation, as he had the rest. Was his mentor's agreement a ploy to shock him out of his misery? But he saw Riander was utterly serious. Riander spoke again.

"Though you will feel insulted at this, I must tell you that you're still very much a child of the Rule, Adelrune. You have kept the absurd idea throughout your training that a knight must be flawless to be worthy. I don't know where you picked this up, for certainly I never said anything of the sort. You conveniently forget Sir Ancelin who slew a dozen of his dearest companions, Sir Actavaron who seduced his best friend's wife, Sir Cobalt who stole and lied in the streets of Avyona for a year, and too many others for me to count."

"But—"

"A man may be flawed and still good. A man may have committed a fault and still be reckoned worthy. What did you expect? That my training would enable you to behave as a saint in all circumstances? The Rule might make such a claim on behalf of its epopts, but you know better than anyone that it is a lie. I tell you this now: for the rest of your life you shall be haunted by the decisions you took and those you didn't take, by the acts you will wish you had not performed and by those you will wish you had. Sir Lominarch spared the life of Ysalva, who later destroyed the only remaining copy of the Scarlet Principles, which might have saved the Order of the Wyvern in its hour of need. Yet had he killed her, he would have been a murderer."

"That is no fair comparison," retorted Adelrune. "Keokle

could never have affected events in that way. And Lominarch did the right thing at any rate: he spared Ysalva's life, he did not kill her."

"But why did he do that? Don't you remember? I told you the story: he spared Ysalva because she was young and pretty, and he itched to lie with her. His mercy came from his loins; not his heart and certainly not his brain. Where did your judgement of the toymaker come from, Adelrune? From the core of yourself. You did not think; you felt no pity, only anger. It was wrong to kill him, and yet I cannot believe it could have been avoided. Had I been in your place, I would have castrated the man before I slew him. It would have been even more wrong; but then, I am only human, as are you."

Adelrune turned his face away. "It is not good enough," he said. "Tell me what I am all you want; *I* know what I am not."

"Sir Aldyve once walked into an inn on the other side of the world," said Riander, "and he was asked, as all newcomers were, to explain who he was. He spent the better part of an hour describing all the facets of himself, and in the end was forcibly shut up by having a sausage thrust into his mouth. He was later heard to remark 'What would they have done if they had asked me to tell them who I was *not!*' "

Adelrune smiled, amused despite himself. "I suspect you to have made up that story on the spot," he said.

"Aldyve knew himself better than you do. *I* know you, Adelrune; would you dare deny it? I know all you are. My old friend's gift lives in me; I could see to the depths of your soul when you showed up at my door, on that early spring day; I could sense what you had the potential to become. You have fulfilled your promises, the dark ones as well as the light."

Adelrune put his hand before his eyes, and a tear seeped beneath his fingers.

"I wish," he said, "that I had not killed him. He deserved to be punished, but the fate I meted out was excessive."

"Yes, it was. But just as I willingly forgave Lominarch his weakness, I forgive you yours. And I say this to you: whether you believe in destiny or not, by your very calling, assuredly more than one occasion to atone will come to you. But though you rescue a thousand prisoners, though you redress a thousand wrongs, you will never undo what you did. And you will never be truly forgiven until you forgive yourself."

Adelrune took his hand away from his eyes, nodded. "You are right," he admitted. "Though I still feel that I should have stayed in Faudace. Never have read the *Book of Knights.* That way I would have avoided doing evil."

"It is much too late for such wishes. Adelrune of Faudace, I, Riander, your mentor, now tell you this: you are a knight from this moment on. Kneel, Sir Adelrune, that you may properly be dubbed."

Adelrune, vanquished, kneeled. Riander struck him on the shoulders with tremendous force. Through the pain he heard Riander ordering him to stand. He rose to his feet.

"You, Sir Adelrune, have gained in your trials your armor, your shield, your weapon, and your mount. Your training is hereby at an end. From this moment onward, you are the Knight Adelrune of Faudace."

Adelrune bowed his head, remained so for a long time. Riander spoke again, in a normal voice. "Never have I been more proud of one of my students. Will you not allow yourself to feel a little of that pride?"

Adelrune raised his head. "I was thinking of Sir Aldyve's story. It is a good one. As always, you are as wise as anyone could wish." He paused. "Yes. Yes, I do feel a little of that pride. I have wanted nearly all my life to be a knight. Perhaps I was afraid of it coming true, after all the waiting. It is not exactly as I had expected it. Nothing ever is. But tell me one last thing. What now? What should I do?"

Riander smiled, took Adelrune's arm, led him toward the front of the room.

"The world is vast. It is full of people, full of doings and battles and magic. Anywhere you go, you will find the world waiting for you. There are a thousand injustices to repair, a thousand battles to join—or to prevent, a thousand stories to be written. There is no Rule to bind you anymore, only the mystery of the world itself."

They had reached the front of the endless parlor. The sun had set and the whole combe now lay in shadow. At that moment came a knock at the front door. Riander went to open it and saw a boy, maybe sixteen, wearing an ill-fitting, tattered chain mail surcoat at least a hundred years old. In his hands the boy clutched a roll of parchment.

"Sir? You're Riander? My name is Thybalt. I wish to become a knight. The Book said you'd ask for a list of accomplishments. This is it. If you would read it. . . ."

Riander took the scroll, read it carefully, beginning to end, three times. Then he looked at the boy who stood quaking on his doorstep. "And what is your purpose, Thybalt, that you should need to become a knight?"

"Every spring, the Red Duke's roughs come down from the hills, they loot and rob, and if anyone resists them they kill him. I've vowed to defend my village. The next time they come I'll send them screaming back to their master."

Riander nodded gravely to Thybalt. "Yes. Yes, I will accept you as an apprentice."

He led Thybalt gently into the parlor. The boy saw Adelrune, halted in uncertainty. "Good evening, sir," he said.

"Good evening to you," said Adelrune. He met Riander's gaze, said softly: "It is time I went, is it not?"

"You might stay a while. It would be no trouble."

"No. I owe it to Thybalt."

"Sir?" Thybalt was astonished enough to speak.

"Good luck, Thybalt," said Adelrune. "In Riander I believe you have the best teacher a knight-aspirant could hope for. Perhaps you and I will meet again one day."

He went out of Riander's house, mounted Griffin, and rode out of the combe. Riander and Thybalt stood in the doorway watching him leave.

"Who was that?" asked Thybalt.

"It was Sir Adelrune of Faudace."

"Sir Adelrune! The Book . . . the Book spoke of him."

"I am not surprised it did."

"Where is he going?"

"Not even he knows."

They stood in silence then, watching the figure of Adelrune ride out of the valley and vanish into the night, into the wide world.